FORGIVE ME, MR. HUNTER

T. N. CULLEN

Jackie,
I hope you
enjoy it!
Cheers!
Tom C.

 FriesenPress

Suite 300 - 990 Fort St
Victoria, BC, V8V 3K2
Canada

www.friesenpress.com

Edited by Claire Mulligan and Cindy Cullen

ISBN
978-1-5255-2102-7 (Hardcover)
978-1-5255-2103-4 (Paperback)
978-1-5255-2104-1 (eBook)

1. *JUVENILE FICTION, SOCIAL ISSUES, EMOTIONS & FEELINGS*

Distributed to the trade by The Ingram Book Company

TABLE OF CONTENTS

There can be no friendship without confidence,
and no confidence without integrity.

—Samuel Johnson

We must accept finite disappointment, but never
lose infinite hope.

—Martin Luther King, Jr.

CHAPTER 1
Days of Innocence: Summer 1986

I was small, as was my world. To an outsider my existence would have appeared to be one with constraints and boundaries. Maybe it was, but that was okay with me. It was the only world I had ever known—happy, carefree, and uncomplicated. I was certain it would go on forever.

It never occurred to me there might be obstacles along the way.

"Obstacles, or challenges, usually come from mistakes we make," my mother had explained to me. "And they're just opportunities for learning."

Maybe so, but I discovered far too soon, before my fifth birthday, that some obstacles can also be life altering.

I was four, almost five. Summertime in Victoria. The sun rose early and the brilliant rays streaming through the windows were like an invitation. I couldn't wait to venture out on my trike.

"Stay on the sidewalks or driveways, and don't go too far. I need to see you from the living room window," my mother would say. That meant I could go no more than three houses in either direction of our house. A small world, but to me it was as vast as Canada.

"Okay. Where's dad today?" I would ask. It was important for me to know this.

"He's in St. John's."

"St. John's. Okay."

Maynard, my ancient, rusty, red tricycle, was like a good friend. I knew his every scrape and rust mark by heart. I loved how the battered, colourful plastic streamers made a cool whirring sound in the breeze. The bent wheels wobbled on a frame that had to be welded together almost weekly. My mother offered to buy me a new trike. I flatly refused. There was no replacement for Maynard.

At almost five, I had outgrown Maynard. My knees were constantly bruised from knocking against the handlebars as I pedaled frantically up and down the sidewalk and in and out of driveways. Each driveway was a new city that depended on where my father was traveling that week.

When my father was away, there was an emptiness in my life that I couldn't explain. I was sad and happy at the same time. I cherished the limited time I spent with my father, but it was always more peaceful when he was gone. And my mother was a happier person.

When my parents argued, which was pretty much all the time, I would disappear into my room and cover my ears. But they were so loud that nothing could block them out completely.

"If you would stop your damn drinking, maybe we could do something as a family!" I remember my mother screaming.

"If you would stop your bloody nagging, I wouldn't have to drink!" was my father's return.

When the screaming finally stopped, I would go sit in the living room just to be near my father. He said very little to me. He smoked, drank beer, and watched TV, and never left his chair. I just sat and watched his every move.

Sunday mornings at church were the only times I could be certain my parents would get along. For that reason, I looked forward to church.

My father sold hospital equipment right across Canada, so he was away most of the time in places like Vancouver, Calgary, Edmonton, Winnipeg, Toronto, Montreal, and even St. John's.

Using an atlas, my mother had gone over Canada's geography with me a hundred times so that I would know where my father was. Not many four-year-olds knew all the major cities in Canada, but I had a map in my head that allowed me to make all the necessary stops en route to anywhere.

That week it was St. John's. Now that was something. Victoria to St. John's is about a zillion kilometers one way, and, of course, another zillion back.

So, when I was on Maynard that day, I made a stop in Hagen's driveway—that was Winnipeg; then Hunter's carport—that was Toronto; and then I finally entered forbidden territory. I went out of my mother's view to get to Kline's driveway—St. John's. It was such a novelty being in Kline's driveway that I stayed a while to sightsee, refuel, and what not.

Big mistake. Soon enough, my mother noticed I was out of sight. She bolted out of the house in curlers, nightgown, and bare feet. That was something to see, my mother doing the hundred-meter dash at Olympic speed in bare feet. I would have laughed if she hadn't yanked on my ears as she dragged me back home, still astride Maynard. Ears just weren't made for that kind of tugging, especially my big ones. The pain wasn't worth the trip to St. John's, believe me.

My mother never stayed angry for long, and I never stopped loving her. I always felt safe and protected. But I enjoyed pushing the boundaries from time to time, and my memory was a little short, so it certainly wasn't my last trip to Kline's driveway.

CHAPTER 2
My Friend Mr. Hunter

Mr. Hunter was my favourite person to visit. In fact, he was my favourite person in the whole world.

Turning left out of my driveway, his place was Toronto, only three houses away, just within my legal limit. His garage was in the back alley, but I could also access it by going through his front yard and opening the gate to the backyard. This was out of my mother's vision, but I was certain she knew exactly where I was since she could see Maynard parked outside the gate. It was the only 'out-of-view' time that didn't cause my mother to come chasing after me.

Mr. Hunter was a handyman. He did shift work at the local Victoria shipyard for a living, and he spent every spare minute of his day in his workshop. Whenever I heard the familiar muffled banging and sawing noises, I made a beeline for Mr. Hunter's.

I was always a welcome guest. Whatever he was doing, any time of the day, at any stage of a project, he would shut it all down the moment I walked in the always-open door. He was genuinely happy to see me, too. I could tell by his voice and his mannerisms. It was easy to tell when adults were faking excitement; their faces always gave them away. The fakers would sound excited but they would not really smile. At most, they'd show a quick smile that died instantly. Mr. Hunter always had a twinkle in his eye and a full smile that showed all his crooked, stained teeth.

It was hard to tell how old he was. He definitely looked a lot older than my parents. I know he was bald on top, but he usually covered that with a baseball cap which was always turned backwards while he worked. Grey hair stuck out on both sides, and Mr. Hunter was constantly tucking it in behind his ears.

In the shop, it was always grey-striped overalls. That's all I had ever seen him wear. It was either the same pair or else he had several pairs that were exactly the same. He always had a pencil in his breast pocket and a tape measure attached to a loop at his waist.

I don't think he had any kids of his own. He never talked about them if he did.

I remember one particular summer day when I raced over to his garage. When I heard the familiar hammering, my excitement was indescribable. And Mr. Hunter was equally excited to tell me all about his current project.

"Axel Poomer! It's great to see you! I'd forget to even take a break unless you popped in. How in the world are you?"

"Fine, thanks," I returned, beaming.

"Tell me what you think of this entertainment center I'm making for the wife," he said, standing proudly in front of his creation. I felt proud for him; it truly was a magnificent piece of work as far as I could tell. Everything Mr. Hunter made was a masterpiece. I was certain of it.

"I think it's real nice," I replied, feeling the smoothly-sanded surface. Then we talked. Talked about anything. About nothing. He asked me endless questions about my life, like what I wanted to be when I grew up, what my favourite cartoon was, how my girlfriend Sally was doing—he teased me about her; she lived

FORGIVE ME, MR. HUNTER

down the street and came over to play sometimes—and where my father was that week.

I would lose track of time whenever I was with Mr. Hunter. I was so fully immersed in his kindness and in the simple belief that he valued me. I was always late getting home after visiting there, but my mother never said a word about that. She would just smile and say that she figured I was visiting Mr. Hunter again, adding, "One day you'll be a handyman just like him."

"I hope so."

CHAPTER 3
1995: Two Connections

This is the third week in my sixth foster home, and my fourth dysfunctional home in a row. Four in a row! Now that's something. For anyone keeping score, that has to be some kind of a record. I'm not really a stats guy, and living with four whacko families in a row is really nothing to write home about, so to speak.

School is a safe haven. It's one of the few places where I find a little peace of mind in my life. My escape from reality for the past few years has been reading, so academically I'm ahead of most people my age. I don't do a lot of writing, but teachers tell me that I express myself well when I do. Oddly enough, I use a dictionary regularly. I like knowing the meanings of big words.

I read almost anything I can get my hands on. In fourth and fifth grades, I read all the *Hardy Boys* book written. Frank and Joe became a part of my persona back then, and I dreamed every night that I would become the best detective in the world. But I moved on to broader horizons with stories that were powerful enough to make me cry like *Where the Red Fern Grows*, *Bridge to Terabithia*, and *Black Beauty*. I read *Treasure Island* and *Huckleberry Finn* three times each, and I most recently discovered a penchant for darker-themed novels such as *The Outsiders* and *Lord of the Flies*.

Pacific Shores Middle School is a big ancient brick building with an institutional look. It's located in the municipality of Vic-East, near the border of Victoria proper. Vic-East has negative connotations for some people because it's an older part of Greater Victoria, and many of the houses are run down. It's a lot more affordable than most other parts of Victoria, and I actually like living in this part of the capital city. I feel more at home with people who don't have their noses in the air while driving around in a Mercedes Benz or a BMW.

I always arrive at school with ringing in my ears from the screaming and rampaging of my foster dad, Flick. His real name is Cliff but he landed the permanent nick name because of his habit of flicking his head. Likely, it started years earlier as a convenient way to get bangs out of his eyes. The hair vanished, but the flicking stayed.

Despite the raucous voices of all the middle-schoolers, the ringing in my ears disappears the moment I walk through the front doors of the school. Having been here just a few weeks, it still feels new to me. I haven't made any real connections yet, but that's mostly my own fault. It's a struggle for me to work up the courage to initiate a conversation with anyone. I mingle a bit and listen to conversations, but everyone seems to be established with groups of friends and they don't readily welcome outsiders into their cliques. I'm okay with that. I like observing and taking mental notes.

I'm tall and slender—some say I'm lanky—and my worn-out blue jeans are still as loose and baggy as the day I got them, but now they're high enough off the ground to stay dry in a significant flood. I know people mock me behind my back, but I really don't care. I just pull back my long, straight, dark brown hair, tuck it behind my big ears and ignore anyone with a superior attitude.

I saunter into my classroom, heels dragging, but Mrs. Watson greets me warmly. I have her for homeroom, English, Socials and Math.

"Good morning, Axel. You look like you're carrying the weight of the world on your shoulders, or maybe you just need about one more hour of sleep." She smiles and I smile back.

"Just one?" I reply. "I think maybe a week would be a start." She nods in her understanding way. I walk to my desk with a little more bounce in my step.

She knows all about me and my foster-kid life. I sense she pities me and that's why she gives me lots of breaks. If she had any idea about the dark cloud that consumes my every waking minute, and has for the past nine years or so, I doubt she'd still be so understanding.

No matter what anyone might say, I'm responsible for my own actions. I would give anything to change one particular event of my past, but that kind of thinking is a waste of time. It's also hard keeping it to myself. But whenever I ask myself who I could trust to tell about my life-changing incident, the answer is always the same: nobody. Mrs. Watson might be the exception. She actually reminds me of my mother, the way she takes things in stride. I suppose she's somewhere between forty and fifty, a little older than my mother would be.

1986

My father was in Winnipeg that week, so I didn't have to ride Maynard beyond my legal limit in the neighbourhood. I checked into Hagen's driveway. From there I heard Mr. Hunter working in his garage, so off to Toronto I went. That day he was working on a car engine. I heard grunting and groaning, twisting wrenches, and a little cursing. Eventually he pulled out a big greasy metal part and threw it into the wooden crate he used for garbage. I watched for a while before he noticed I was there.

"Axel, I didn't even hear you come in! How are you, my little friend?" he yelled as he threw down his tools and gave a full-toothed smile.

"Fine, thanks."

"Boy, this classic baby is giving me headaches like you wouldn't believe. '57 Chevy, about thirty-years-old now. I thought it would just be a simple tune-up, but I see now that I've gotta put in a new starter as well. And something tells me I'm gonna run into more problems before I'm done. And there's enough grease on this darn engine to fill an oil well."

He shook his head and sighed, then chuckled to himself. "Oh, it's all good, Axel," he continued. "I shouldn't complain, but you're a good listener, so I'll keep on complaining unless you tell me to stop." He nodded at me like it was my cue to speak.

"I don't mind," I said. I never really thought of Mr. Hunter as a complainer. My mother often told me not to complain about things like eating peas or having a bath. Those were things to complain about, things that would make life happier if they just disappeared. But Mr. Hunter was just doing what he loved: being a handyman.

"I didn't think you would. You're a good boy, Axel. Hey, how about flexing those muscles of yours and giving me a hand with this bin. We'll just slide it right out the door."

It looked too heavy to budge, but I was willing to give it a try.

"Now, bend your knees a little like this," he explained as he demonstrated, "and get your body up against it, and I'll count to three, and on three just push like you were a front-end loader."

I had no idea what a front-end loader was, but the crate slid across the garage floor like it was on rollers. Once outside, we tipped the bin and dumped out all the greasy, scrap pieces right on top of a pile of junk that was heaped against the weathered picket fence of his backyard.

"That oughta do it, Axel. Good job! And this is another big headache," he complained as he tossed some of the stray pieces of scrap back onto the pile. "One day I'll have to deal with this mess. It's like a boar's nest back here. But that's for another time, my friend. There's only so many hours in a day, and twenty-four is not enough."

He talked about other things, but I fixated on his comment about not enough time to get things done. How I wished I could help him get things done! If I could make Mr. Hunter's life easier, I would be the happiest kid alive.

"Well, Axel, I'd better get back to work here. This here is a friend's car, and he needs it back soon."

"Oh," I replied. "I thought it was your car."

"No such luck, my friend. The wife always gives me a hard time about that because I never seem to find the time to do my own repairs. Oh, she's a good woman, Axel. She and I have always agreed on one main thing. And that one thing is this: always do as much good as you can for other people. Because, Axel, if you always do good things for others, good things will come back to you. Remember that."

I did remember that. I repeated his advice over and over in my head until it was etched on my brain as if with a thick, black marker. All that night I thought about good things I could do for Mr. Hunter. Lying on my pillow, my mind raced out of control, playing out one scenario after another, imagining me doing tasks that would help Mr. Hunter feel that there were enough hours in a day. Even tasks that were beyond my reach.

I thought about sneaking into his garage and finishing all the mechanical work with the Chevy. I imagined his look of surprise. But how do people do mechanical work? The thought of removing a part from a car engine, let alone replacing it, was too overwhelming.

Or maybe I could build him the most amazing piece of furniture imaginable. One that would serve a hundred purposes so he would never have to build again. But how would I even start? What tools would I use? I had no idea. All of my great ideas hit stumbling blocks. I was getting frustrated.

And then it hit me. It was so doable, even for me. It would save Mr. Hunter time and headaches. Surely, he would be grateful for the favour. I played the scenario in my head. I pictured me completing the task and seeing Mr. Hunter's reaction. I was convinced I had finally come up with my first great idea to do something good.

I take a seat at my desk. The bell rings, and here we go. News is discussed, plus a lot of personal events are shared, then instructions start coming at us, and by that time I'm deep in the ozone. I drift off to places unknown, but I always end up in the same place: deep inside a black cloud, fighting my way out to find blue sky.

I've mastered this altered state of mind. I can somehow come up with answers when called upon, and still not lose my place in my imaginary world. Today I'm surveying the class and using the information I know to put myself in their places, in their lives. Then I compare them with my own life.

First, I dwell on Frank. He's an enigma; maybe a hair taller than five feet, about a hundred pounds soaking wet, dark brown skin, straight, dark hair to his shoulders, and dark, penetrating eyes. Though diminutive, he's fearless and his huge attitude intimidates guys twice his size.

His mantra is: "If you don't like me, change me." He says it, then he steps forward with arms wide open, and gives a laser glare that makes his opponents shudder and retreat. It's really something to see, and I've witnessed it four times now. I always shake my head in disgust when those bigger guys don't take a swipe at the intruding rodent. Instead, they always crumble and take flight, leaving their dignity behind.

I've heard stories about Frank, sort of school folklore. And judging from his character, I can't help but believe they're true. Apparently, his parents are big-time drunks, and, when they're on a bender, Frank becomes their human punching bag. So, he spends a lot of time on the streets. And he often gets the crap beat out of him there as well. Maybe he should add one more word to his mantra: *please.* "If you don't like me, *please* change me."

When I compare my life with Frank's, I think I would choose mine, minus the black cloud. I get yelled at and put down, but I don't get the living crap beat out of me.

I continue daydreaming, considering people like Will the well-to-do, uppity snob, or Chelsea the most popular girl I know. I wonder about that, too. How would I deal with popularity like hers? Not that I'll ever have to worry about it. Popularity comes with expectations. You're expected to be nice, fashionable, athletic, good-looking. Basically, to be somebody I wouldn't want to be. Too much pressure.

Chelsea seems well-suited for that role but, she doesn't look that happy to me. She has an amazing smile, but I never see her laughing. Kids flock around her in the halls, yet I always see her walking home alone. I have to admit that she's someone I'd like to get to know better, but she's out of my league.

"So, what do we have to do with these two fractions in order to add them? Axel?" Mrs. Watson notices when I drift away and likes to catch me off guard.

"Oh, you'd have to find a common denominator," I reply without missing a beat. Then I glance at the board and quickly add, "For those fractions, the LCD would be twelve."

"Very good, Axel. Thank you." She nods and smiles. "So you are paying attention."

I continue to drift off. Before I know it, the recess bell goes. I join the rush into the hallway and head to my locker for a snack.

Everyone is congregating around the lockers. I'm squeezing my way through a small crowd when I feel a sudden jolt from behind. I'm pushed so hard that I lose my balance and bang my head into the lockers. Giving my head a shake, I turn to see Frank, a big grin on his face.

"Hey, I'm real sorry, buddy," he says. "Just lost my balance. No big deal, eh?"

The smirk on his face makes my blood boil. "Lost your balance, my ass!" I scream. "What the hell!" I lose complete control of my temper and start calling him every name in the book, including the one I know he hates: WOP.

My mouth just keeps letting loose until there he is, in my face, arms wide open: "If you don't like me, change me." Then he gives me the famous glare.

Suddenly, this all feels surreal. It's just happening so fast. There's no time to think, but two things race through my mind. The first one is *how did I get myself into this?* The second is *how do I get out of it?* It had always been Frank and somebody else, with me as the observer. I should have known that it would only be a matter of time before it was my turn. Now I'm the one being watched. I'm so focused on those beady eyes that are making me shake, that I barely notice the gathering audience.

My knees buckle, but I still tower over Frank. I nervously push my long bangs back and away from my eyes. I tell myself to stay put, not to retreat, as if Frank were a cougar I just encountered in the wild.

"Change me," he says again, then steps so close that I can barely move. At this point my mind goes blank and my fists take on a life of their own.

I punch him hard. Blood instantly shoots out of his nose. I punch him again and again. His eyes are puffing out; his lips are bleeding. I just keep punching Frank until, thankfully, several kids jump in to wrestle me back. After that, it's all a blur. I hear the principal's booming voice as he disperses the crowd, and the next thing I know, I'm in Mr. Hagan's office. Frank arrives a few minutes later after receiving some medical attention.

Mr. Hagan doesn't seem too interested in hearing our stories. Apparently, a few witnesses came forward right away and let him know that Frank was the instigator.

"Is what I'm hearing true?" he asks Frank. "That you started this whole thing?"

Frank is barely able to speak, but manages a mumbled "yes."

Mr. Hagan looks directly at Frank and grimaces. "Are you going to be okay, son?"

"Yes."

"Well, I hope so. I'd say you've learned a valuable lesson here. And I hope you have as well," he adds, looking me up and down. "You obviously came out of this a little better than Frank here, but you need to find a better way to deal with a confrontation like this."

"Yes, sir," I reply meekly.

Very business-like, he starts to fill out suspension forms while we watch and wait anxiously in complete silence.

I'm starting to regain my senses. Out the corner of my eye, I see Frank sitting with an ice pack on his eye and a blood-satu-rated Kleenex up his nose. The side of his face is badly swollen as well. It takes me a minute to realize that I was the one to inflict the damage.

I'm not proud of that fact. I actually feel sorry for Frank. I know I can justify it because he started it, but I feel upset for having lost control. It doesn't happen often, but I always hate myself afterward when it does.

"Well, boys," says Mr. Hagan as he puts down his pen, "I'm going to give you the light touch. The school year is just getting under way, and I really don't like the idea of you having to miss classes. But I have to be consistent so that everyone realizes there are consequences for fighting. I'm giving you just a two-day suspension, and that's counting today. So just today and tomorrow. Then I want to see you both back here with level heads and a focus on your grades. Agreed?"

"Yes," we both reply.

"Thanks, Mr. Hagan," I add as I stand up to leave.

"Okay, Axel. You keep your cool from now on, right?"

"Right."

Walking through the doors of the school two days later, I'm fully expecting to be accosted by Frank. From what I've seen, he's not the kind of guy who can let a beating like that just go away. I'm certain he'll be looking for a rematch to save face, so to speak.

As if in answer, Frank is the first guy I see. He's actually waiting for me at the front door. Swollen face and black eye, he does his best to smile and comes forward with his hand out.

"Friends?" he says.

"Friends," I reply, shaking his hand and breathing a sigh of relief. Now I can't help but chuckle to myself when I think about his mantra. I think I really did change him. Oddly enough, Frank is now the first connection I've made at this school.

Friday doesn't come soon enough. School is going fine, but there's nothing like the freedom of a weekend. On my walk home, I somehow redirect myself to Zellers, about eight blocks off the beaten track. Even though I don't have any money to spend, I like to wander around the store and make a wish list.

Approaching the stereo department, I see a familiar face. It's Eric. He's in some of my classes. He's tall and skinny with a severely pock-marked face and a permanent goofy expression, like he's on the verge of explosive laughter. And because he's always loud and outspoken, he comes across as the most self-confident person you could ever meet.

Eric spots me right away. He seems unusually pleased to see me, especially since we're not friends.

"Hey, Axel! Good to see you, buddy. Hey, we're in some classes together, right?"

"Right," I reply. "How's it going?"

"Couldn't be better, buddy. I'm looking at stereo systems and I'm thinking how rad it'd be to have one of these babies. Like how cool would it be to have a thirty-watt amp with some bad-ass speakers?" He's very animated, talking loud and fast about stereo features I know nothing about.

Soon he has me following him over to the electronics section where he drools over every amplifier and speaker in the store. He checks out each product, then checks the supply of boxed items on the shelves below. He continues to talk faster and faster and doesn't miss a beat while he pulls out the boxes he wants and sets them aside.

Before I can even attempt to refuse, I'm carrying a box that Eric almost throws at me. It's a Sony amplifier. He then stacks two speaker boxes in his arms and leads the way. I'm led to believe that we're heading to the check-out. I'm wrong, and I'm completely baffled as I continue to follow Eric's directions. As he

19

leads the way in behind the checkout area, big boxes in hands, I naively ask where we're going.

"Just gotta get these out to the parking lot to save everyone a little time and trouble, then we'll pop back in to take care of things."

"Are you sure?" I ask incredulously, but too confused and shaky to push the issue. I've never seen a store purchase done this way, and I have a really bad gut feeling about this transaction. But here I am following the leader like a lost sheep.

Eric has that goofy look on his face and I think for a second that he's going to break out laughing and tell me that this is all a joke. That doesn't happen. He's excited, but serious.

"Right through here," he directs me as the door automatically slides open. There are no security guards in sight, and the check-out ladies are all preoccupied with customers. What we are doing apparently looks perfectly normal to everyone else. I guess the adage 'avoid suspicion by doing the obvious' has some merit after all.

We exit the store and shuffle through the parking lot like Olympic speed walkers. I hear footsteps right behind me. It must be a security guard who's going to take me down! I glance quickly behind me. Relief! The footsteps are just those of regular shoppers.

It's clear to me now that we aren't regular shoppers. We aren't going back in to pay. We're thieves, and this is no small theft. When we reach the end of the lot, Eric sets the boxes down and uses them as a bench.

I'm dumbfounded. "What the hell!" I cry. "You're really not going back?"

"Are you kidding?" he returns, half smiling. "Hey, they'll never miss this stereo. It's no big deal. But listen, I gotta run across the street to make a call. My buddy will be by to pick up the parcels. Just stick around to watch 'em, and I'll be right back."

Before I have a chance to respond, he's gone like a flash. So I decide to follow suit and race home. I'm guessing that the stereo will end up at Eric's house as planned. When I think about it, that stereo is really half mine. But then again, if the crime ever catches up with Eric, the stereo is all his. He can have it. And good or bad, Eric is now my second official school connection.

I believe I know a little about Eric's home life, at least from the rumours that fly around the school. I don't like to make judgements based on rumours, but after you hear the same stories a number of times, it's hard not to believe they're true. The word is that Eric's father is in prison for either murder or attempted murder. People talk about him as if he's not part of the human race, just a monster who should rot in jail.

I don't see it that way. I'll bet he's just a regular guy who made a huge mistake and probably regrets it. I picture him in his cell contemplating life on the outside, making plans for restitution, and hoping to show everyone that he's a much better person than they ever imagined. I'm all for forgiveness, but I keep that to myself since few people seem to feel the same way. Deep down I hope that many people feel leniency is a good thing.

Another rumour about Eric's family is that his mother is a drug dealer. So, one parent is in jail, and the other one is heading in that direction. And Eric seems to be on his own path of self-destruction, but who wouldn't be in his situation? I would definitely choose my life over his.

CHAPTER 4
Helping Mr. Hunter

1986

I worked out my plan carefully. It was going to be great. I would help Mr. Hunter, and it would be my first good deed in life.

As I rode Maynard the next day, I didn't care about where my father was and whose driveway I needed to negotiate. Rather, my thoughts were consumed by the burning desire to do something good for Mr. Hunter. Did I want anything in return? I don't think so. If Mr. Hunter were genuinely pleased with me, if he really felt I had done him a favour, that would be my payback.

As I rode in and out of driveways, my plan began to take form. And it was the perfect plan. It was simple, certainly easy enough for one small guy to execute. It would help Mr. Hunter get rid of one of his headaches: the junk pile. I would simply dispose of the eyesore that was building up outside his garage. I smiled to myself. I could see Mr. Hunter sporting his huge smile when he found out that Axel Poomer was his secret helper.

As far as I could tell, the details of the plan were simple and flawless. To start with, I needed some matches, and I knew exactly where to find lots of those. Being a smoker, my father kept a supply of wooden matches in a drawer beside the kitchen sink.

I was forbidden to play with matches. My mother had scolded me a few times for even touching them, and so I knew that I would have to somehow sneak them out of the house. I convinced myself I would not really be breaking the rules, because this was not 'play.' This was serious. Helping my friend was serious business. I had watched my father light his cigarettes many times. He would push open the box, remove a match, close the box, strike the match on the side of the box with the dark-brown stripe, and sparks would shoot up, followed by a steady flame that he would hold to the end of his cigarette. When the cigarette was burning red, he would blow out the match and throw it into an overflowing ashtray with a hundred other discarded cigarettes and matches.

It would be easy. I pedaled faster than ever before in my excitement to get home and execute my plan. But my exuberance was short-lived. It dissipated the moment I walked in the door and my mother announced that I was just in time for my nap.

"But Mom," I pleaded, "I'm not even tired. Do I have to?"

"You know you don't do well without your naps. Naps give you more energy to ride Maynard, and they just make you a better boy."

"But Mom," I whined, and continued to whine until I was given an ultimatum of nap-time or a spanking. I had experienced just one spanking and it had been from my father. This was not long after my fourth birthday, and I don't even remember what I had done to deserve it, but my rear end was aching for a long time after several whacks with a wooden paddle. I couldn't imagine my mother actually using that paddle on me, but I wasn't about to test her. It was nap time.

My mother always cuddled up with me for naps, and she usually ended up sleeping longer than I did. If I were restless,

she would sing me a lullaby. It was always the same lullaby, and it was easy to be lulled to sleep with her soft voice
and the familiar lyrics that always started with several lines of 'laloo':

> *Laloo laloo laloo laloo laloo la.*
> *Go to sleep my darling little chicky*
> *Or the fox will catch you if you don't,*
> *Hushabye, rockabye mama's little darling,*
> *Mama's little lullaby a coo.*
> *Laloo laloo laloo laloo laloo la,*
> *Underneath the silvr'y shining moon,*
> *Hushaby, rockabye, mama's little darling,*
> *Mama's little lullaby a coo.*

I was definitely restless with so much on my mind. My mother sang the lullaby, but sleep was not in the cards for me on that particular day, no matter how many times she repeated the verses. Over and over again she sang them. I stayed still, pretending to sleep, but really just waiting impatiently for her voice to slowly die off. Then there was the familiar deep, steady, rhythmical breathing that I recognized as the sound of her fading away to sleep.

Slowly, carefully, I slid away from her embrace. I listened closely for any change in her breathing pattern, then tiptoed out of the bedroom. Wasting no time, I grabbed the matches, and off I ran to Mr. Hunter's.

Fearing that someone might take the matches away if they saw me, I went through our backyard to the back alley. All the garages in the neighbourhood were accessible via the alley. It was a hot, sunny day late in the summer, and most of the lawns had turned yellow. I always heard sprinklers on at night-time, and found it odd that nobody seemed to water during the heat of the day when the grass must have been thirsty.

Mr. Hunter's garage door was closed, and it was all quiet inside. I looked around at all the neighbouring yards. Not a soul stirred. The pile of junk reached half way up the fence and spread along several pickets. My stomach churned. I needed to pee. It made no sense. This was the moment I had been waiting for. I had to finish the task, the favour for Mr. Hunter that would make him proud.

I pushed open the box, picked out a match, and struck it on the side. Nothing happened. I struck it again and again. A few sparks flew, and then the match head broke off. Another match. This time I struck it more firmly. It flared up and stayed lit. Wide-eyed and gripping the match tightly between my thumb and forefinger, I stared at the steady flame and lowered it to the junk pile. Something caught fire. Flames shot up, but quickly died away.

I lit another match and held it to a greasy cardboard box near the bottom-center of the pile. It caught fire. Plumes of black smoke billowed upward. Success! Pleased with myself and certain that this flame would catch, I sauntered down the alley to survey the neighbour situation. I looked into the backyards of at least half a dozen houses. All were clear and quiet.

I turned to look back at Mr. Hunter's. My heart dropped to my stomach. Flames were shooting high above the fence, engulfing the fence itself. This was impossible. How did my small fire become a raging bonfire in just seconds?

I couldn't move. I swallowed hard and tried to ignore my increasing light-headedness. Above the rising flames were huge clouds of black smoke. Hell came to mind. As a regular church goer, I knew about the never-ending fires of hell, and I was sure I had just brought hell to earth.

I stared blankly at the matchbox still in my hands, and hoped against hope that my fire would miraculously go out. I watched in a hypnotic trance, then shuffled slowly towards the conflagration, drawn like a magnet. By the time I reached the burning pile it had seized hold of the garage, like some monster with fiery jaws.

People ran from their houses, converging on the scene. Someone yelled out about a garden hose and the fire department. A few men barked out orders above the frantic jabbering, then got everyone to back up.

Then, above the din I heard a noise coming from inside the garage, a car engine starting, or trying to. I heard it turning over and over like a stubborn beast crying in pain. Then. Muffled screaming and inarticulate shouting. It was Mr. Hunter.

He sounded hysterical. Out of control. I had never seen Mr. Hunter out of control. What was he was doing in the garage? He needed to get out of there. Flames were now eating away at the whole front of the garage, including the roof. The few would-be heroes with garden hoses were useless.

I heard more panicked yelling from Mr. Hunter as he tried desperately to get his friend's car started and out of the inferno. The whole scene was a living nightmare. People watched helplessly, some of them crying. Wailing sirens in the distance grew rapidly closer. Flames grew higher and spread quickly. And then it happened.

A deafening explosion from within the garage blew the large sliding door open and shattered the windows. People screamed in agony as flying shards struck their faces and arms.

The chaos was terrifying. Intense heat burned my forehead. Oily smoke filled my lungs. I was choking half to death and wanted to cry. No tears came. I couldn't take any more.

Praying for an escape from the madness, I clamped my hands over my ears, dropping the matchbox—it might as well have been a hand grenade. I felt like I was going to explode. The crime weapon was on the ground. I bent to retrieve it. Too late.

"Hey, there, young man," a deep male voice bellowed. "What are you doing with those? Why in God's name are you carrying a box of matches?"

"What the hell!" a woman yelled. "Did you start this?"

I slowly backed up and escaped into the mob. I saw an opening and ran. I didn't get far before another small explosion stopped me dead in my tracks. The crowd hushed, then—gasps of horror. I couldn't bring myself to turn around.

I glanced over my shoulder. Everybody was paying attention to the fire, not to me. I was free to run away, but my feet wouldn't move. I couldn't watch, yet I couldn't escape the madness. I wanted to die right then and there. I wanted God to throw me into the burning fires of hell where I belonged.

I screamed over the crowd. "Run, Mr. Hunter! Get out! Hurry! Run, run!" I continued to shriek at the top of my lungs until I ran out of breath and fell on my knees, sobbing uncontrollably. Through the clamour of voices and fire I thought I heard a muffled reply, but it might have been my imagination.

I stopped crying and strained my ears. Still on my knees, I squeezed my eyes shut and drifted to another world a million galaxies away. I was walking hand-in-hand with Mr. Hunter, explaining to him that I was only trying to help him get things done. I told him that I only wanted to do something good, just for him, so that he would be proud of me.

Just as I had come to expect, Mr. Hunter, in my daydream, was kind and understanding. His reply was the one I hoped and prayed for. He said that I was a good boy. Deep down, I knew I was not, but I buried that final thought in my guilt-ridden brain:

Mr. Hunter said I was a good boy. I just had to somehow convince myself that it was true.

The firemen arrived and the crowd dispersed, but not before the man who had yelled at me pointed me out to the fire chief. He carried me, unresisting, over to a fire truck. The match box was ripped from my hands. "Did you start this fire?" he asked. Tears rolling down my face, I nodded like a puppet as he fired more questions at me.

"You stay right here!" he yelled, and threw me into the back seat while he and his men continued to fight the fire.

It was a living nightmare. I watched out the car window through glazed eyes. I didn't even notice when the fire was at last put out. The fire chief returned, and I was jarred back to reality.

He grabbed my arms and shook me violently until my whole story came out in blubbering sobs. When I finished, he stared at me in disbelief for what felt like several minutes. Then he scolded me with such intensity that I wet myself. All I remember about the scolding was how he emphasized that a man had died in that fire.

"A man," I thought. "The man has a name." I wanted to interrupt him so I could tell him the man's name, and that he was my best friend. But he wasn't interested in hearing anything from me. His tirade continued as he drove me home where he dragged me to the front door of my house. He knocked hard several times before my mother finally appeared in her housecoat.

"Oh, my goodness!" she yelled, her eyes bugging out of her head, and her hand over her mouth. "Has Axel done something wrong?"

"Do you know where your son has been?" the fire chief asked sternly.

"Well, I was just having a quick nap, and it looks like my little monster escaped."

That triggered a volcanic eruption in the chief. He berated my mother, who was struck dumb by the chief's perplexing, unfathomable story. He swore, too. The worst words I'd ever heard.

She cried and shook her head at me in disbelief. The part that really confused me was that he was blaming her for the whole thing. That made no sense to me. Mom was napping the whole time, so how could she be blamed? Only one person was responsible for killing Mr. Hunter, and it wasn't my mother.

I wished and prayed for a new life after that and, in a strange way, my prayers were answered. But not the way I wanted them answered. The fire had caused an irreparable rift in the neighbourhood. My mother was now an outcast, unable to show her face in public.

My father received all the news long distance somewhere in his travels. He had an unusual way of dealing with it. He simply didn't return. Ever. Turned out he had been doing a lot more than building sales in the hospital industry. He had been building a new family in Toronto as well. So, with all the bad things happening in Victoria, I guess he figured it was the right time to tell my mother about his other life. He was wrong.

It was the last thing my mother needed to hear. She went pretty crazy. Within weeks she was put into some kind of mental institution.

It was not the new life I had prayed for. That was strike three for me. The three most important people in my life were now gone: my mother, my father, and Mr. Hunter. So where did that leave me? In foster care, and weighed down by a huge, black cloud of guilt.

Over the next few years, I begged and pleaded to see my mother. For the first year I was told that she was not allowed to see me. I cried a lot that year. After that she disappeared from the face of the earth. Nobody knew her whereabouts. She had been released into the care of some trauma center, but she left for a routine unsupervised walk one evening and never returned. A lot of people searched for a long time, but she was not to be found.

Even more confusing to me, my father never made any attempt to find her. He did make infrequent attempts to phone me, but his interests were clearly elsewhere.

With him being on the road so much, it was always Mom who had dealt with child-rearing issues and all the decision-making. He had always conveniently avoided the real challenges of parenthood like diapers, toilet training, fevers and temper-tantrums of the terrible twos and threes. He mastered avoidance, so why was I surprised he avoided something as monumental as this?

Our family was a shattered mess. And to my father, I was likely nothing but an obstacle. He had a new woman and two new kids in Toronto to look after.

Each phone conversation ended with a promise to come and see me soon. The first six or seven times my spirits were lifted by those promises. It was not easy coming to grips with the reality that he simply was not coming back. I was let down and left in a state of confusion and despair. Eventually I gave up on ever seeing my father again, and I wouldn't answer his calls.

CHAPTER 5
Life with Flick

Friday morning. I wake up to my radio alarm, and Billy Joel is singing "Vienna Waits for You." I like the lyrics and sing along softly while I work the crusties out of my eyes. My bedroom is downstairs in the basement. It's small, dark and musty, but my room is private, which is more than my older foster brothers Ted and Ben can say about theirs. They share a large bedroom upstairs, and they resent me for having my own. It wasn't my decision. They have Flick to thank for that. But they have a healthy fear of their dad, so it's easier to take it out on me.

Ted and Ben are sixteen and seventeen respectively, and they're both big boys, I would guess about two hundred pounds each. Fortunately, they don't actually get physical with me, but they do try to play mind games. They're not the sharpest tools in the shed, though, so they never come up with anything original. I play mind games with them as well, but they don't know it.

My favourite one is giving them cold showers. When Flick had the hot water tank replaced, I watched the plumber install it and discovered that the main taps for hot and cold water, the ones that shut off the water to the whole house, were right there. Now, when I feel the need for a little entertainment, I wait until I hear one of them stomping around in the bathroom upstairs.

Once the shower is running, I slowly turn off the hot water. Listening to them scream like little girls makes me split a gut. Then I turn the water back on, wait to hear the water running again, and play the game for a few more rounds before retreating to my room. They never catch on.

Ted and Ben's big thing is to put me down with worn-out one-liners about my big ears or about my too-small clothes. Quips like: "Hey, Dumbo, you gonna fly away?" or "Don't go climbing trees today unless you trim those ears first" or "At least you don't have to worry about a flood with those pants."

I keep a straight face but sometimes have to fight off tears, because they do bother me. But I'll never let on. I've always been self-conscious about my ears, and I've always envied people who have fashionable clothes. In fact, I'm secretly saving up my allowance to buy new clothes. That day can't come soon enough.

Outside of the house, I don't exist for them, and that suits me just fine.

Halfway through the song, I'm about to nod off again when explosive pounding on the door makes me leap right out of the covers. It's Flick's wakeup call.

"Get the hell up, you bonehead! If you're not ready in twenty minutes you bloody well walk to school!"

"Okay, I appreciate that," I reply sarcastically.

He opens the door to reveal his amazing, tattooed beer-gut hanging over his pyjama bottoms. "Don't be a smart-ass, or I'll come in there and kick *your* smart-ass." He waves a finger at me and flicks his bald head before retreating.

I don't want to test Flick's threat, even though he has yet to lay a hand on me. I get up and use the tiny downstairs shower. My designated bathroom is an exercise in space economy with a shower, a toilet and a sink in a space of about ten square feet. I have to rest my feet in the shower basin when I sit on the throne. But at least it's private.

Just as I'm about to come up the stairs, I hear Ted or Ben running the shower, so I play my little water game to pick up my spirits before surfacing for breakfast. As usual, I have to fend for myself. My foster mother, Margaret, sleeps in until long after everyone is gone. She's a screamer like Flick, so I appreciate every minute she sleeps.

I put some bread in the toaster just as Ted and Flick appear, and here we go. "You're gonna have to start getting your own ass out of bed, buddy. If you're gonna be a part of this family, get the hell on the same page!" Flick starts in.

"Okay, I get it," I mumble.

"Oh, okay, you get it, do you? Nothing is *okay* here as far as I'm concerned! Never mind giving me the okay, just bloody well get your lazy butt moving, and we'll all be okay!" He flicks his head and glares at me.

I butter my toast and decide not to respond. It's no use anyway. Flick is not what one might call a conversationalist. He just likes to hear himself speak, or yell. I dwell on his comment about being a part of his family. What a concept. I remember what it was like being a part of a real family, and I remind myself often that my mother loved me unconditionally.

My father did as well, I think, but he lost his commitment somewhere along the line. It's my mother's image, how she embraced me in her loving arms and sang me to sleep, that I cling onto like a life preserver to guide me through all the rough waters in my life.

I also fixate on the idea that Mr. Hunter is always watching me from above, and that I will one day earn his forgiveness. I haven't been to church for several years, but I want to believe that God is up there helping me out as well. I remember my mother telling me that He can perform miracles. I didn't know what a miracle was then; I know now.

In the foster world, you can't choose your family. The case worker finds someone who has an opening, and that's where you go. The interviews are a farce. Everything sounds wonderful and rosy when the foster parents are in front of the case workers. They play the game well, but I can tell who's in it for the money as soon as they open their mouths. I'm pretty sure Flick and Margaret are in it for the money.

I'm never included in the decision-making. If I were, I'd likely be homeless. Sometimes I seriously believe that being homeless would be better than dealing with my arrogant, self-serving foster parents.

But I need to regroup here. I'm just angry, and who am I to be so critical anyway? I have to remind myself about how this all came to be, about how I created the black cloud that weighs me down. I shouldn't complain. For now, it's a roof over my head and, as I always tell myself, it could be worse.

I will say this for the ministry: they are true to their word. They said that the circumstances surrounding my family break-up, specifically the fire incident, would stay confidential. I was far too young to ever have my name, and therefore our family name, published for what the papers described as an accidental fire.

We lived back then in the western communities, and none of my foster homes have been anywhere near there. To my knowledge, I've never crossed paths with any of our former neighbours. Besides, I believe that once the news spread that Mom had gone crazy and was sent away, the story was pretty well closed. So, my foster parents think I'm merely the victim of a nasty breakup. End of story.

Looking agitated as he pours his cereal, Ted says, "So what the hell is with that new water tank anyway? Having a shower is a bloody test. Starts fine, then it's so freakin' cold, I have to turn it off. Then it's fine, then it's cold, and holy crap! Something's really screwed up!"

I can't help it. I burst out laughing.

"What the hell is with you?" Ted yells, holding up a clenched fist. "That's funny to you? You need to work on your sense of humour, you freakin' idiot."

Then Flick starts in on me, and it's a tag team of ganging up on Axel while I gobble down my toast and toss back a glass of milk. I'm so amused by the success of my water game that I couldn't care less, even though my ears are ringing from the abuse.

Flick manages a gas station. He hates his job. I've heard him say it a hundred times already. And he's usually in a rage about something from the time he wakes up until the time he leaves the house. I think he should change jobs.

He's used the ride to school as leverage to keep me under his control for a few weeks now, but that's already worn thin for me. I'd rather walk. It's only thirty minutes at my strolling pace, and it helps to clear my mind.

So, when I tell Flick that I'd actually like to walk, it really throws a wrench into his whole being. His leverage is gone. This pisses him off even more. He slams the door on the way out.

As I walk to school, I wonder if Flick yells to himself all the way to the gas station. I wonder what it would be like having Flick for a boss.

CHAPTER 6
My Story Starter

My thoughts are a million miles away as Mrs. Watson reads ancient history from an ancient textbook: "Homo habilis fashioned tools from rocks, walked slightly stooped and showed no evidence of wearing clothes. Their existence was limited to warm climates because they had not yet discovered fire." *Discovered fire ... fire in ancient times ... fire in modern times ... fire ... fire ... fire.* I obsess about fire until the class ends.

"Let's leave it there for today. We'll finish the chapter and related questions tomorrow. Let's put our books away quickly before I change my mind," says Mrs. Watson with a cryptic grin. The class gives a collective cheer. Books fly off the desks. Most land on the floor. "Excuse me!" she calls above the high-spirited chatter. "I think your lockers are a better place for the texts, thank you!"

She waits patiently on her stool at the front of the class until everyone has settled down. "Okay, I need your undivided attention. So please, pencils and pens down, and let's get the creative juices flowing. We're going to start our Writer's Workshop." She pauses for the expected moans and groans and a few under-the-breath *I hate writing* comments.

Before continuing, Mrs. Watson makes eye contact with all the distractors.

"Now, tell me this. Why do you hate writing?"

Several hands wave. The responses are similar and predictable:

"We always get topics that I hate and I can't write about something I hate" or "Writing sucks. When is creative writing ever going to be useful in my life?" or "When I write something I like, by the time I do it over and over again, proofreading and editing and all that garbage, I end up hating it."

Then Chelsea says something that resonates with me. "I like writing because I can escape from everything. It's an outlet for all my thoughts, and I find it relaxing when I sit down at night and write."

"Thanks for that, Chelsea. Tell us, what sort of writing do you like to do?" Mrs. Watson asks with a big smile.

"I just write whatever comes to mind. Maybe it's about something that happened at school, or about a soccer game. Sometimes I just write down my opinions. I keep a journal. I'm also in the middle of a short story, but that's been a project for a while now."

"Well, Chelsea, you just saved me a lot of time explaining Writer's Workshop, because what you're doing is exactly what we do in Writer's Workshop. We find topics that interest us, and we just write. I'm not the one who supplies the topics; you people are. And you get to choose which projects you really want to perfect by going through all that proofreading and editing *garbage* that Joel was referring to."

There is some chuckling, but she now has our undivided attention. Usually writing is a mindless activity for me. I procrastinate, but I always complete the assignments, mainly to keep my grades up. But I think I can embrace Writer's Workshop.

"So, let's get started," says Mrs. Watson. "What we need is a topic, an opening sentence, or perhaps a title to start a personal anecdote. Now before your hands start waving, let me explain that a personal anecdote is simply a story about you. The reason we start there is because every one of you has a story to tell.

"It doesn't have to be something exciting or eventful. You have all lived for about thirteen years, so you have lots of stories. Think of a childhood memory, something you've talked about, laughed about, cried about, sweated about. Maybe it's something you hide deep down because it was embarrassing, but it could make for a good story." She pauses. "Okay, I'll start off by telling you one about me."

Mrs. Watson opens up a notebook and begins reading aloud her own personal anecdote. It's about a time when she was very young, and she was tobogganing in a stranger's yard because it had a nice slope. She was with a friend, and when the owner of the house came out, Mrs. Watson ran for her life, but her friend didn't follow.

She then tells about her reluctance to come back to face this old woman who was now talking to her friend. Fearing the worst, she made her way back, but almost wet herself. The lady asked her to put out her hand. She closed her eyes and, reluctantly, offered her hand to the lady. That's when the magic happened. The lady put money in her hand, then thanked her for using her yard because it gave her great joy to hear kids laughing and playing.

"So, you see," she finished, "your anecdote does not have to be something outrageously exciting or eventful. It just needs to be an event that means something to you. That lady's comment stayed with me forever. And to someone else it might not have been important at all. To think that I could give someone that much joy and I didn't even know it. That is a memory I treasure."

The class silently reflects on her story, and the creative wheels start turning. Some students are already writing, and others are chewing on their pencils while they dig into their memory banks for a meaningful story.

Looking pleased with the reaction, Mrs. Watson continues. "Okay, you have the idea now, so I'm going to give you about ten minutes to come up with just an idea. That's all I want for now, your idea for a story. Go back in time, or it could even be a recent event, and when I call on you I want you to tell us either the first line of your story or perhaps a title. Remember that the first line is the one that ropes the reader in."

It's an animated ten minutes with everyone wanting to share their story with friends. I listen while each person tries to outdo the next one in an effort to be heard. The noise builds up until it reaches a crescendo and nobody can really hear a thing. My own thoughts are drowned out by the clamour. It's not that I don't have a story, it's that I can't imagine sharing it with the class.

"Okay, time's up!" yells Mrs. Watson. She is ready with a pen and a class list. "I'm going to go through the list, and when I call out your name I would like you to tell me the first line of your story or the title. Nothing more for now. And remember, writers need listeners, so please listen to each person's response."

Mrs. Watson goes through the list. Poomer is on the bottom half, so my turn won't come for a while. The topics all sound pretty mundane, but I guess if they have meaning for the individuals, then it's all that counts. One by one, they deliver their first lines:

"It was the worst birthday party anyone could ever imagine."

"It was the final soccer match of the season, and I was playing with a fever."

"We were going skiing when my dad hit a deer with his truck."

Frank's is predictable: "I waited in the parking lot for this guy to come out for a fight." Eric's is interesting: "After waiting for my whole life, I finally got the stereo of my dreams." I make a mental note to talk to him about his story. If it's the one I'm thinking of, the one that involves me, he'll need to change the names to protect the guilty. Better yet, I might coerce him into telling a different story altogether.

Then it's Chelsea's turn: "I was playing in a soccer tournament up island when I met a guy who I thought was the nicest guy in the world." I wonder what she means by that. *Was* he actually the nicest guy in the world or did she just think he was, and he turned out to be a dud? I don't want to admit it, but I feel a pang of jealousy. It doesn't make any sense. Chelsea and I have had casual conversations, but that's it. Nothing even close to intimacy has ever occurred, not that I would mind if it ever did. I wonder what it'd be like to be the boy in her story.

Those thoughts take me on a tangent while Mrs. Watson continues down the list. I'm lost in my dream world when my name is called. "Axel?"

"Yes?"

"Your first line, please."

"Oh, right, my first line." I breathe deeply and sigh. "Well, um, my first line is like, uh, well ... I don't really know how to put it."

"Oh, come on, Axel. It doesn't have to be anything complicated. Just give us something so I know that you're ready to start writing."

I clear my throat and squeeze my hands together. All eyes are on me. I know I can make this all go away by simply making up a first line. I can always change it later.

"Axel, we're waiting. First line, please. If you really need more time, I could come back to you after Terry." Terry Williams is the last person on the class list, and his name is not far from mine, so there won't be much time anyway.

This started out as a simple exercise, and now I am feeling the weight of the world on me. I try some self-talk: "*Axel, just relax and come up with something. You're being an idiot and everyone is watching. The sooner you give her a line, the sooner all the attention goes away. Just quit sweating it and do like everyone else did. They're waiting.*"

"Axel, shall I move on and come back?" asks Mrs. Watson, sounding more impatient than ever before.

"Um, no. I, uh ... I have something."

"Okay, good."

I stare off into space, unconsciously grinding my teeth. I see Mr. Hunter. He's in his garage greeting me with a smile, then suddenly he's a ball of fire. I try to erase the second image, but it continues to grow. I can physically feel the heat of the fireball; beads of sweat form on my forehead. I wipe them away with my sleeve and start drumming with my ruler. Kids in class start laughing. They all look like Mr. Hunter. I drum louder and louder until Mrs. Watson runs out of patience.

"Axel!" she yells. "What in the world is wrong with you?" That's the first time she has ever yelled at me. I feel like crying. "Just give us the line and for goodness sake, let's move on!"

I clear my throat. My eyes bug out of my head. With no further hesitation, using the same volume as Mrs. Watson, I yell out my answer. "I was just four years old, almost five, when I murdered my best friend!"

CHAPTER 7
Regrets

"I really don't know why I said that," I say to Mr. Davis, our school counsellor. "I just, well, I guess I felt that I had to give Mrs. Watson a story topic and I couldn't think of one," I lie.

"Okay, pardon me for just a second, Axel," he says. He stares into a computer monitor and frowns in frustration as he types. "I'm just trying to shut this silly thing off. I think I'm one of the last holdouts in the district, but I'm slowly learning."

I wait patiently while he experiments with the new technology. I find myself staring at a large coffee stain just below the pocket of his new-looking yellow shirt. Mr. Davis constantly strokes his goatee while he plays with the computer. His goatee is thick, black, and well-groomed; it seems to make up for his thin, greying hair.

"You know," he says calmly, "ten years ago nobody would've dreamed that these would be everywhere. But here we are in 1995, and they're taking over the world." Another pause. "There, it's off. Nothing to it. Whew!"

He removes his reading glasses and takes a deep breath. "Right," he starts. "I think I understand where you're coming from, Axel. What I'm hearing you say is that you felt pressured, so you gave a response that just came out of left field to please Mrs. Watson. Does that make sense?"

"Yeah, it does."

"Okay, Axel. But tell me how you think your particular response made Mrs. Watson feel?"

"I think, uh …" I pause to reflect on that. How might she have felt? I try to put myself in her place and imagine a student telling me that he wants to write about a murder he committed. I think I would kick him out of the class for being a smart-ass, and probably send him to the counsellor, if not the principal's office. "I think it made her feel offended," I answer.

Mr. Davis nods. "Offended. That's probably an accurate word to use, Axel. Why do you think she might feel offended?"

"Because it's a total lie, and it sounds awful."

"I would have to agree with you that it sounds awful, Axel. But I don't think I'd call you a liar. That might be a little unfair." He strokes his goatee while he analyzes me. "Yes, you did make up your story starter, but I guess we could say that it was just fiction. If you were making something up for a writing project, that doesn't make you a liar. Does that make sense to you?"

"Um, yes, I guess it does make sense. But I really do see why Mrs. Watson was offended. It was supposed to be a story about ourselves. A murder topic does sound ridiculous, and I think she was pretty surprised. I think I offended her. Her and maybe the whole class. In fact, I know I did. She's never been upset with me before."

"By the sound of it, this is clearly a one-off for you, Axel. You sound like a sincere guy, and I really like the way you can see the other side, Mrs. Watson's side, of this situation." He rubs his goatee again, and then writes something down on a notepad.

"Quite an imagination, Axel," he continues. "Murdered your best friend when you were four, almost five. Do you see where there might be some concern about the theme of your story, even though it's fabricated? I mean, we see in the news some nasty things happening in schools: shootings, beatings, and so on. So your topic, as ridiculous as it may seem to you, triggers alarms and red flags. And it clearly got a rise out of Mrs. Watson."

He pauses to give me a chance to respond, but I'm speechless.

"So now, where do we go with this, right? I don't think we could classify this as a case that requires my immediate attention. Unless you actually have thoughts about hurting someone. Not the case, right?"

"Right. That would be the last thing on my mind." I can hear my own voice increasing in volume. "I would never think about hurting anyone! I would only think about saving someone!" I'm close to hyperventilating.

"Okay, Axel. Take some deep breaths," Mr. Davis says calmly. He waits patiently for me to compose myself. "I believe what you said, Axel. It would be a great thing if we could all save someone, wouldn't it?"

I nod in agreement.

"Axel, everyone makes mistakes, even good people like you. So you made a mistake. I think we can all live with that. Sometimes good things come from those mistakes, like me getting to know you better."

I continue to nod and attempt to mumble a thank you but nothing comes out.

"So, please do me a favour," he continues. "If you're put on the spot again, and you need to come up with a bogus topic to satisfy your teacher, try something that doesn't give her a heart attack."

I laugh and choke at the same time. "Yeah, I will, for sure."

"Now, besides giving Mrs. Watson the apology she obviously deserves, here's my assignment for you, Axel. First, never stop looking for ways to save someone—doing something good will always have its rewards. And second, please come by and talk to me at least once a week, just to talk. It would make my day."

Shivers run down my spine. "Thanks, Mr. Davis, I will," I sputter. His advice is basically the same advice that Mr. Hunter gave me and asked me to remember: *Do all the good I can do and good things will come back to me.* It's more than a coincidence to me.

And to think that I actually made his day by coming in to talk. Amazing. I'm sure I had just ruined Mrs. Watson's day, so maybe this is how the world is balanced. I make eye contact as I leave. Mr. Davis has a genuine smile, just like Mr. Hunter's. And his teeth, like Mr. Hunter's, aren't what you'd call perfect.

I think I have just found a person I can really talk to. More importantly, I have found someone who will listen to me. Just minutes before this I was a sorry, shameful idiot being sent away from class. Now I can't wipe the smile from my face.

It was the second morning block when I had my outburst, and I'm in no hurry to return to class. I take my time writing out an apology for Mrs. Watson. I also write out an apology of sorts that I can read to the class if I get the chance. I know that I'll be the hot topic of gossip, so I sneak off the school grounds to avoid everyone during lunch break, and then I try to sneak back in when the bell goes.

Frank reminds me that these kinds of things don't go away quickly. "Hey, it's the murderer!" he shouts the moment I walk back into the school. "Everyone run for cover! Lock down!"

"Okay, Frank. I get it. No need to scare everyone off. It's only Axel the sorry twit who screwed up. But if I do write that story, I'll be sure to make you my main character."

There's a lot more teasing to work through before I make my way back to the classroom. And I cringe at the thought of having to face Mrs. Watson. I hesitate at the entrance and stick my head in to see where she is.

She sees me instantly. "Axel, it's good to see you again," she says calmly. There's no anger in her voice whatsoever. In fact, she sounds light-hearted and welcoming. "Come on in here where you belong."

I wait for the steady stream of kids to enter the classroom, then I walk right up and hand her the apology note before taking a seat at my desk. She opens it and reads it right away. When she has read the whole note, she starts to put it down, then holds it up to reread it. Then she stares blankly at the paper while the whole class watches in silence.

The tension is palpable as she methodically folds it back up and carefully tucks it in her sweater pocket. Then she fumbles in her purse for a Kleenex, and turns away to wipe her eyes and blow her nose.

I wrote in my note that I was sorry for being so rude and disruptive, and all the things I knew she would expect me to say. What she might not have expected was the part where I went *"deep down"* for something meaningful to say. I told her that she reminded me of my mother, even though I could hardly remember her now. But I said that what I do remember about my mother is that she was eternally understanding and always kind.

After composing herself, she comes by my desk and quietly thanks me. She also tells me that I have made her day.

I suddenly feel that the world is a great place to be. I have the ability to make someone's day. Twice in one day. Now that's something. Feeling unusually confident, I put up my hand.

Mrs. Watson looks at me cryptically. "Yes, Axel?"

"I actually do have a starting sentence for my story."

"Oh, you do," she replies, mockingly. "Well, let's hear it."

"Okay. The plumber showed me how to turn off the hot and cold water to the whole house, and that's when the fun began."

CHAPTER 8
Fireworks and Heroes

I was never big on Hallowe'en. I participated because it was the thing to do, but I was never a big fan of candy. But throw some fireworks into the mix and I'm there. Eric tells me at school that day that he has bought a ton of Roman candles, and he wants me to come out with him to fire them off.

"I've got about fifty of 'em!" he says. "So you should come over and meet me on Sunday and we'll have a real show!"

"Wow! Fifty? That must've cost a fortune! Where did you get them all?" I ask. But as soon as the words leave my mouth, I regret broaching the topic.

"Oh, places. Don't worry about that," he replies with a smirk. "Are you in or not?"

"Yeah, sure, I'm in." If they are stolen, which I'm sure they are, at least this time I will only be an accessory after the crime.

"Okay, I'll tell you what," Eric continues. "We'll get started when it's good and dark, maybe about seven. Do you know where I live over on Bryden?"

"Yeah, I've been by your place." It's only three blocks away. "Should I come by your place at seven?"

"Yeah, good. But, uh, maybe don't actually, um, come up to the house," he stumbles. "Just, uh, wait near the corner and I'll meet you there."

"Okay, sure." There's probably a good reason why he's uncomfortable about inviting me, or maybe visitors in general, into his place. And I really don't care. I'm just looking forward to the fireworks.

Sunday arrives, and the fireworks start, but not the Hallowe'en kind. Flick is in a rage about the Quebec referendum. He's an armchair politician who, according to his own self, would be the 'best damn leader this country could ever have.' Now that's something to ponder: Flick as Prime Minister. He does have the prerequisites to qualify as a third world dictator, but that's where it ends. He'd have to have tight security to speak in public.

"Why the hell did Chretien even stick his nose in this business?" he screams as he waves his fist at the news anchor on TV. "He should've just let 'em get the hell out of Canada. Just carve out the whole damn province and let 'em drift away!"

Then Margaret gets in on the act, and the two of them seem about to renounce their Canadian citizenships. That wouldn't be a national disaster.

They rave about this while I make myself a sandwich for supper. We had talked quite a bit about the Quebec referendum in school. Mrs. Watson said that she wasn't really allowed to give her political opinions, so we discussed all the issues around a province suddenly leaving Canada. She did explain that the reason we all have to take French is because we're a bilingual country, and that the French are a huge part of our history and culture.

Besides the possibility of not having to take French again, there aren't any pros that make sense to me. It isn't like the visual Flick is suggesting, where the province would be physically removed. It would be like having a country within a country, and Canada would have this strange division.

I think about the days when I rode Maynard in and out of driveways. I remember that Montreal was a driveway I was afraid to go to since it was next door to Hunter's and out of my mother's sight. Now it's amusing to think that I might have been stopping in a foreign country on the way to St. John's. And we missed having that foreign country by less than one percent. Close call!

Ted and Ben enter the kitchen, shaking their heads as the rampage continues in the living room.

"Well," Ted starts, "at least Dad seems to have forgotten about this morning.

"Yeah, thank God for that," adds Ben.

"What happened this morning?" I ask.

"What? Where the hell were you?" snaps Ted.

"Lucky Axel," says Ben. "He was gone before the party started."

"Party?" Now I'm even more interested.

"Yeah, party. A Dad rage party. He got up late, said his alarm didn't go off, and holy crap, he doesn't like being late. We were all late, except I guess for you."

I just about spit out my food, then quickly step out of the kitchen to contain my laughter. My silly prank actually worked even better than I imagined. Music to my big ears! The previous day was a set-up I just couldn't pass by. The whole house was vacated by the time I came up for breakfast. Even Margaret had gone to an early hair appointment. I guess Flick drove her. I'd never had the morning to myself, and I cherished every peaceful second of it.

As I was on my way out, it dawned on me that the chances of me having another peaceful morning were slim to none, and a brilliant thought popped into my head.

I still had some time, so I stepped back in the house to put my clever plan into action. Nothing complicated. I simply went into Flick and Margaret's bedroom and set the alarm ahead one hour. The whole house operated on Flick's morning schedule, so if he didn't get up, nobody would. Nobody but me, that is.

My prank was successful. Everyone slept in, and it was peaceful. Two in a row! I had thought about waking up Flick, but I knew that somehow it would end up in disaster, so I decided to let the sleeping bull lie. I was gone before anyone stirred and thought nothing more about it all day. Until now.

Having control again, I step back into the kitchen and ask Ted and Ben what they're doing for Hallowe'en.

"We'll be shootin' off some fireworks at Connor's, and then he's having a big bonfire," says Ben. "Not for little twits with big ears, though."

"Oh, good one," I chirp. "I'll be shooting off my own fireworks anyway."

Ted wags his finger at me. "Well, be sure to count your fingers when you're done."

"Thanks for the tip," I counter.

The doorbell rings. "Trick-or-treat!"

Flick and Margaret suddenly go quiet, and I slip out the back door while they hand out treats. They never really question my whereabouts at night as long as I'm home by nine o'clock and in bed by ten. Being Hallowe'en and a Sunday, I'm sure an extra hour thrown in won't make a big difference.

The sidewalks are buzzing with trick or treaters. Lots of ghosts, scarecrows, witches, and strangely painted faces. There's no shortage of wild screaming, but it's all fun. Even though I was never able to generate that kind of excitement for Hallowe'en when I was younger, I'm actually enjoying it tonight. Something about the innocent wildness of the evening appeals to me.

It's a perfect evening with near freezing temperature, a starry sky, and a gentle breeze. I dodge kids all the way to Bryden Avenue where I plant myself on a rock wall near the corner, close enough to Eric's house that I can see his front door. It's a few minutes to seven, so I figure my wait will be short if Eric is reasonably punctual.

Right at seven o'clock a dark-coloured car pulls up in front of Eric's house, and two large men wearing black leather biker jackets jump out. They stand near their car and look around suspiciously. When there's a reprieve from trick or treaters, they walk up to the front door and knock loudly. Eric's mother is there in a flash. She hands them a paper bag.

One of the men reaches into his pocket and pulls out something to give to her in exchange. The transaction takes no more than fifteen seconds. Before another group of kids crosses their path, they are back in the car and smoking the tires as though making a clean getaway. As the car races pass me, the man in the passenger's seat scowls in a way that freezes me on the spot.

I'm pretty sure there wasn't candy in that bag. I think about the rumours that circulate about Eric's mother, and I wonder now if they're more than just rumours.

About five minutes later another car pulls up. This time it's just one woman who gets out. With the aid of a street light, I see that she's tall and slender with long, scraggly hair. She's wearing a short-sleeved t-shirt, clearly underdressed for the weather. I can't tell her age, but she walks with a limp that makes her look old. Like the two men, she surveys the whole neighbourhood carefully and waits for the kids to disperse before approaching the house.

Again, there is a paper bag and something exchanged. This all takes about fifteen seconds, then she's on her way. No smoking tires this time. She drives away casually, like she's in a school zone. I feel like an ogling idiot when she makes eye contact and smiles on the way by.

The rumours are confirmed.

I think about Eric, and what it must be like living in that kind of environment. Men and women from all walks of life coming to the front door, likely at all hours of the day and night, looking for something to get them high. And when they get that bag in their hands, what if they decide that their end of the deal is off? How would Eric's mother deal with that?

Or what if they are really desperate and decide that they want the whole stash? I wouldn't want to try and stop those biker-looking guys from taking what they damn well want. I guess there is some honour in the trade, but I've also heard about deals gone bad–like deadly bad.

A door slams shut. I turn to see Eric jogging out of his front yard wearing a backpack. He looks agitated, even with the goofy grin on his face.

"Hey, sorry I'm late, Axel. Got sort of tied up with helping my mom, trick or treaters and stuff."

"That's no problem," I reply. I'm not about to pry into his life, even though I'm aching to find out more about those transactions. "Lots of kids stuffing their bags full of candy tonight."

"Yeah, so, hey, follow me. We'll head over to Front Street and go toward the mall, and shoot some of these off on the way."

Cedar Ridge is an ancient strip mall that services Vic-East. It has the essentials: a Chinese convenience store, a dry cleaner and laundry mat, a thrift store, a second-hand book store, and a few other odd merchants in the mix whose doors I have never even considered entering. As we walk, Eric pulls a handful of Roman candles out of his pack.

"Now, remember the rules we heard from Constable Boyd," Eric says sarcastically. "Always have an adult to supervise, bury the fireworks firmly in the ground, and stand well away as soon as you light the fuse."

"Okay, so we're zero for three on that count. How do you really want to do them?"

"Well," continues Eric, "we just change things around and use Eric's rules. Eric's rules are sort of the opposite of the real rules. Like you're the supervisor, we bury them in our fists, and we hold on bloody tight while the fireballs blast out."

We both have a good laugh about Eric's rules. "How many balls are in these?" I ask.

"Ten. These are the expensive ones. So when you get it lit, count 'em, 'cause you don't wanna let go until they're all out. These babies will burn like hell if you hit yourself. And just don't aim the tube at me either."

"Don't worry, I won't."

Eric hands one to me and takes out a book of matches. "Now hold your fuse against mine," he directs. He lights a match and holds it down to the fuses. They both crackle to life instantly. "Now hold it up so they don't hit any kids!" he yells excitedly.

A colourful ball shoots out from each of our candles, high into the air. The reverse thrust that accompanies the blast surprises me. It knocks the tube right out of my hand.

"You idiot!" screams Eric. "You have to hold on tight! Grab it, quick!"

I bend to pick it up just as another ball shoots out. "Watch out!" Eric yells. He tries to stay focused on his own candle, pointing it upward, while he panics about mine. I keep trying to grab the moving target, but each time I get close another fireball shoots out, narrowly missing me each time.

Eric is laughing at that point. "Just leave it," he says. Let it blow itself out and just watch where it's pointing and get the hell out of the way. There's no kids around right now so don't worry about it."

"Thank God for that," I add. So we watch and dodge fireballs until we count ten.

"Okay, so now you know what not to do, right?" Eric chides. "Like don't let go of the tube. Like hold on for dear life, right?"

"Yeah, I got it. It won't happen again, believe me." As soon as I say that, the reality of the situation hits home. I'm playing with fire. And fire is at the root of the black cloud that follows me everywhere. It was fire that did more than just burn my best friend.

But here I am, playing with fireworks, even though I know all about the potential dangers. I paid close attention to Constable Boyd who recently did a presentation at the school. I was shocked when he showed slides of kids who had been badly burned by them.

Some nasty shots! I had to turn away for most of them. He told us about the chemistry of fireworks, how it has its own oxygen supply and will continue to burn until it's used up, even in water. Now that's something.

"You know what?" I say. "Being the idiot that I am, I'm gonna just be the assistant guy. I'll just be the lighter guy. You take out the Roman candle, I light it, and you let it blast. That way we stay focused on just one at a time and we don't have to dodge bullets at the same time."

FORGIVE ME, MR. HUNTER

"Hey, that sounds like a good idea. Not that I don't trust you," he mocks. "I love shootin' off these things. So here, you take these."

Eric hands me the book of matches, and we continue on our Hallowe'en escapades. It's like an assembly line with me lighting candle after candle and Eric shooting them off, always being careful to hold them firmly upwards. But, true to his unpredictable nature, he's soon aiming the fireballs every which way, not just straight up in the air as originally planned. He starts using random objects for target practice, like stop signs, fire hydrants, and trees. When some of the fireworks ricochet in the direction of trick or treaters, I start to worry.

"Hey, Eric, do you think maybe we should keep them going up so we don't hit anyone?" I reason.

"Hey, don't worry about that. I'm not gonna hit anyone. This is sure a hell of a lot more fun than just firing them straight up," he replies, just as a fireball deflects off a nearby tree and lands at his feet. "Whoa!" he howls. "That was damn close!"

"Yeah, that was too damn close," I agree. "And I don't think we want them to get that close to the kids, right?"

"You got a point, but ..." Before Eric can finish his sentence, two fireballs fly right at us. One lands on my jacket. I flick it off, but not before it burns a small hole near the right pocket.

I can see the culprits across the street, but I can't make out their faces. They don't look all that big, probably close to our age.

"Hey, assholes!" I yell. "What the hell do you think you're doing? You burned a frickin' hole in my jacket!"

"Oh, get over it, and don't call us assholes, asshole!" one of them screams back. "You guys started it! You almost got me in the bloody head!" Then more fireballs come at us and we drop to the ground to avoid being hit.

"Get some candles out, fast!" I say to Eric as I scramble to light a match while flat on my back. He holds out one in each hand, and I light them instantly. Then Eric stands up and the battle is on. He looks like a western gun fighter with a pistol in each hand, and his aim is true. The first ball hits one of the guys in the gut. He frantically brushes it away. Eric takes full advantage of the opening.

He walks towards the guys with fireballs blasting and now they're on the run, calling Eric a shithead as they trip over trick-or-treaters in their scramble to escape the barrage. Eric is relentless. He keeps them on the run until all twenty balls have been fired. The kids on the sidewalk disperse onto lawns, screaming at the top of their lungs.

"Get a life, you dorks!" Eric yells. He waves the spent candles at the two bodies disappearing into the night. When it's clear that the whole episode is over, he starts making his way back. He barely steps onto the road when a black SUV pulls up and blocks his way. Red and blue lights start flashing.

Oh, no, I think. Or did I say that out loud? *The cops. We're hooped.*

Two uniformed officers step out of the ghost vehicle and order Eric to stop and come over.

Eric shuffles over sheepishly. I hear him trying to apologize. "Hey, officers, I'm really sorry, but these guys were shootin' these—"

"—Be quiet!" yells one of the officers. I can't make out what is being said after that. The two of them take turns lecturing Eric in low tones while he just keeps his head down and nods every now and then. Next, they confiscate his backpack and stuff Eric in the back seat of their vehicle.

I want to jump in and save my friend, but they're gone in a flash. What could I have done anyway? I would have incriminated myself, and then it would have been both of us in that backseat.

So here I am, Eric's accomplice once again, but at least I'm free. Now I feel a little guilty about the whole thing. After all, Eric had invited me out for this adventure. He had supplied all the Roman candles, and he'd been willing to share them with me. And he'd been defending the both of us from those two idiots. I have to admire him for his reckless courage.

My blood boils. I pace while my mind races. It was because of those twits that Eric is now on his way to the police station. Yet they are still out there somewhere, probably having a good laugh. That really rubs me the wrong way. My adrenaline surges. Revenge, that's what I need. It will be two against one, but I'm willing to take my chances.

I jog in the direction I saw them run. Everything is back to normal. The sidewalks are crowded with kids, so I stick to the edges of the street. The two guys are nowhere in sight. I pick up the pace and turn right onto Chambers Street, thinking that's where I'd go. I'm not exactly a fitness machine, and I'm gasping for breath.

Nevertheless, I keep pushing myself, adrenaline keeping my legs moving. About two blocks down Chambers I see a commotion that stops me in my tracks. Under a bright street light, I see someone in a pumpkin costume, clearly older than the kids, running and yelling frantically at someone. The pumpkin has a female voice.

"You assholes!" she screams. "Give that bag back, you scumbags!" She seems to have the same sentiment for her scumbags that I have for mine. It makes me chuckle, but I feel her frustration. I'm about to offer my assistance when, coincidence of coincidences, the *scumbags* I'm looking for come running in my direction, one of them with a full pillowcase of candy.

The pumpkin is not far behind, but she's losing ground. Good thing the scumbags are running right to me. I jump onto the sidewalk to cut them off. They're too busy watching what's happening behind them to notice me. I stay focused on the one with the bag.

Just as he's approaching me, I drop down and stick out my leg. He whirls to see what's in front of him, and then I kick sideways and take out both his feet at once. With an "oomph!" he is flat on his face, the wind knocked out of him. He writhes in pain and gasps for breath. His faithful accomplice sprints into the chaotic scene, glances at his downed partner, and keeps on going.

I pick up the pillowcase and hold it out to the fuming pumpkin, who stumbles in like a miscued actor. She breathes hard, still furious. She ignores the bag and, instead, kicks the scumbag in the ribs, then calls him every lowlife name in the book.

"That was my little sister's candy, you spineless frickin' worm!" she shrieks. And that's only the beginning. I watch her with admiration, then I realize who this pumpkin is: Chelsea! The always popular Chelsea, berating the candy thief with language I never imagined would come out of her mouth. It's a different side of Chelsea, a real human side, and I'm liking it. And I must admit, she's a fine-looking pumpkin.

The guy attempts to get up. He shakes his head and tries to get his breath, blood running from his nose. When he sees me, he comes to life.

"Axel," he sputters, still struggling to breathe. "So it was you. You just wait ... you're dead meat."

Now I recognize him. It's Donny Cox, a guy from one of the other grade eight classes. I don't really know him, but I do know that you don't want to be on his bad list. Not so much because of him, but because of his notorious big brothers.

Anyway, I can't dwell on that at the moment. My adrenaline is still flowing and right now I have the upper hand. "Yeah, well, bring it on," I finish.

Then Chelsea, all calm now, comes over to me and smiles, orange face-paint tears running down her cheeks. It's a big, glorious smile that makes me shiver inside. "Axel, thank you! Thank you so much for what you did. That ... that thing," she scowls at Donny still squirming on the ground. "That lame brain came up from behind and snatched my sister's bag. I mean, what's with that? That's just unbelievable."

She takes a deep breath and faces me again. "Anyway, enough about him. You saved the night, Axel. My sister would've been destroyed if he got away, and ... and, just thank you." Then she gives me the biggest hug ever.

I'm caught off-guard, but no complaints from me. She almost squeezes the wind out of me. Then she takes the bag from my hand and gives it to her little sister, who has been waiting quietly behind her. "Thanks again, Axel. I'll see you at school."

"Hey, not a problem," I reply. "Really not a problem. I'm just glad your sister got her candy back."

"You take care, Axel," she finishes.

"Yeah, thanks. You, too."

CHAPTER 9
Promise Not To Tell

After that magic moment with Chelsea, I can't even consider going home. I feel funny inside, uplifted and confused at the same time. It's still early, so I take a long walk. The ocean is not far away from Vic-East, so I head in that direction, towards the Ocean Boulevard Bridge.

I'm so deep in thought, I don't even hear the noisy kids still collecting candy. The cold night air keeps me moving at a brisk pace. A city block disappears behind me in a few short minutes.

Soon I'm on Ocean Boulevard Drive, close to the bridge, where a windy path leads me down to an oceanside walkway. I take a seat on the first bench I come across. I'm all alone on the walkway. Normally I'd be wary of shady characters. Not tonight.

Small, whispering waves roll onto the shore, not twenty feet in front of me. The Inner Harbour is filled with flashing beacons and an array of colourful lights from surrounding hotels and the Parliament Buildings. The Empress Hotel is the most stunning and majestic of them all. Then I spot a noisy float plane making a slow landing just beneath a falling star.

I've seen the ocean and the Inner Harbour hundreds of times, but tonight it's like I'm seeing it all for the first time. So beautiful.

I reflect further on the evening. Was Chelsea's embrace anything more than a simple, genuine thank you? I hope so.

When you have no confidence, you can't imagine actually being in a relationship. Tonight, for the first time, I feel that maybe, just maybe it could happen, that anything is possible.

My thoughts turn to Eric and friendships. I seem to always have acquaintances, but never close friends. That's my fault. If I suspect someone wants in on my deep, dark secrets, I play the avoidance game, and the friendship never evolves.

Today I'm wondering about the true meaning of friendship. Is Eric a friend or an acquaintance? I enjoy hanging out with him. He's funny. He's generous. And tonight he proved his loyalty all the way to the police station.

He's a little rough around the edges, but I think he has good heart. Eric is also a thief, but, hey, no one is perfect. Look at me. So then the question is: What can I offer as a friend in return? I'm not sure, but I believe I'm ready to peel off a few layers to find out.

Monday morning after Hallowe'en is a little quieter at school than usual. Half the students are still in bed. The ones that do show up, like me, are fighting to keep their eyes open. I wasn't out too late, but I was wide-awake half the night thinking about Chelsea and Eric.

Still worried about Eric, wondering whether he actually spent the night in the slammer, I see the answer coming my way: Eric, with a goofy look on his face.

He wags his finger at me.

"What?" I ask. "What's that supposed to mean? And what the heck happened to you, anyway?"

"To me? The real question is: what happened to you? Tell me about it, Axel. And don't forget about the part with Chelsea, lover boy." Then he does something that he rarely does. He laughs whole-heartedly. It's a real belly laugh, so great a thing to see, for two reasons. First, having seen a small sample his life, I can understand why he doesn't laugh a lot. Second, if he's so happy, his night with the police could not have been that bad.

"Okay, slow down, buddy," I respond, patting Eric on the back. "So, what exactly did you hear about me anyway? And where did you hear it from?"

"It was on the radio, on the Q, where else?" he replies, then doubles over with another fit of laughter.

"Oh, ha, ha. Good one. So you're not going to tell me?"

Eric composes himself. "Let's just say that there are no secrets around these parts. Jared and Tyler were out gettin' candy, and they saw the whole thing. You know, like Chelsea mauling you and giving you goo-goo eyes. And hey, the best part! Way to go with taking that jerk down! That part was icing on the cake. Man, I wish I could've seen that. I heard it was Donny, right?"

"Yup, Donny Cox. Threatened me while he was down for the count, too."

"Don't listen to that chicken shit. That guy's nothing but talk."

"Yeah, but what about his big brothers?"

"They're just big losers. Don't sweat it, man."

"I won't, for now. Life goes on, I guess. But you haven't told me about your night. What did the cops do?"

Eric clenches his fists and grimaces. "Ah, it was nothin' really. They just lectured me and took the candles away."

"And that was it?" I say incredulously.

"Well, pretty much, I guess. They forced me to take a ride home with them so they could hand me over to my mom. Like she wants to deal with cops, right?"

"Oh, so, uh, was she, you know, okay with everything?"

"No. God, I screwed things up for her. Hey, come over here so I can tell you something, in private."

I follow Eric to a small nook in between the lockers where there is just enough room for two people. What I'm about to hear can't be good news.

Eric grips my arm. He's dead serious. I've never seen him like this. "Can you keep a secret? I mean like a *real* secret? Like one where you don't tell even one person? Can you promise me that?"

I don't hesitate. "I promise." I brace myself. But I'm keen to help. This is my first opportunity to be real friend and return his loyalty.

"Okay, listen. My mom hates it when the police come around. She's had some really bad experiences with those guys. Most of it was when my dad was around. Long story, but he's in jail for a while. Mom's just trying to make money so her and I don't get our asses kicked onto the streets. Now, she'd kill me if she knew I told anyone, so shhh, right?"

I nod. He looks around nervously for eavesdroppers. I wait anxiously for the next line.

"Okay, here it is. She's making extra cash selling drugs. Not the real serious ones," he adds defensively. "Like it's not meth and stuff like that. You know, not the stuff that people cook up in their basements, and who the hell knows what goes in it? It's all clean stuff, grass and hash and stuff, and maybe a little snort, but nobody gets hurt, you know."

"Oh," I say. I don't know what else I *can* say. I'm shocked, even though I was already convinced that the rumours about all this were true.

"So, now my mom is all freaked out," Eric continues. "The cops drop me off just as some guy is handing some cash to her. Of course, they get suspicious and start firing questions at the guy.

The idiot has guilt written all over 'im. He can barely speak. I'm thinking he's screwed for sure. But he keeps mumbling and stuttering until the cops get impatient and talk to my mom instead."

Eric continues to race through his story, barely taking time to breathe. "They told her all about me and the Roman candles, and how I was a real public nuisance and how she needed to give me more supervision. That got Mom really irritated, and when she gets irritated she usually flips out. So she starts telling off the cops, saying they didn't have the right to tell her how to run her life, and that I was the greatest kid a mother could have, and this is nothing compared to the thugs and murderers and rapists out there, and they should be spending more time on that stuff, and on and on and on."

"That sounds a little weird," I comment. "She's mouthing off to the cops when they actually came to scorn *her* out."

"Yeah, weird is one way to look at it. The cops didn't know what the hell just hit 'em. It was actually pretty funny, but I didn't dare laugh. If they'd been around for any of the heyday crap with my dad, they'd know about thugs and all that stuff. And they'd know why my mom was blowing off steam.

"Anyway, the good thing was that my mom flipping out gave the guy who just bought the drugs a chance to get the hell out of there. So he gets away, and the cops finally leave our place, but they left with a warning that really pissed off my mom. They said that they're watching our place closely. So now she's really scared about getting busted. I'm scared, too. We're up the creek if she gets busted."

"Yeah, I guess I'd be worried, too," I agree. "I sure hope it all just goes away."

The bell sounds and Eric steps away from the nook. He gives me a high five, stares at me solemnly and says, "Promise, right?"

"Promise."

CHAPTER 10
Do All the Good I Can Do

I keep my word with Eric. I feel like a character in a spy novel, like an international spy, in a life and death situation. Under pressure, torture, and the threat of death, how would I fare? I imagine my fingernails being yanked out, or worse, if I don't tell. And if I do tell, they'll still kill me, or maybe my own people would, for cracking under pressure. But that's just fiction. Eric's situation is real.

Deep down I know Eric's mom is a walking disaster. She's a drug dealer, under surveillance by the cops. If her drug deals go bad, their lives will be in the gutter. And if the drug deals continue, their lives are still in the gutter. They can't win. And now that Eric has made me a keeper of this disastrous secret, I want to help make things right. Though I have no idea how.

It's the last block of the day. I'm tired of yawning, tired of watching everyone else yawn. Chelsea is the only thing that keeps me awake. Every time I see her, she waves and smiles.

Mrs. Watson sighs over her listless class.

"Okay, people, let's have a discussion about something that might perk you up: our field trip at the end of the year."

The class gives a resounding cheer; everyone is awake once again. The field trip is to Playland in Vancouver. We're to fundraise to offset the costs. Never too early to get things started.

Mrs. Watson raises her eyebrows and smiles. "Good. I thought some of you had stopped breathing." She writes on the chalkboard: *How do we know when we are privileged?*

A few hands go up. "Yes, Richard?"

Richard is a tubby, smart guy with strong opinions. And he likes to suck on the ends of his long red hair. Thankfully, he always sits at the back. Whenever he asks a question, it becomes a heated discussion. "What does that question have to do with our field trip," he queries.

"Good point, Richard," replies Mrs. Watson. "So, let me ask you this: would you say it's a privilege to go on a field trip?"

"Well, not really. It's something that most grade eights do."

"I find that line of reasoning very interesting." She walks to the back of the classroom. Then looks at Richard. "So then, do you feel that it's a right for you to go on a field trip?"

Richard fidgets and looks around the class for support. He likes debating, so he's well aware of the difference between valid and vague arguments. "Um, well, when you put it that way," he stumbles, "I have to say that, no, it's not a right. It's a privilege. I guess we can't demand that we go on this field trip, but we'd probably rebel if we didn't."

"Yeah! We'd rebel!" the class shouts. Someone pounds on their desk and everyone follows suit.

Mrs. Watson holds up her hands to quell the commotion. When she has once again regained control, she just laughs.

"You guys are very funny," she says. "But I'm a little concerned about that outburst. I sense a lot of followers in the crowd, and not many leaders. But I suppose you have the *right* to be followers, and it should be your *privilege* to have Richard as your leader."

"Yeah, King Richard!" someone yells. Now the whole class chants: "King Richard! King Richard!"

Richard takes a bow while holding back his long hair.

"Okay," continues Mrs. Watson. "We strayed, but that's okay. Now, back to my question on the board. You people obviously understand the difference between a right and a privilege. The field trip to Science World is a privilege, for sure, but I want to take us beyond that. Let's think about our lives in general, and then let's compare them to the lives of millions of people in third-world countries. What things do we have that much less fortunate people in the world would consider privileges?"

Eric is first to put up his hand. "Eric, what do you think?" He catches my eye and nods. I nod and shrug in return.

"Well," Eric responds, "Not everybody here is really privileged. I think our world's just different from theirs. So, like maybe they would be privileged if they had food every day, but here everyone just expects that. Most people in Canada don't even have to think about getting food because it's just there all the time because we're a richer country."

"Some good points, Eric, but ..."

Eric continues before Mrs. Watson can finish her sentence. "But not everyone in Canada is rich like people in poor countries might think. There's a lot of poor people here. So, if we live in a country where food and clothes and stuff are just expected, then why doesn't everyone have those things, like all the time?"

Eric gives me thumbs up. I'd never heard him speak his mind like that before, and I'm impressed, but also concerned. Mrs. Watson surveys the class for a response as a low murmur spreads.

"Anyone?" she asks.

Lots of jabbering, but nobody is willing to jump into the discussion. Am I the only one who knows Eric's desperate situation? How close to the bone his speech was? I know where Mrs. Watson is taking the discussion, and I don't want Eric to incriminate himself any further, so I raise my hand.

Mrs. Watson looks relieved. "Axel, we'd love to hear your thoughts."

"I agree with a lot of what Eric is saying. I know that not everyone in Victoria has money, but I think in most of the third world countries it's pretty common to have next to nothing. I think they would see us as being privileged if all we have to do is go to the grocery store to get food. I mean, I've seen those ads for starving kids on TV, and it looks pretty sad if that's really what it's like."

"Thanks, Axel," says Mrs. Watson. "How many of you have seen those ads that Axel is referring to?"

Pretty much the whole class raises their hands.

"Okay, that's great. So you have an idea of what I'm talking about. Now, I'd like you to watch this short video. I warn you that much of the information is quite alarming, but I believe it's important that we understand the reality of life in other parts of our world."

She turns on the TV and pushes the video cassette into the VCR. It starts right away with a title in large black letters: *Nutrition Solution: We Can Save the World*, and bleak background music. It looks just like the ads on TV, but it's more intense.

Shabbily-dressed, emaciated black children, flies swarming their faces, hold out empty bowls. The landscape is barren. The commentator talks about a persistent drought that has plagued the country for close to a decade. Housing is non-existent save for some primitive lean-tos. Education is only a dream. Day-to-day survival is their way of life.

The video ends with a plea to help those children. "For just one dollar a day, only thirty dollars a month, you can save one of these children from starvation and thirst. There is no need for any one of these children to suffer from malnutrition or lack of water when we have so much to give. But we must act now. We're losing hundreds of these beautiful children each and every day. The more we can give, the more lives we can save and those sad faces will turn into grateful smiles. So please donate today to Nutrition Solution."

The ads on TV never hit a nerve like this one did. I've never really thought about how privileged I am. I have a lump in my throat. So many poor helpless kids who have no hope in their lives. My problems seem insignificant compared to theirs.

I do have a daily struggle with my huge black cloud of guilt, but I don't have to fight for food or water to stay alive.

It suddenly dawns on me, like a beaming ray of optimism, that this could be the solution to my problem. If I can save one of those children, I will be doing something good. *Do all the good you can do.* As clear as the day he said it, I can hear Mr. Hunter giving me that advice.

Mrs. Watson brings me back to earth. "Okay, so that's what we're going to be thinking about when we do our fundraising for the field trip. We're going to sell chocolate almonds, and while you will be benefitting from your sales, so will some far less-privileged children on the other side of the world.

"That's how people in first world countries like Canada share the wealth with third world countries." She holds up a case of chocolate almonds. "These are what we'll be selling. People love them. They really sell themselves."

"How much are they?" someone yells out.

"The almonds sell for just two dollars. But they cost us one dollar each, so our profit is obviously one dollar per box. Now, out of that dollar, here is how we decided to break it down: ten percent will go into the general fund to cover costs that we may have overlooked. That's just ten cents per box. Fifty percent will go towards your own personal field trip costs, which we calculated at about fifty dollars, plus spending money. And you're allowed to bank money with us for spending money. So how much is now left over?"

Frank actually raises his hand.

"Yes, Frank."

"That leaves almost a half a box of almonds for me out of every one I sell," he quips.

That triggers an outburst of laughter from the class.

"Okay, thank you, Frank. Remind me not to go into business with you. You'd eat all the profits," Mrs. Watson returns. More laughter and Frank turns red. "Okay, so who has the answer? Yes, Shelly?"

Shelly is a quiet, prim girl. "Forty percent is still left over, and that's forty cents."

"Thank you, Shelly. You're right. So that forty cents will go to the Nutrition Solution charity, and we'll see how many kids we can save as a class."

I pull out my calculator. I want to know how many boxes I would need to sell to save one child. The answer is seventy-five. Now that's something. I sell seventy-five boxes of chocolate almonds, which supposedly sell themselves anyway, and one child is saved. If I sell a hundred and fifty boxes, two kids are saved. Seven hundred and fifty boxes saves ten kids! My heart starts racing.

After all these years, I believe I've just stumbled on the solution that might clear my black cloud. I hope Mr. Hunter is listening. "*This is for you,*" I whisper under my breath. "*I am going to save more children than you can imagine. I'm going to do all I can do*

Forgive Me, Mr. Hunter

for others, just like you said, and it's all going to be in your name. And you'll be proud of me. All I want in return is for you to be proud of me, and for you to forgive me."

"Listen up, everyone," directs Mrs. Watson. "The bell is going to go soon, so I would like everyone to sign out a case of almonds to start selling. Plus, I have these envelopes for you to use to collect the money."

She tells us the safety rules about selling door-to-door, how to look after the money, and so on. "And note, there are thirty-six boxes to a case, so be sure to bring in the full seventy-two dollars when everything is sold. We will do all the accounting at school."

The bell sounds and everyone scrambles out the door with their case of almonds, anxious to be first to make a sale. I'm opening my locker when Frank approaches me.

"Hey, Axel. What do you think about me and you selling together?"

"Hey, Frank. Um, selling together, eh?" My first instinct is to say no. I'm now on a personal mission to save children, and I need to do it entirely on my own. But then again, what difference would it make if we work together? Seventy-five boxes will save one child whether if it's accomplished with one person or a hundred people. And combining sales with a partner, logically, should speed up the whole process. I've never been a real team player, but for all the right reasons that is about to change. "Yeah, sure, let's do it."

Then, as if in answer, Eric stops by and asks us if we'd like to buy a box of almonds.

"No, thanks. Got an oversupply. Sorry," I return, tongue in cheek.

"Hey, I was thinking," says Eric. "Now, no jokes about that, okay?"

"Beat me to the draw," I return.

"But seriously, I was thinking that it would be a good idea if we sold these almonds together. Are you up for that?" asks Eric.

Frank and I look at each other and shrug. Then Frank speaks up. "Hey, Axel and me were just talking about that. We're gonna sell together. So, it's up to you I guess, Axel. But I don't mind if there's three of us if you don't."

Why not one more partner? "Well, I guess we're all sales partners then," I say. "Let's get in touch a little later on today and we'll figure it all out."

We all shake hands, and then Frank and Eric take off.

I dawdle at my locker, feeling inspired. But, as I've learned from experience, things change quickly in this unpredictable world.

My case of almonds is suddenly kicked from my grasp and skids down the hallway, still in one piece. I turn. It's Donny Cox.

"Hey, tripper, feel the end of *my* boot!" he yells with a crazed look, launching his foot into my upper leg. My quads cramp with pain.

"You bastard!" I return. His other foot is coming towards me. I grab it in mid-air and hurl him backwards. He hits the floor hard. I'm psyched for an all-out brawl. I'm about to pounce, but he waves at me in self-defence and actually starts to cry.

"Leave me alone, you asshole!" he shrieks.

I stand over him still shaking with anger, and give a fake jab to his head.

"You pathetic piece of crap!" I yell. "Stealing candy from babies? What a scumbag!" I'm stealing lines from Chelsea. I think he sees the irony of the whole scenario. He was down for the count then, and here he is looking up at me from the ground again.

I continue to lambast him with insults, feeling no pity for the teary-eyed weasel. I'm hitting my stride when a thundering voice stops me dead mid-sentence.

"Axel, stop this instant! Leave that poor boy alone!" It's Mr. Murray, the vice-principal.

CHAPTER 11
Mr. Davis

"I really don't know why I said that," I explain to Mr. Davis.

"Well, Axel, according to Mr. Murray, you were very creative with your choice of words, and you were about to beat on Donny Cox while he was already flat on his back. I can't imagine what Donny could have done to deserve that." Mr. Davis calmly strokes his goatee.

I'm ready to spill all the beans about Donny, but I catch myself. "Yeah, well, I don't really know what to say. Donny's not my favourite guy in the world. He did some things that put me off I guess."

This is a real dilemma. If Mr. Davis has the facts about the Hallowe'en incident, he'll understand where I'm coming from. But ratting out Donny is a little below me. Donny is the last guy on Earth that I want to protect; it's my personal principles at stake. Not his reputation.

Mr. Davis nods and replies, "I would've bet on that. And you know what? I might have done the same thing at your age, under the circumstances. You don't have to tell me the details. I'm more interested in just having a good conversation with you. That okay with you?"

"Yeah, sure. I'm happy to talk," I reply, breathing a sigh of relief.

"Great. I love it when things are going well for students, but life has the tendency to throw in a few road blocks, and it's my job to clear the roadway."

Smiling, I reply, "Yeah, I get it. I've had a few of those road blocks lately."

Mr. Davis grins and looks me in the eyes. "Maybe so, but it looks like you're keeping your head above water." He pauses. "So Axel, take me back a little here. Tell me a little about yourself."

I look around his office while I think. On the wall behind Mr. Davis' chair is a large framed picture of him with a lady, I presume his wife, and two young boys. They're at a lake. They wear bathing suits and big smiles. A canoe sits on the beach beside them. They're going on a family adventure. I feel envious.

"That's a nice picture," I state. "How old are your boys?"

"You mean my two little goofballs?" he replies, turning around to point to the picture. "That one there on the right is Theo. He's four and a half, and Richard is five and a half. We had them pretty close together. They're smiling like little angels there, but believe me, they can be little brats." He says this with a twinkle in his eye.

"Looks like you guys were having a good time there."

"Yes, we were, for sure. That was taken just last summer. I do love spending time with those guys, and my wife, of course. I guess that's what summers are for, right?" He pauses, but I have no reply. "Do you have any brothers or sisters, Axel?"

"No, it's just me. I always wanted one, though, at least when I was little. Especially a big brother, but a little one would've been good, too. Now it's too late anyway."

Mr. Davis chuckles. "Well, I guess that's a family matter. I'm sure your mom is busy."

"You'd have to ask her, wherever she is."

Mr. Davis winces. "Are you not living with your mother, Axel?"

"No."

"Are you with your father then?"

I shift nervously in my chair. I'm confused. I thought the counsellors knew everything about all the kids in the school. Mrs. Watson knows, at least about my living in foster homes. Maybe, I decide, he does know but he wants it first hand. If that's the case, this is a waste of time.

"Um, Mr. Davis," I say, "have you read my file?" I've seen my file before. It was on a teacher's desk last year, and I happened to see my name on the tab. It was a thick file, too.

"No, I haven't. I probably get a few hundred files at the beginning of the year, and it would take a ton of time to go through them all. There's just not enough time in a day. And, quite honestly, your name has never come forward. Should I have a look?" he asks.

My mind is stuck on his point of never having enough time in a day. That was Mr. Hunter's line, the one that I'll never forget. That was where it all started: me wanting to help Mr. Hunter to get things done. My hands shake. I force myself to focus.

"Well, I don't know," I finally reply. "I'm not sure it would change anything if you did look at it. Probably nothing serious in it really. I'm living in a foster home."

"How long have you been in foster care?"

"About nine years."

Mr. Davis sits upright. "Nine years? So you've been in foster care since you were in kindergarten?"

"Yeah, a little before I was in kindergarten. Lots of different homes, too."

"And your parents, are they in the picture at all?" he asks, but then jumps in before I can respond. "Sorry, Axel, maybe I shouldn't be asking you that. I don't know anything about the circumstances of your parents. Are they—"

"—Mr. Davis, it's all okay," I cut in. "I don't mind just telling you about my family. Yes, I've been in foster care for a long time, way too long. But it's all out of my control. Are my parents still alive? My dad is, but I can't say for sure about my mom. She was in a mental trauma centre a long time ago. I haven't heard anything about her for seven or eight years. I sure hope she's still alive because she's the main reason I keep going. I'd give anything to see her again. And my dad probably still lives in Toronto, but I haven't talked to him for about two years."

Mr. Davis gives a small smile. "You're an amazing boy, Axel. You come to school each day and, from my short discussion with Mrs. Watson the other day, I gather that you're a very bright student. But what you've been through would be enough to send most kids in a direction that often puts them on the street, and sometimes in jail." He pauses, nodding his head. "I really admire you. You have the drive and courage that we don't see often enough."

"Well, thanks," is all I can muster for a reply. I feel like laughing and crying at the same time, but I don't want to cry in front of Mr. Davis, so I swallow hard and avoid his eyes.

"Thank you, too," he says softly. "You probably recall that I asked you to come in and chat with me any time because it would make my day. You might think I say that to every student but, believe me, I don't. I said it because I meant it, and here you are making my prediction come true. You just made my day, in a big way."

He looks at me like a professional football coach does after a star player completes a winning touchdown. He might even pat me on the back.

"Thanks," I repeat. "I'm glad I came to talk."

"Well, me, too. Please tell me to back off if I'm prodding too much. I'm interested in knowing why you haven't talked to your dad for so long."

"I don't mind telling you more," I say. And I really don't mind. This talk with Mr. Davis is feeling good, maybe even therapeutic. All this stuff has been bottled up inside me for far too long.

I've always thought that I could deal with everything in my life, and that nobody else could possibly help me anyway. That fake confidence is really a flimsy barrier I've kept in place to protect me from facing reality. Now it's being stripped away, and Mr. Davis is offering me a suit of armour.

"My dad lives in Toronto," I continue. "At least he was there the last time I talked to him. He has a new wife and a new family. You see, something bad happened just before I went into foster care, and I guess he didn't want to deal with it. He was there one day, and gone the next.

"I talked to him on the phone a few times. I always thought he'd come back and take me to Toronto to live with him. He made promises and promises until I wanted to stick those promises up his ass. I hate my dad now, and I don't care if I ever see him again." My knuckles are white from clenching my fists.

"I'm really sorry to hear that, Axel. Your anger is understandable. Never came back? That makes no sense to me. I'm guessing he had some serious issues of his own."

"Yeah, I guess. I remember my parents having some pretty good screaming matches. He drank quite a bit and he was away a lot. I don't think that helped."

"I suppose not," Mr. Davis replies calmly. "Anyway, that was out of your control. But were there no relatives to help out?"

"My mom has a sister, my aunt, who lives in Winnipeg, but she has enough problems of her own without a problem nephew coming into her life; depression and drugs and stuff. And my dad was an only child, so no uncles or aunts on his side. And my grandparents were either too sick or too poor to have a grandchild come to live with them. It was my grandparents on my mom's side who got me into foster care. And they all live in Alberta, so I don't have much contact with any of them either."

"I see. So foster care was really the only option." Then, sounding more optimistic, he adds, "And it can be a good option in many cases."

"I guess that's true," I agree. "I haven't had the best luck with my foster homes, but I guess I can say that I've never had to live on the streets."

"That's a good attitude, Axel. The glass is still half full for you, and that just amazes me." He pauses again. "So now, about this 'something bad' that happened to cause the family breakup. Was it anything you want to talk about?"

"It was something I did," I state flatly.

Mr. Davis almost leaps out of his chair. "Axel, please don't go down that road. Kids usually blame themselves. They think that all the fighting they witnessed was because of stress they caused, and that things would have been different if they hadn't been around, and so on. But that's never the case."

"Maybe that's the right thing to say to them, but my case is different. I mean, I did something really bad, and it changed everything."

"But you weren't even in kindergarten," Mr. Davis adds. "How could you be responsible for your parents breaking up before you had even lost all your baby teeth, for goodness sake?"

"Yeah, well, I just know I am." Beads of sweat form on my forehead. "I can't talk about it anymore, but I'm pretty sure you'd feel different if I ever told you."

"I can't imagine that, Axel, but, okay, I'll leave that topic alone for now."

"Thanks."

"But before you go, let's finish our discussion about Donny. Do you expect a follow-up battle between you and him?"

"I don't know. Hey, is this just between you and me?"

"Everything we discuss is completely confidential, Axel. I'd only tell someone if I had your full permission."

"Okay, good. So, I can see why he wants to pound on me. He wants to prove that he can even the score no matter what. Maybe that has to happen before he'll go away. I don't want to rat him out, but he did a really stupid bonehead thing on Hallowe'en, and I was the one who stopped him. Totally separate, he also fired some Roman candles at me and my friend, and we fired some shots right back. But my friend was the only one who got nabbed by the cops, so that made me angry. But I guess we only have ourselves to blame for that."

"A pretty wild night," Mr. Davis comments.

"It was," I agree. "Anyway, he did the really stupid lowlife thing after that, and in the end he got hurt, thanks to me. And I think he was embarrassed, too. So he was trying to pay me back yesterday. I was caught by surprise. He was the one who attacked me. Actually, he kicked my almond box out of my hands, and then he came at me with his boots."

My heart races as I continue my story. "So, I was really just defending myself. But Mr. Murray only saw the tail-end of the whole thing, so I must've looked like the ass-kickin' bad guy to him. And he wouldn't listen to my explanation, so that was that. If he stays away from me, I'll gladly stay away from him. My life really doesn't need someone like Donny in it right now."

"Hmmm," says Mr. Davis. "I'm sure Donny will think twice about coming at you again. If I'd been beaten up twice by the same guy, I'd move on. But do avoid another confrontation with him, if at all possible. Mr. Murray could easily have suspended

you, but he decided to refer you to me instead. I'm going to tell
Mr. Murray that his decision was not in vain. This has been far
more fruitful than a suspension."

"Thanks, Mr. Davis. I appreciate that."

"Thank you, Axel." Then with a beaming smile, he says, "And
please, come by any time to make my day again."

"I will, for sure."

My stars have aligned, I decide, as I walk home with my box of
almonds. I didn't get suspended, I had a positive talk with Mr.
Davis that lifted my spirits, and I've put into perspective the
incident with Donny.

When I think about Donny himself, I feel no anger at all. Sure,
he did a boneheaded thing by stealing that bag of candy, and he
is a slimy guy in my opinion. But still, he's no longer the object
of my anger.

My anger is an invisible monster that shows up when I least
expect it. I felt it rearing its head when I told Mr. Davis that I
hated my dad. And I felt it again when I told him that I would
give anything to see my mother again.

I'd like to be rid of that monster. If I feel the anger building
up again, I will go right away to talk it out with Mr. Davis. I have
a real friend I can lean on, and he seems more than happy to be
leaned on, so why wouldn't I?

My glass is half full for one more important reason: I have
in my possession the means to do something good. This case of
almonds alone is almost enough to save one child. I hope Mr.
Hunter is watching me now.

CHAPTER 12
Plan C

It takes a few days for Frank, Eric and I to finally arrange our chocolate almond sales door-to-door. But soon into our campaign we realize that we started too late. "Oh, sorry, we just bought some from some school kids the other day," is the line that is repeated over and over. We do make some sales, but we're not going to be saving many starving children at the rate we're going, let alone pay our field trip expenses.

"This sucks," says Frank as we tally up our sales for the first day. "Sold ten boxes. Wow! What a frickin' waste of time this is. That's like ten bucks profit between the three of us, and we don't even get to keep it all. We gotta give some to those skin-and-bone kids in the video who live a frickin' million miles away, because we've gotta solve all their problems, too."

"Yeah, this does suck," agrees Eric. "I can sure as hell think of better ways to spend my time, like maybe watching ice melt."

What did I expect from these two? Frank's comment about the poor kids in the video bothers me, but this isn't the right time to stand on my moral pedestal. I have to agree that it's been a depressing day of sales.

"Well, look guys," I say as I open a box of almonds for ourselves, "it's only the first day, so we can't throw in the towel yet."

"Yeah, and now we're eating all the profits, too," adds Eric, filling his face with a large handful.

Then Frank pipes up. "I don't really give a damn. If I don't sell these, I just don't go to Playland. What's new? I never get to go anywhere anyway, so what the hell difference does it make?"

I'm not about to let this all fall apart so soon. But trying to keep the team in the game feels like a losing battle. I try to stay positive. A little pep talk.

"Okay, you guys, we're all in the same boat here and nobody's happy about it, but we've gotta give it at least one more shot. I say we try going a little out of this neighbourhood where maybe they haven't been sold yet. What've we got to lose?"

Frank and Eric gripe a bit more, then reluctantly give in. Before they have a change of heart, I suggest we head home and rest up for round two.

I go over sales strategies in my head all night. The door-to-door idea might have been a good idea if we'd been the first ones out there. But we can't turn back the clock. We'll go ahead with Plan B, the idea we agreed upon for tomorrow. If that doesn't work, I now have a Plan C.

The next day it's like pulling teeth getting Frank and Eric to walk the seven or eight blocks to get to new territory. New neighbourhood, but it feels pretty much the same as the old one, except for the rudeness. People in this part of town are door slammers. They tell us that we're interrupting their day and then Slam!

Add to that, snarling pit bulls and Rottweilers guard every other yard. After about three hours, we call it a day. We doubled our sales from the previous day, but it's still not enough.

"Oh, good," says Eric sarcastically. "Now we have just about enough to get one of us on the ferry. The other two can just swim, I guess."

"I don't mind swimming," I quip. "And you know what? I'm gonna be the first one to say that this whole door-to-door selling is crap. That was our Plan B, and I say we shred the whole thing. But Plan C could save us all."

"Plan B. Plan C. Where do all these stupid plans come from?" whines Frank.

"From me," I reply. "Plan C is where we go to a big business, like maybe Canadian Tire, and set up a table just outside the entrance. We'll have hundreds of customers walking right by us. No door knocking. No people getting pissed off because we interrupted their supper or a stupid hockey game. And no dogs to watch for."

Eric's eyes light up. "I'm game for that!" he says, leading the way with a spring in his step. Frank jumps in close behind and states, "We've wasted enough time getting' nowhere, and I'd really like to get rid of these things before I go home. Let's go."

"Well, hold on, you guys!" I yell. They stop. "I don't want to pour cold water on this, but we can't just go and set up without permission. We have to phone the manager and set up a time that they'll allow us to be there. I made a call to Canadian Tire last night to find out how it all works. They need to make sure that we're selling for a good cause. I told him it was for the Nutrition Solution charity, plus for a school field trip. He said that it all sounds good. All I have to do now is phone him again to get a day and time. I wanted to see how we did today before I even brought up this idea."

"Well, now you see how we did, so let's do it," says Frank, looking anxious.

"I'm in," adds Eric.

"Okay. I'm with you guys. When do you want to sell?" I ask.
We settle on Thursday.

"Okay," I say, "and what if sales are great? Do you want to pick any other days as well?"

Eric replies, "If it goes that good, let's sell Friday and Saturday, too. Hell, if sales are good, why not make as much cash as we can?" I can practically see the dollar signs in his eyes.

Frank jumps right in. "I can make it any day you guys want."

"Done deal," I finish. "I'll call as soon as I get home and I'll let you guys know."

I make all the calls that night and etch everything in stone. Thursday and Friday late afternoons, but we'll have to let the manager know if the plans change since he's reserving the spot for us.

Thursday after school, armed with our cases of chocolate almonds, we race over to Canadian Tire. It's close to the Ocean Boulevard Bridge, about a twenty-minute walk at our exuberant pace. The manager has a table ready for us to set up. We're in business in no time. I made a small information poster that we tape to the table.

It's a huge success. We sell out in less than two hours. Sixty-six boxes. Frank and Eric do a victory dance that has customers in stitches. I don't join in, but I'm over-joyed. And relieved.

"We're back here tomorrow, for sure!" proclaims Eric.

Frank pumps his fists and yells, "And let's bring a lot more than we had tonight!"

Our luck has changed. I'm almost levitating with the positive vibes. "That's a great idea!" I say. "Let's check with Mrs. Watson and see if we can get maybe two cases each."

We high-five until our hands are sore, then call it a night.

Unbeknownst to my partners, I threw in two dollars of my allowance to cover the bar we devoured. So when we submit our earnings on Friday, the books balance perfectly. Mrs. Watson is hesitant about giving each of us more than one case at a time, but we beg and plead and reassure her that she can trust us and that we'll have the money in her hands by Monday.

When the last bell of the day rings, we rush out the door with our two cases each, arriving at Canadian Tire in record time. The weather is cooperating: no rain, mild, and just a light breeze. It's Friday, paycheques are in pockets. I bet people will be throwing money at us. And they do.

We're selling two and three boxes at a time, with tips to top it off. We started at four o'clock and we're sold out by six. It's all so simple. Set up shop, people come, we make money, they get a chocolate fix, and everybody's happy.

"Looks like I'll be going to Playland after all," says Frank. "Who the hell would've guessed that?"

"Not me, that's for sure," replies Eric. "But here, you take this," he adds, handing me the envelope. It's bursting with cash. "I don't trust that kind of moola sitting around at my house. So you take care of it. You're the banker." He laughs, and it's wholly genuine.

"Yeah," Frank agrees, "You don't want cash like this sitting around my place either. The old man would drink it up in no time."

"Okay," I say. "I'll look after the cash, but don't be surprised if I show up wearing a Rolex watch and a tuxedo."

"Yeah, right," says Eric with a friendly shove. "It better all be there on Monday. And, hey, what about next week? We've gotta do this again. Why don't you call up the manager again and see if we can come back? No sense quittin' while we're ahead, right?"

Frank nods excitedly. "Let's make more!" he yells.

"Sure," I say. "I'll call tonight, you guys. Leave it with me and I'll let you know what he says."

Arriving home, I phone the Canadian Tire manger and tell him about our success raising a lot of money for the charity. I ask to reserve our spot for the following Thursday and Friday. He congratulates me, and says those days are not a problem, but explains that after that he has obligations to other groups.

Thrilled, I run downstairs and hide the envelope under my bed. Thankfully, nobody ever ventures inside my boar's nest of a room.

Then I do a calculation. Frank and Eric are focused on their personal profits, but I'm more interested in the charity. Any way we look at it, the numbers are good. We've now sold three hundred and twenty-four boxes of almonds! We've paid for our trips and then some, so Eric and Frank will be happy to hear that.

More importantly, Nutrition Solution will get a good chunk of the proceeds. We have enough money to save four kids, and part of a fifth. Four kids and counting. Now that's something! I flop down on the bed and stare at the ceiling. Visions of laughing, satiated children in Africa fill my head.

And we aren't done. I believe I'm getting close to the point where Mr. Hunter might forgive me.

CHAPTER 13
The Phone Call

Sunday evening, shortly after supper time, the phone rings. Flick answers it in the living room. His voice is loud enough to shake the house off its foundation. I'm still in the kitchen doing my own dishes. I don't intend to eavesdrop, but Flick's tone changes so quickly and drastically, that it catches my attention.

He keeps repeating the same lines: "Oh, I see" or "oh, yes, for sure."

There's a pause while the caller asks a question, then Flick's response: "Oh, he's doing just great ... Yes, he's really a good boy, goes to school and does his chores." Flick is giving me accolades? This really piques my curiosity. The conversation continues. "... Oh, we're very happy with him here, couldn't ask for a nicer kid ... Yes, I think he'd be very happy to hear from you."

I freeze. My hands tremble. The conversation goes on for a few more minutes, but I'm no longer listening in. Who could it be? I can think of only three possibilities: my grandparents, my father, or—I can't really conceive of the possibility—my mother.

Before I have time to organize my thoughts, Flick stomps into the kitchen. "Just one second, he's right here in the kitchen doing dishes, being the good boy that he is," he finishes. He hands me the portable phone with raised eyebrows, then flicks his head.

I stare at the phone while composing myself. Flicks hovers, as if determined to be part of the conversation. I cover the mouthpiece and say, "Please. Please, Flick."

Flick nods and backs out the door.

"Hello," I say, my voice cracking, which is happening more and more as it slowly shifts about an octave lower.

"Axel? Hello, son, it's me. Your, uh, well, it's your dad."

"Dad? Really. It's you," I reply flatly. I'm beset with a million emotions.

"Axel, it's me. Honest. How have you been keeping, son?"

My ears aren't deceiving me. He did say 'son.' Fathers pick up their kids at school, so I hear that a lot. To me, when a father addresses his kid using 'son' it says a lot. There's a bond, a connection, a closeness that those fathers and sons have, and I always watch it with envy. I picture some of those fathers, so different from mine. Why does he think he can call me that? We're not 'close' at all. In any way.

"Where are you?" I ask.

"I'm in Toronto, same place, same old house I've always been in out here. Nothing much to tell here, but I haven't been in touch for a while, so I wanted to know how things were going."

Now I'm pissed. It was two foster homes ago that we had last spoken. "Yeah, well, I'm doing fine, I guess. Haven't heard from you in almost two years. How did you even find me?"

"Well, I had to jump through a few hoops to get that information," he answers enthusiastically. "I contacted the social services ministry in B.C. and I had to fax some personal documents to prove who I was before they'd release that information. I had talked to your foster dad, I believe his name is Cliff—"

"—Flick," I interrupt.

"Oh, sorry. Flick. I must have misheard him. I talked to Flick about a week ago to introduce myself, and just to see if everything was okay. He sounded a little suspicious, or maybe just guarded, and didn't really want to share much information. He was much friendlier this time. Anyway, I asked him to tell you I'd be calling soon. Did he mention that to you?"

"No, Flick and I don't talk much. But I don't mind. It's fine here. I'm fine," I add. So he went out of his way to find me. So what. He's still five thousand kilometers away. He's been useless to me.

"I'm delighted to hear that, Axel. You sound good. Your voice is changing a little; you sound so grown up. How tall are you now?"

"I guess about five-six or so. I haven't measured for a while. But dad ... uh," I fumble for the right words without being blatantly rude. "Um, listen. It's, uh, good to hear from you, but, you know, I've got a lot of work to catch up on and I'd better get at it."

"Axel, please don't hang up just yet. Listen, please. I've been thinking about you a lot, and I really wanted this phone call to come out right."

I wait.

Dead silence. Then I hear sniffling and nose blowing.

"I can understand if you're angry with me," he continues. "I've done some soul-searching and I realize, I know deep inside ... deep inside ..." More silence and then muffled background noises. I picture my father, phone in hand, struggling to find the right words to say to me, a stranger more than a son, to make up for nine lost years. Why's he the one crying?

After a long pause, he asks, "Are you still there, Axel?"

"Yeah," I reply, on the verge of tears myself.

"So, listen, what I'm trying to say is that I've been working hard to just, well, to make me a better person. I know that my drinking has been at the root of my problems, and I've been going to AA meetings. And through those meetings I've had to come to terms with a lot of things." A lengthy pause with more sniffling. "And, what I really want to say is that I realize I've failed you."

What more can either one of us say? I agree he's failed me, but I've moved on. Haven't I?

For the first six years or so, I struggled to come to terms with his sudden abandonment, finally tucking the matter away in a nice little compartment of suppression with a foolproof padlock. And that's where it's been hiding, safe and sound, for the past three years. The elusive key to the lock is hidden away so well, even I have no idea where it is.

"Well, I guess that's good that you're getting everything sorted out. But don't worry about me. I'm okay," I respond unconvincingly.

"Yeah, I guess you are. You sound pretty darn good to me. I just wish, more than anything now, that I had sorted out my own life sooner. I wish I could've been there for you, son."

"Yeah, well, that's in the past, right? Can't change that now. So look, I gotta go and—"

"—You're right, son," he cuts in. "We can't change the past, but I sure as hell wish I could. So, listen, Axel, another reason I called you. I applied for a job in Vancouver, and there's a good chance I'll get it. If I do, I'll be moving out west in the near future, and I'd love to see you."

"Vancouver, eh? That's not far from the island."

"Just a ferry ride away," he replies, upbeat.

"Dad, it's been good talking to you, and if you get that job I guess I'll be seeing you." I'm not falling for his promises again.

"Not just a guess, son. I'll be seeing you for sure."

"Okay, see you," I finish.

"You take good care, son. I'll be in touch. You can count on that."

He hangs up. His last line resonates like a hollow drum. How many times have I heard that line from him? How many phone calls ended just like that? And how many times have I been let down? The answer is: every time. So why will this time be any different?

It takes the rest of the night to find a space in my little compartment for that phone call. Fortunately, other things rekindle my spirits, like the cash-stuffed envelope under my bed.

CHAPTER 14
Big Sales

I hand the money envelope to Mrs. Watson first thing Monday morning. She's shocked. She counts it and does the calculations, then announces how much we've made for ourselves and for the charity.

"You boys have made just over one hundred and sixty dollars for yourselves, and just under one hundred and thirty dollars for Nutrition Solution. Very impressive!"

I tell her that we've secured a few more days for sales at Canadian Tire, and that I'm certain we can sell three cases each if she'll let us take that many. She needs no further convincing.

"But you really don't need to sell any more," she says resignedly. "You've already covered all your field trip costs, plus you have a little spending money."

"But what about the charity? Their costs are never covered," I reason. "Plus, I guess a little more spending money would never hurt, right?"

"Now, how can I argue with that? There always seems to be a few dozen cases that I end up sending back. Why not sell them if we can? And I respect your attitude about the charity, Axel! If you guys want three cases each, I'll stick my neck out again and approve it."

"Thanks a lot, Mrs. Watson. We don't actually get the spot to sell until Thursday, so we'll maybe just wait until then to pick them up, if that's okay."

"That's just fine. I'll hold them until Thursday."

Thursday is one of those days at school when the energy is palpable. Maybe it's a full moon. People fly into lockers, guys roughhouse in the hallways, girls laugh and talk loudly, and teachers yell above the commotion trying to dampen it all. The decibels in the building make Flick's yelling seem tame.

Despite my ringing ears, I'm in the thick of it with Eric and Frank. Frank jumps on my back and challenges me to knock him off. I twist and turn until I almost puke, then I run backwards to slam him into the lockers. He falls off. Eric eggs us on with some hooting and hollering, but doesn't join in the action. Something is up with him.

I'm trying not to read faces so much these day. It gets in the way of going with the flow. Still, I can't help noticing how Eric's expression changes: anxiety is written all over his face.

"Hey, Eric, are you pumped for the sales today?" I ask.

"For sure! Can't wait to see that cash rolling in." He sounds like himself.

"Yeah, me, too."

"Hey, I was thinking though," Eric starts, then pauses. "Ah, nah, you wouldn't go for it."

"Wouldn't go for what?" I prod. "You never know. What's up?"

"Well, okay. Like, if we're making more for our own spending money out of all the sales, what would you think if I just kind of borrowed some of that part, and then just paid it all back later. I mean it's really mine anyway, right? So it shouldn't make any difference."

So that's it. Eric needs money. But he's putting me on the spot, looking for my approval for something that's not my decision to make.

"Oh, I get it," I reply. "Well, I don't know, Eric. You know, if you really need to borrow some cash, I could dig into my allowance and you could just pay me back later."

"Thanks. I appreciate the offer, buddy, but I wouldn't feel right about taking money from you. I'd rather just deal with my own bank, if you know what I mean."

"Yeah, I get that. It's just that Mrs. Watson was pretty strict about us handing in all the cash so she could do all the calculating. I don't think she'd like the idea of us holding back our share since it's all supposed to be for the field trip. I think she might get herself in trouble if she allowed everyone to do that."

Eric nods, frowning. "Hmmm. Yeah, I suppose. Well, look, I just thought I'd ask, but it's no big deal really. I'll be fine without it."

He doesn't sound convincing, but it's a dead-end discussion. The bell rings. I haul books and my lunch bag out of my backpack to put in my locker.

Eric stops me just as I'm about to open my lock. "Hey, just a sec," he says. "You're not gonna believe this, but I just noticed that I completely forgot to pack my lunch. Like, what an idiot I am! And I always have a snack before first class. Damn!"

I can't bear the thought of my friend begging for food. I jump in before he can pop the question, saving him face, as they say.

"Hey, you're in luck because I actually packed more than I can eat today. You'd be doing me a favour if you could help me eat some of it." I hold out my lunch bag.

"You're full of crap," Eric says with a friendly shove.

"No, I'm serious." I hand him half of my ham and cheese sandwich and a chocolate chip cookie. "Please, take these so I won't have to bring anything home today. I had a massive break-fast and I won't be able to eat everything. They hate it when I have leftovers, and I hate dealing with anything they hate."

Relieved, Eric smiles and pats me on the back. "Okay, buddy. Glad to help you out then."

Our luck with perfect weather conditions has run out. A steady, light drizzle accompanies us all the way to Canadian Tire, and thick, rolling grey storm clouds accumulate. In addition to the usual tables, the manager brings out two large patio umbrellas, so we're reasonably well-protected from the wind and rain.

The cases are fairly saturated, but the almond boxes are still in good condition. We pile all nine cases on the tables and go to work. Our poster is damaged beyond repair, so we rely on our verbal sales pitch: "Almonds for charity! Save kids in Africa and treat yourself at the same time!"

The ominous weather proves more of a blessing than a curse. Two-thirds of the shoppers are more interested in getting out of the rain and into a warm, dry store than they are in buying almonds. But the other third take pity on us and buy up our product like it's going out of style. Some are repeat customers from the previous week, and they treat us like old friends. The supply of almonds diminishes at a decent pace. By six o'clock we're down to just under three cases.

"I'm gettin' cold," says Frank. "I think we should pack it in for today."

Cold and wet, Eric needs little convincing to call it a day. "Yeah," he agrees. "We still have tomorrow to sell the rest. I wouldn't mind bringing my body temperature back up to a little above the freezing point." He laughs at his own remark. "Plus, I'm bloody starving! Hope you guys don't mind." He rips open a box of almonds and pours in a mouthful. "Just take it out of my share," he says, almost choking on the almonds.

"Fine by me," says Frank.

I shrug. We can always adjust for being one box short.

Three more customers buy almonds just as I'm about to pack it up. I look beyond our little sales area. The parking lot is filling up.

"You know, you guys," I reason, "I'm damn cold, too, but look at all the cars just coming in now. I say let's give it another half hour max and see how much we can unload. I mean, the less we have to carry back, the better, right? And I'm afraid it will all get soaking wet and then we won't be able to sell it anyway. What do you guys think?"

"I'm timing us starting right now," says Eric, looking at his watch. "Thirty minutes. Go!"

Frank just shrugs and nods his assent.

Customers drop by in threes and fours, and we take turns using our pressure sales tactics, emphasizing the Nutrition Solution charity. It works like a charm. Thirty minutes pass and we have a little more than one case remaining. Eric reminds us of the time, but doesn't force the issue since sales are still going strong. With no further discussion, we ramp up our sales pitches until every last box is sold.

"There!" exclaims Eric. "It's seven o'clock and we're done! Just like me." He gives us high fives. Then he steps out from under the umbrellas, rain striking his held-out hands. "And the timing couldn't be better. It's just pissing out here. Let's get our asses home!"

Frank gathers up the empty cases and carries them to the garbage bin beside the store. Eric and I take down the umbrellas and carry them inside the entrance. I make sure all the money is stuffed carefully inside the large manila envelope now bulging with loonies, toonies and bills.

It's far too big to fit in any of our pockets, so I tuck it inside my jacket and hold it in place under my armpit to keep it out of the rain. The manager comes by just as we're about to make our exit. We thank him profusely. He shakes our hands and says he's happy that it all went well. We can call him any time for future sales, he adds.

We walk in the dark, the rain pummelling us. We try to calculate in our heads how much money is in the envelope.

"We had nine cases and there's thirty-six boxes in a case, so what's nine times thirty-six?" I ask.

"Are you kidding?" Frank says, laughing. "Me and math don't get along. I'm leaving that one up to you guys."

"Count me out, too," says Eric. "Go for it, Axel."

"Well, let's see," I say aloud. "Just do nine times three, that's twenty-seven, so just put on the zero and nine times thirty is two hundred and seventy. And add on nine times six."

"Fifty-six!" Eric yells. "I know that one."

"Right, well, close anyway," I remark politely. "Fifty-four actually. So just add two hundred and seventy and fifty-four and we get, uh … three hundred and twenty-four. Can you believe that? We sold three hundred and twenty-four boxes of almonds in one day? That's gotta be a record!"

"So then, give us the number," says an anxious Frank. "How much money do we have?"

"Well, two bucks a box, so just multiply it by two. That's six hundred and forty-eight bucks. No wonder that envelope is bursting with cash!"

"Minus two bucks for the one I inhaled," blurts Eric. He smacks his lips and pounds his chest. "*We are the champions, my friend,*" he declares, quoting some Queen lyrics.

FORGIVE ME, MR. HUNTER

"No time for losers," Frank joins in.

Before we know it, the three of us are singing in the rain at the top of our lungs: *"We are the champions, my friend, and we'll keep on fighting 'til the end, we are the champions, we are the champions ..."*

We get stuck on that line, singing it louder and louder. Passersby stare at us. People peep from their windows. We're oblivious. We're on a high, seizing the moment, in a world of our own, and nothing else matters.

More kids in Africa are now about to be saved! That thought gets me singing even louder than my partners.

We turn onto Chambers Street, bouncing along, still singing high-spiritedly. Suddenly, two large, dark-hooded figures leap out from behind a cedar hedge and block our way, just like in some horror movie. The three of us jump right out of our skin.

"Hi guys. Know who we are?" one of them asks. They pace around us like hyenas honing in on their prey.

"No," I reply nervously. "Who are you?"

"Well, Mr. Ears, we're your worst enemies. Sure hope your sales went real good tonight 'cause it'll be your last chance to use your big mouths to sell anything. And if you think this is just bad luck meeting us here, think again. We followed your asses all the way from Canadian Tire. And hey, get your money back for those singing lessons. Jesus, you suck."

"Oh, sorry," I say to appease him, and then look frantically for an opening to make a run for it. I'm racking my brain to put a name to the voice or to the partial face, to either face, but I'm drawing blanks.

They are clearly a little older than us and way bigger. So even though we outnumber them, it won't help. I look over at Frank and Eric. Both of them appear to be paralyzed with fear.

"Don't apologize to us, scrapper," the same guy retorts. "You see, we got a little problem that we'd like to solve, and that problem has to do with a relative. That's the guy you need to apologize to."

"I don't understand, I—"

"—Shut your face!" he snaps. "You'll figure it out soon enough. I'll give you a hint: Hallowe'en, fireballs, tripping and knocking the wind out of the guy, and pushing him on his ass at school. Need any more hints?"

I didn't. The moment I've been dreading has arrived. Donny Cox's brothers have caught up with me. This is not going to end well. At least they're not indicating any interest in robbing us. The only possible consolation I can think of.

"Look, you guys, you only have one side of the story and—"

"—Who the hell said you could speak, Spock? You just keep your mouth shut. We didn't go through all this trouble to sit around here and have a gab session with you guys. And I can tell that you guessed who we are. That's right, Donny's brothers. Oh, I guess I should've introduced us," he adds sarcastically. "I'm Daryl and that's Devon. You'll wanna remember our names, I'm sure. And too bad for you dudes," he continues, referring to Eric and Frank, "but you're friends with this asshole, and now you get to help him."

Frank, desperate, faces Daryl, the one doing all the talking. He stands tall, arms wide open, and says the line I haven't heard since the day I'd had it out with him: "If you don't like me, change me."

Daryl and Devon look at each other and erupt into wild laughter.

"Change you?" Daryl says mockingly. "You mean change your diaper?"

I can't believe what I'm seeing and hearing. Courage is one thing, but stupidity is another. Sometimes courage and stupidity can work together, but this is not one of those times. This is just stupidity.

Frank steps closer to Daryl and repeats his line with conviction: "Really, if you don't like me, change me."

Daryl winds up, his right hand reaching way back somewhere into the next municipality, and then twists his body, adding more leverage to the punch.

His blow would have flattened Muhammad Ali, let alone Frank. Frank drops. I watch, helpless. Frank doesn't move.

I hurl myself at the thugs with whatever I have. Eric follows my lead.

I leap at Daryl first, knocking him to the ground. I punch him a few times before he recovers. That's it for my offence. Now I focus on defence. I take a few solid blows to my face before I put my arms up for protection and duck down. But that leaves open my sides and lower back. He punches and kicks relentlessly, wherever he can find an opening.

There's sharp, intense pain each time he connects. I bend lower and lower, hoping it will come to an end. I pull my hands from my face for just one second. Smack! Another fist in the eye. My gut tells me to give up and collapse.

Instead, I give a blood-curdling scream and run for it. I'm tackled from behind before I get twenty feet. Eric is beside me. He's curled up in a fetal position on the wet grass, Devon pounding on his back. It's an endless nightmare; we're going to die if it doesn't end now.

"Okay, you guys!" I scream. "I'm sorry, okay? I'm sorry! I'll never touch your brother again! Please leave us alone! I'm sorry!"

The pounding magically stops. Has my pleading gotten to them? No. A car has stopped. The lone male driver trains a flashlight on us through his partly-open window. He moves the beam from one person to another and back again, finally training a steady beam on prostrate Frank. I have no idea how much of the fight he witnessed, but he's created enough of a distraction to throw off our attackers and save us from the critical ward.

"Okay, you punks, you keep the hell away from Donny," Daryl warns, struggling to catch his breath. "Remember that!" He glances at the driver of the car and yanks the hoodie over his face. "Let's get the hell outta here!" He grabs his brother and hauls him down Chambers.

The man in the car rolls his window down and asks us if we're okay.

I look down at Frank and then back to the man. "Um, yeah, we're fine," I reply. It hurts my whole face just to speak. "We were just, uh, play fighting and my friend there is just tired now." It sounds feeble, but it's better we keep this whole incident to ourselves.

"But thanks for stopping," I add. I keep my face out of the beam of light. My pounded-meat face might cause the man to pry further.

"Okay, you're sure everything is fine then?" he asks one more time, turning off his flashlight.

I fight to keep talking. "Uh, yeah, we're just heading home now. But thanks again."

"Okay, you're welcome, boys. You guys are going to catch pneumonia out here. Hope you don't have far to go."

"No, just around the corner," I lie.

"Night, boys," he says, and drives away.

So here we are, three sorry, drenched, whipped souls licking our wounds in the pouring rain on a dark, miserable night on Chambers Street. I feel my face. The right cheekbone is swollen to the size of a grapefruit, and the vision in that eye is blurry.

My spine and ribs feel like they've been run over by a Mack truck. But I'm still standing and able to walk, which is more than I can say for Frank. He's still flat on the ground, face up, his body twitching involuntarily. He somehow turned himself over. That's a good sign; at least he's still alive.

Eric is also watching Frank, and probably thinking the same thing. He limps over and drapes his arm around my neck. I'm not sure if it's just a friendly gesture, or whether he needs me for balance.

"Donny's brothers," Eric says flatly. "Two frickin' arseholes. I'm gonna get those bastards back if it's the last thing I do."

"It just might be the last thing you do," I respond, speaking slowly, trying to ignore the pain. "I'd like nothing more ... than to see them get the living crap beat out of 'em ... but it won't be you and me doing it, that's for sure. Anyway ... right now we've got Frank to worry about. Let's see if we can get him up."

I kneel down beside Frank and shake his head lightly. "Frank, wake up," I coax. "Come on Frank, say something to us."

Eric joins me and the two of us sit Frank upright, slap his cheeks and pat his back. He groans. Makes a guttural noise.

"Keep patting his back," I say to Eric. "He's coming around."

"Yeah, I guess you could say that," replies Eric. "He doesn't sound so good, though."

The rain, now pelting down, creates puddles in the grass and floods the sidewalks. We're all soaked, but the cool water running down my face is soothing. Frank's groans increase and his legs jerk. He kicks his feet like he's riding a bicycle on the ground.

"That's great, Frank!" I encourage him. "Keep moving, buddy. Keep those feet moving. Try to stand up. Here, we'll give you a hand." Eric and I take an armpit each and lift him up. This time it's us who groan in pain, then we both let loose primal screams, like weight lifters do at the end of a great lift. We try to laugh, but the pain puts a quick damper to that.

We hold Frank carefully until he can stay up on his own. Moments later he utters his first coherent words.

"Crap, you guys," he says laboriously. "What the hell's goin' on? I can't see straight."

"Just close your eyes and relax," orders Eric. "But keep talkin' if you can. And don't worry. Axel and me won't let you fall. Maybe try walking a little."

"My head ... damn ... it's pounding. Where are we?" he mumbles.

"Frank, it's your buddies Axel and Eric. Remember?" I respond. "We just came from Canadian Tire and we're on our way home, and we just had a bit of a problem with a couple of guys, but they're gone now and we're going to get you home, pronto."

"Yeah, home," he moans. "Get me home ... I need to lie down. Frickin' head ... I feel like I'm dyin'."

Eric shakes his head, half smiling. "Don't worry, you're not dying. Not for another eighty years at least. Hey, just hold on to Axel and me. We're not doing so great ourselves, but we're gonna keep you moving."

We drape Frank's arms around our necks and start hauling him in the direction of his house. It's the blind leading the blind but, despite our own excruciating pain, we're better off than Frank.

It's the longest five blocks in the history of mankind. Time drags on as we three cripples hobble down the sidewalk at a snail's pace. I use every last ounce of my reserves to stay focused and keep moving so we can get Frank safely home.

Finally. Frank's house. I knock loudly, then open the door without waiting for an answer. Frank's father appears. He's unshaven, dressed in pyjama bottoms and a white undershirt over a mass of grey chest hair. He clutches a glass of whiskey in one hand, a stir stick in the other. His double chin jiggles when he speaks.

"Hello, boys!" he greets us gruffly. He reminds me of Flick, but with more hair. He's shiny bald on top with grey, mad-doctor-looking hair on the sides. Like Flick, he has a fat gut that protrudes from his undershirt.

"What the hell have we got here?" he continues loudly. "You guys look like you just had a battle with a tornado and you lost!" He laughs through a wheezing cough and takes a drink. "Frankie, what in God's name did you get yourself into, huh? You been in a fight or something? And look at you," he adds, shifting his attention to me.

I'm too mesmerized by this beast of a father to say anything. He laughs again, this time almost choking to death, his face turning beet red. At one point I thought he'd stopped breathing. Amazingly, he didn't spill a drop of his whiskey.

"Jesus, you guys look like hell run over," he continues. "You're not gonna get any girls that way!" He laughs, amused by his own so-called wit. But his dark eyes are not laughing. They're glazed-over, unblinking. Makes me shiver inside. And the alcohol on his breath is enough to intoxicate anyone within a ten-foot radius.

"Uh, Frank had a bit of a fall and we just wanted to bring him home. I think he needs to lie down," I say timidly.

"You clumsy ass!" he says to Frank. "Can't even stay up on your own two feet, you idiot. Serves you right! Ahh, damn kids these days. I'll give you a damn good reason to fall down, all right!" He smacks Frank on the back of his head.

Frank grimaces. "Ow, Dad! My head really hurts. Please don't touch it."

"Oh, quit your damn whining!" he bellows. "That was nothin' but a love tap. I'm just playin' here, fellas!" He pats Frank lightly on the head. Then he guzzles down his drink. "Well, look, you guys, you can head on home now and I'll take good care of Frankie. And stay out of those nasty wind storms!" His laugh turns to a wheezy, phlegmy cough as he shuffles us out the door.

I look at Eric, too stunned to speak. Maybe dropping Frank off at home was a bad idea. Frank had told me that his father liked to punch him when he was drinking. It's still early in the evening and his dad is already pissed. No special occasion, I'll bet. I just hope and pray that he'll come around enough to give Frank the care he needs.

"I don't know," I say to Eric as we walk away. "I get a bad feeling about his dad."

"You said it. Me, too. Man, If I had a dad like that, I'd run the hell away."

"Yeah, I guess. It's a tough one, though. Where do you go, right?"

Eric ponders my question. "Where *do* you go? I guess you end up on the streets, unless someone's willing to take you in. I don't think I'd choose the streets, though. There's a lot of crap going on out there." He sounds like the voice of experience.

"A lot of crap, all right," I agree. "Like Donny's brothers kind of crap. I can't believe what just happened. I feel like we've been up for at least two days. Like, was it actually tonight that we were singing together? Was it today that we set a new record for sales? I can't believe it. It feels like a week ago already."

I shake my head in disbelief. "There we were high-fiving each other and stuffing wads of cash into the envelope and ..." I stop and reach inside my jacket. I can't feel the envelope. I rip off my jacket and pat myself up and down. I pace frantically back and forth, checking the ground everywhere.

"Are you okay?" asks Eric.

It's dark and drizzly, so Eric can't see that I must be pale as bone. "Nooo!" I scream.

Eric grips my shoulders. "What the hell is wrong with you?"

"The envelope! That's what's wrong! It's gone! The frickin' envelope fell out of my jacket!"

CHAPTER 15
Big Brothers

I awake to my alarm at 7:30 Friday morning. I'm stiff, sore and sick to my stomach over the missing envelope. Eric and I had spent hours tracing and retracing our steps between Frank's house and the scene of the fight before conceding that the envelope was really gone. At times, we were both in so much pain that we were literally crawling on the sidewalk. I was cold and exhausted.

I barely remember coming home. I do remember that Flick, slightly drunk, spotted me trying to sneak downstairs. He showed no concern for my well-being, just asked about my "pretty face." I was too tired to conjure up a believable story, so I told him the truth, or at least a half-truth.

I told him we were jumped by a couple of thugs wearing black hoodies and that I didn't recognize them. He asked me if we fought back. I just laughed. I don't even know why I laughed. Maybe I was on the verge of one of those nervous breakdowns. Flick stared at me like I was going crazy. He seemed pissed off, too. But at least the interrogation ended there.

I didn't mention the envelope. The two stories were unrelated anyway. The envelope had likely fallen out either sometime during the fight with Daryl or during the walk to Frank's place.

But the Cox brothers are crossed off my list of suspects. They left the scene when the car pulled up; if the envelope had been in their hands, I would've seen it for sure.

My brain aches. I can't think anymore. I read where I left off in "The Giver" by Lois Lowry. I feel like Jonas, loaded with emotions I'd rather not deal with. But I'd rather be part of the 'sameness' where all pain and strife has been eliminated.

I reach for my cassette case and find David Bowie. I always have "Space Oddity" rewound and ready to play. I put it in the machine. The song starts and I escape to places unknown, floating in outer space, running aimlessly in a sea of nothingness, bouncing from planet to planet. ... *Ground control to Major Tom* ...

Where do I go from here? I ask myself. I can barely walk, I look like I just went ten rounds with Ali, and those are the positives. They're just superficial wounds and they will heal. ... *take your protein pills and put your helmet on* ...

I can think of no reason to move forward. ... *check ignition and may God's love be with you* ... Over six hundred dollars! How will I ever pay that back? The almond-selling campaign is ending on Monday. All the money is supposed to be in by Tuesday. I'll be happy if I'm even walking by Tuesday. And what about all the kids in Africa that I was going to save? ... *you've really made the grade* ...

I really hope Mr. Hunter is not watching me now. Not when I'm like this. I'd like to ask him to take a hiatus, but I don't know if that's possible. I've let him down in a big way. ... *now it's time to leave the capsule if you dare* ...

I had nothing but good intentions and it was all going so incredibly well. I thought I was actually winning the race, and now I'm right back at the starting line again. The starting line. How many times have I been there now?

Every time I move to a new foster home it's a new starting line, so that's nothing new. But what would the finish line look like anyway? Is that the point in time where everything in life is solved? Is that even possible? I think that must be when you're dead. Or if you're not dead, you'd be the walking dead.

I feel like the lying down dead. But I know my moods well, and I remind myself that I get like this when I'm exhausted and beaten down. I need to somehow look beyond this. I need to ask myself why it's important to move on. One obvious reason is to save those kids in Africa. But to do that, I have to recover the lost money or somehow make it up.

Also, I'm angry at myself for being so self-absorbed. What about Frank and Eric? We're a team, so I need to be a team player. *... I'm stepping through the door... and there's nothing I can do ...*

But there has to be something I can do. What about the team? I owe it to them. That ass-kicking was meant solely for me. I was the one who kicked Donny's butt. Just me, on my own. It was really just bad luck, bad fate, unfortunate timing, whatever you want to call it, that Frank and Eric happened to be with me. I was the target of the hit men, and they were the collateral damage. I owe it to them to get back on my feet and find a way to move forward. I owe them everything. ... *Can you hear me, Major Tom? Can you hear me, Major Tom?*

I turn off my music and lurch out of bed, but the pain is too much. "Ahhhh!" I yell louder than I intended, surprising myself.

It's my back, my legs, my head, my entire body. I won't be going to school today, that's for sure.

Seconds later, Ted and Ben appear at my bedroom door. They knock, then come barging right in.

"What the hell is the matter?" asks Ben. "It sounded like you're dying down here."

"Oh, sorry, you guys, I didn't mean to be that loud."

Ted peers at me lying here in my bed. He scrunches up his face. "You're one hell of a mess. Did you get run over by a truck or something?"

"Yeah, something like that. I don't think it would feel any worse than this." Weird. They aren't cracking any jokes about me or ridiculing me or anything that I've come to expect from them. It isn't normal.

"Seriously," says Ben. "Who the hell did this to you? And don't give us some bullshit story. Dad told us you got jumped last night, and we thought it was a bunch of crap. Did you really?"

"Yup," I reply. "It's no bull, I really did."

"You need some ice for that eye," Ted says matter-of-factly. "I'll get some." He returns in no time with ice wrapped in a dish towel.

"Thanks, Ted," I say, my spirits lifting. I'm liking this sudden interest in my well-being. I hold the towel on my sore eye. The coolness gives me instant relief. "I guess you guys have to get to school soon," I add. "Don't think I'll be going too far today myself."

"No, you're in no shape to do nothin'," agrees Ted. "But let's get back to where we were. What about these guys who beat the hell out of you? Anyone you know, or anyone we know?"

I hesitate to rat out the Cox brothers. I should just let it go. I can't deal with those guys again; it'd be like a death wish.

"Uh ... well ... I don't think so. Couldn't really tell who they were. They had black hoodies and it was dark and, well, there wasn't much of a chance for us to really see anything."

"You said 'us.' Who else was with you?" asks Ted.

"My two buddies, Frank and Eric. They got it pretty bad, too. Especially Frank."

"I don't get it," says Ben. "Who the hell would do that? Do you have any enemies out there? Like, who have you been pissing off?"

"Um, yeah, well, I guess someone doesn't like me, or all of us. But I don't know what their problem was."

"Did they rob you guys or anything?" Ted jumps in anxiously. "Like there must've been a reason."

"No, they didn't take anything."

"Didn't take anything?" repeats Ben. "So these goons are out there beating the snot out of kids for fun? Just don't make sense to me. If that's what they think is fun, I think they need a little tuning up themselves. How old were these guys anyway?"

"Um, I guess about your age or so. Couldn't tell for sure."

"So if they're about our age," reasons Ben, "then they probably go to Vic-East High. If they do, we'd know 'em, right Ted?"

"For sure. You and me pretty well know every guy at Vic-East. But maybe those guys don't go to school."

All this bantering is amusing. I'm relishing every minute of it. Ted and Ben are in my bedroom treating me like a real human being. Just being included in the conversation gives me a rare sense of belonging, especially with me being the centre of attention.

Guys at school talk about their brothers who beat the crap out of them regularly, and how those same brothers always go to bat for them if someone else beats them up. It's like protecting their property, like an age-old unwritten family code that confuses outsiders.

I'm feeling that family code in action right now. I've never been their whipping boy, but being ridiculed and shunned is a close second. Now, amazingly, they're chomping at the bit to seek revenge for me.

"Okay, Axel," continues Ben, "try to remember something about these guys. Like how tall were they or how big?"

"Okay, let me think." I wipe the water from the melting ice off my face. I replay the events in my head, fixating on the part where Daryl does the introductions.

It was the sarcasm, the evilness in his voice that makes me shiver even now: *You'll wanna remember our names, for sure.*

I'm drifting away when Ben nudges me. "Stay with us, Axel!" he says. "Tell us something about these guys."

I'm still in a dreamlike state. "Oh, yeah, well, I'd say Daryl was the bigger of the two. He got me good."

"Daryl?" yells Ted. "Did you say Daryl?"

I'm jolted to full consciousness. "What? Did I say that? Oh, crap, no. I didn't mean that."

"Bullshit! You said Daryl. You damn well know who they were, don't you?" Ben is more excited than angry, like an investigator who just got the elusive lead that will solve the crime. "You mean Cox, don't you? Daryl Cox would do something like this. He's an asshole with a capital 'A'. And who was he with? No wait, let me guess. He had his brother, asshole number two, with him. Devon, right?"

I nod my head, just barely.

"Daryl and Devon Cox! I can't believe it!" Ben rages on. "I always knew they were dickheads, but now they went a notch below that. Those guys kicked the crap out of three grade eights! Boy, they must be proud of themselves. They are dead meat!"

Ted takes over where Ben left off. "I'm gonna squeeze the tiny brains out of their big heads! And hey, tell me again. They did this just for fun, right? Like you guys weren't stirring up crap or anything?"

"Okay, you guys, give me a minute here. Let me fill you in on the whole thing so you know what happened." I close my eyes again and gather my thoughts. "So, I have to go back to Hallowe'en, the night I was going out to shoot off fireworks with my buddy Eric, and ..."

I tell them everything. They get a real charge out of the Roman candle part, and they think the tripping of the candy bag thief is hilarious. Then I recall for them the incident with Donny kicking me and my almond box, and how I sent him flying on his butt in return.

"And Donny did threaten me about his brothers, so I guess it wasn't exactly a complete surprise that they caught up with me. But Frank and Eric didn't really have anything to do with it, and they got it at least as bad as me."

"So, what's with that little punk Donny? That little asshole can't handle his own fights, so he gets his bonehead brothers to look after it?" says Ben, now seething with anger. "You know what, I'm gonna kick his little ass, too!"

"No, you're not," interrupts Ted. "We don't beat on little kids. That's what the Coxes do. We just beat on the big bros, and when Axel is up to it, he can take care of the punk. Sounds like he's done that already a few times," he adds, chuckling.

"Hey, you guys," I interject. "Maybe we should just leave it for now. You know, like I wanna be able to walk the streets again."

"Oh, you'll walk the streets," Ben assures me. "And believe me, you won't have to worry about those boys again. When we finish with them, they'll be in wheelchairs anyway. Right, Ted?"

Ted clenches his fists and punches the air. "They are dead meat, and the last thing they'll wanna do is touch you again."

"You guys, I don't even know what to say."

"Don't need to say a thing," Ben jumps in. "We'll do all the talkin'." They both turn to leave. "And keep that ice on your eye. It looks like hell," he finishes.

I have no choice but to give in. "Okay, will do. Thanks."

I've always wondered what it would be like to have big brothers, and I guess now I know. But I feel uneasy about the whole thing. Sometimes retaliation just breeds more retaliation, and Ted and Ben can't be my fulltime protectors if the Coxes decide to ambush me again.

But the ball is not in my court any longer and, lying here in bed, there's nothing I can do about it. Deep down I'm smiling. Actually, on the outside, too.

The ice is almost melted. I toss the towel on the floor and return to my novel.

CHAPTER 16
Never Say Never

I spend Friday and most of the weekend reading, listening to music and staring at the ceiling in my bedroom. Just thinking and healing. I do manage to limp upstairs periodically for some food, and I also make one phone call on Sunday afternoon. I let the police know about the missing envelope. But before I do, I think about it carefully.

I anticipate a lot of questions about the amount of money and about my credibility in general. Remembering to subtract the box that Eric devoured, the total is six hundred and forty-six dollars. That's no small sum for a thirteen-year-old to be hauling around on a Thursday night.

The officer who takes the call is surprisingly polite and accommodating. I just tell him the truth, that me and two buddies had had a record day of almond sales at Canadian Tire, that it was all for a charity and a field trip, and that the envelope had fallen out of my jacket somewhere on the walk home on that rainy evening. I don't mention the attack. At this point I don't feel that it's a police matter anyway. It's a personal matter.

He says it was a commendable thing we were doing and he feels horrible about the loss. "Come down and fill out a few forms. There's always a chance you'll recover all the money, or maybe some of it," he says. "We always hope there are good, honest people out there, so we never say never."

Never say never. I like that. Maybe there's a slim chance the envelope will show up.

By Monday morning I'm feeling a whole lot better, but I still decide to take one more day off school to let my eye clear up. I walk the six blocks to the police station during normal school lunch hour so it doesn't look like I'm skipping class.

The officer in charge has me fill out a form that requires a complete description of the lost item. This seems pretty basic. I write down: *A large manila envelope full of cash. $646.00 in loonies, toonies, five, ten, and twenty-dollar bills, but just two twenties. 'Almond Sales' on the envelope.* Then there's all my personal information, so they'll know who to contact if it's turned in.

"Do you have any idea approximately where you were when you lost it?" asks the officer.

"Pretty sure I was on Chambers when it fell out of my jacket."

"Was it just last night?" he continues while taking notes.

"Well, actually no. It was on Thursday night, probably about 7:30 or so," I reply.

"Thursday?" he says, looking shocked. "Why did you wait this long to inform us? You know, the sooner someone reports a lost or stolen item, the better the chances are that it gets recovered. I don't want to pour cold water on this, but it might have helped if you'd come to us right away." He notes my disappointment. "But let's not throw in the towel on this. People always surprise me with their kindness and honesty. It doesn't always happen right away either. We've had valuable items returned to us as much as a year later. So never say never, right?"

"Yeah, well, thanks a lot," I reply, and turn to leave.

"Oh, I forgot to ask you," the officer adds before I reach the door. I turn to see a friendly smile as he points at my shiner. "What does the other guy look like?"

I can't help but smile, too. "Oh, he doesn't look too good."

"Yeah, I thought so. Anyway, I hope our next meeting is when I'm handing you an envelope full of money. You take care of yourself and stay away from right hooks."

"I will, for sure. Thanks."

I'm not accustomed to missing school, and it feels strange being out in the neighbourhood when everyone else is in class. I take the long way home, surreptitiously walking by the school grounds to see if there's anyone around who can to fill me in on what's been happening.

The people I hang around with usually go to the far end of the soccer field where large cedar trees provide some privacy. I don't have to search for long. Eric spots me and runs over. He's still limping and his right cheekbone is a swollen mass of purple and yellow.

"Axel!" he cries. "How the hell are you? Shit, the whole school knows about our royal ass-kicking. It was all spineless Donny and his big frickin' mouth. Anyway, your eye still doesn't look so good."

"No, but I'm a lot better than I was on Thursday. You don't look too bad. How are you feeling?"

"Like hell, but I'll live. School's better than hanging around at home, so I decided to come. But hey, did you hear about Frank?"

"No, I haven't talked to anybody since Thursday. Is he okay?" I ask reluctantly.

"Actually, no, he's not. He's in the hospital with a bad concussion. Somebody in the class heard about it; I don't know how. But I'm guessing it was his dad who put him there. That guy was an asshole. You saw him. I wouldn't put it past him to beat the

127

hell out of Frank even when he was already half dead from the freakin' Coxes."

"I wouldn't either," I agree. Just the thought of Frank's father makes my blood boil. "I can't believe that. In the hospital, eh? That really sucks. It must be really bad to have to go to the hospital. Well, we'll have to maybe see if we can visit him."

"So, what are you doing anyway?" asks Eric. "Are you coming back to class?"

"Not today. Giving this eye one more day to heal. But I was just at the cop shop."

Eric raises his hands as if surrendering. "You didn't rat out the Coxes, did you?"

"No, don't worry about that. That's the last thing I would do. But ... I, well, I sort of ..."

"Sort of what? Tell me what you sort of did," Eric insists.

"Well, not even sort of. I actually did. You see, I was caught off-guard when I got home that night and I told Flick that I was jumped by some guys, but that was it. So anyway, he tells my foster brothers and they came down to my bedroom the next morning and kind of forced me to tell the whole story."

"You told them?" Eric yells.

I put my hands up defensively. "Hold on, buddy. It wasn't deliberate. They were actually really pissed that I got beat up, and you guys, too. And I swear that I didn't mean to give any names, but I was right out of it, and it sort of slipped out. But all I said was one name—Daryl— and they figured it all out from there. I guess those guys have a real reputation at the high school."

"So, what does this all mean to us? Your foster brothers know, so now what?" asks Eric resignedly.

"Have you seen Ted and Ben?" I ask.

"Sure, I've seen them around. They're a couple of big dudes."

"Yeah, exactly. They're big, tough dudes and they really didn't like the Cox brothers beating us up, especially us being just grade eights. And you know what, whatever happens, happens. I can't control it now, and anyways, the Coxes getting a taste of their own medicine wouldn't upset me one bit."

"Oh, man!" Eric cracks a wide grin. "I get it! They're gonna kick their asses, right?"

"Let's just say that the odds are pretty good. One thing's for sure; if I was placing a bet on a fight between the Coxes and Ted and Ben, I'd bet my life savings on our side."

Eric suddenly looks solemn. "If they do get the crap kicked out of 'em, they're gonna come after us again, aren't they?"

"That's exactly what I said, and they almost laughed at me. They more or less said not to worry about a thing, that they would take care of everything. So you know what? I'm gonna try to not even think about it. I've got bigger things to worry about, like the envelope, and that's why I was at the cop shop. I figured I should tell them about it in case someone turns it in."

"Oh, sure. What the hell are the odds of that?" Eric scoffs. "If you found an envelope with over six hundred bucks in it, would you actually take it to the cops? I don't think so. I know I sure as hell wouldn't."

"Yeah, well, I'm not holding my breath, but what the hell, it can't hurt to try. Never say never, right?"

I hear the bell ring in the background. "Okay, so I've gotta go," Eric says. "Some of us have classes today."

I chuckle. "Better you than me. But if you want, I'll get a hold of you and maybe we could find a way to get to the hospital to check on Frank."

"Yeah, sure. I'm with you on that. And maybe we can figure out how to make six hundred bucks by tomorrow," he adds sarcastically. "Anyway, yeah, give me a call."

I take my time walking home, ambling along in a world of my own. Frank is in the hospital and that's disturbing to say the least. I replay the events of Thursday night in my head, wondering if we'd missed something about Frank's condition.

We pretty much had to hold him up the whole way to his house, but he was reasonably coherent, even after his dad whacked him in the head. I'd thought that he was recovering. But what if his dad beat him after we left? I don't even want to think about that.

What I need to think about right now is the money. As much as I want to hold onto hope, I know that the odds of someone turning in the envelope to the police are about the same as winning the lottery. So I need to earn some fast cash.

But I have to be realistic. Earning the kind of money we need won't happen overnight. Maybe I can talk Mrs. Watson into some kind of instalment plan and pay her back gradually over a certain period of time. But what's a reasonable amount of time? Two weeks? A month? Two months? No. Not enough time.

I rack my brain. I need a job. It's the only way I can earn extra cash. Just blocks away there are two fast food restaurants and two gas stations.

I try them all. The response is always the same: I'm too young to be hired. Conversation over. The minimum wage is seven dollars an hour, and sometimes a little less for under-agers, but a thirteen-year-old is out of the question.

They're more interested in my eye than in me as an employee. And they look askance at my clothes. Admittedly, I'm not exactly dressed for job hunting, sporting my high-waters, a jacket with a burn hole, and battered running shoes. The stares make me more and more self-conscious of my appearance.

As a last resort, I walk over to Front Street and check out the thrift store. At least there I'm treated with a little more respect.

They pay no attention to my clothes, make no mention of my eye, and they help me as much as possible.

They say that they can't afford to hire me for regular hours, but I can come in Saturday mornings to help sort out the incoming donations. Wages will be around five dollars an hour. That would amount to about twenty dollars a week.

That's well over a hundred bucks a week short of what I need if I'm to pay everything back in a month. I thank them, but say that I'll have to get the okay from my parents first.

A paper route? Nah. Kids at school have *Times-Colonist* routes. With the amount they get paid, nothing less than twenty routes would solve my problem.

I'm about ready to throw in the towel. My ideas' reservoir is tapped out. My inability to repay the money is slapping me in the face, and I hate it. Most problems can be solved with the right amount of patience and perseverance. I get that, but this is just not one of those problems. This one is unique to me. But that doesn't mean I'm about to stop trying.

I'm back at Flick's by about 3:30, and I have the house to myself. Margaret must be out shopping or something. I make myself a peanut butter sandwich and turn on the TV. I've never really watched daytime programs. After going through most of the channels, I can't understand how anyone can spend their time watching all these soaps and talk shows. But I do find one that looks pretty wild and entertaining.

A fat lady hurls chairs and then her clunky shoes at a man a third her size. The audience is egging them on with heckling and taunts. Meanwhile, the stage hands struggle to gain control.

The host stands back, amused. I have to wonder if they're all actors or just ordinary people who crave the limelight despite making complete fools of themselves.

Everyone has their aspirations, and if a measure of fame at any cost is someone's goal, so be it. Regardless, I'm glued to the TV. There's something appealing about the utter chaos, about these out-of-control lives. In a strange way, it gives hope for people like me. The missing envelope is an all-consuming problem, but I haven't completely lost control of my life. At least I'm not hurling chairs. Yet.

I hear a muffled banging noise, so I turn down the volume. I strain my ears. There's a loud knock knock at the front door. My heart skips a beat. I head to the front entrance. Who could it be? At this mid-afternoon hour? The mailman? Or maybe ... I open the door. My heart skips five beats.

CHAPTER 17
Surprise Guest

I can't believe my eyes. "Hey, Chelsea! How's it going?" I say, despite my brain nearly shutting down.

"I'm good, thanks, Axel. But how are you? That's more important," Chelsea replies, staring sympathetically at my eye.

"Oh, I'm doing okay, I guess." I rub my sore eye. "I guess this still looks pretty bad, but it doesn't hurt or anything."

"That's good to hear, Axel."

We look at each other awkwardly until, thankfully, Chelsea breaks the silence.

"Hey, do you mind if I come in, or are you in the middle of something?" she asks.

"Um, no. I mean, yes. I mean, sure, come on in. I'm not doing nothing important." I can't stop stumbling on my words. I feel like slapping myself.

Is this really Chelsea Grant asking to come into my home? I give my head a shake as she comes in and surveys the house while I survey only her.

People gush about meeting movie stars in person and how they look even better than they do on the silver screen. That's Chelsea. I've always thought that she looked good at school, but up close and personal, she's a knock out.

I try not to stare. I feel inadequate. I'm dressed like a slob, and my eye is an ugly mess from the beating. I feebly attempt to cover the battered half of my face.

Chelsea, though, looks perfect, from her medium-length blonde, slightly dishevelled hair down to her faded blue jeans. I really can't believe she's here, in living colour, standing right in front of me.

She clasps her hands together meekly. But Chelsea doesn't seem meek to me. She has something important to say, and my curiosity is running wild.

"Would you like to sit down?" I ask.

"Thanks, Axel, but I'm okay standing for now," she replies, looking more relaxed. "So Axel, why I came is that I want you to, um ..." She grabs my arm. "On second thought, let's sit down." She leads me over to the couch. We sit with only a small space between us. She continues to hold my arm gently.

Chelsea speaks softly. "I want you to know what I've been thinking, so just be patient with me for a minute. I want it to come out right."

"Sure, that's fine," I say, now about to explode with anticipation.

"Okay, listen. I heard what happened last week. Donny was mouthing off about it at school today. I wouldn't expect anything more from that scumbag. And when I heard about it, I just cried."

"You cried? Why?" I ask, surprised and flattered.

"Well, really because of you. I didn't know how bad it was, and I had visions of the worst-case scenarios. I found out that you weren't at school, so that worried me even more. But then I saw Eric, and he filled me in on what happened. That poor guy really took a beating as well, didn't he?"

"Yeah, he did. And so did Frank."

She looks at me with big green-blue eyes and wipes away a tear.

"And look at you," she says. "They really got you good, didn't they? And think about it, Axel. This is all because of me and my sister. It all goes back that stupid scene on Hallowe'en. It's all my fault."

"It's not!" I say sharply. "You can't possibly take the blame for this. All the things that happened that night had one thing in common: Donny. He was actually shooting fireballs at me and Eric before he took that candy bag, so I was out to get him for my own reasons. Then it was actually pretty funny how it all worked out. I mean, you and I were after the same guy and it was really because of you that he fell right into my trap."

"You mean trip," Chelsea quips, perking up.

"Right, my trip." I chuckle. In my mind's eye is a clear picture of Donny on the ground and me standing over him with Chelsea yelling invectives from the sidelines.

Chelsea suddenly reaches for my hand, and I go all tingly inside.

Smiling, she says, "Axel, that's just you, isn't it? That's exactly what I would've expected from you. Even though I know damn well that I had a pretty big part in all of this, you take all the blame yourself. And you know what? That's what I really like about you. Looking out for the other guy and not thinking about yourself. Well, no matter what you say, I still think I'm at least partly responsible for this, not that it changes anything really. But I couldn't hear about all of it and then just do nothing. I don't know, did you think about telling the police or anything?"

"Yeah, I thought about it, but I don't think it's a good idea right now. Anyway, I don't think they'd do anything about a street fight unless we ended up in the hospital." Frank comes to mind. He's in the hospital right now, but I'm certain it's not the Cox brothers who put him there.

"Plus," I add, "the Coxes would just lie about everything, probably say that we mouthed them off and then it would just be our word against theirs."

"Do you think they'd come after you again?" she asks anxiously.

"Actually, no. I think they'll keep their distance from now on, but I can't really say why."

"I sure hope you're right. You know that saying 'what goes around comes around'?"

"Yeah, I've heard it before."

"Well, I believe that's true. Guys like that usually end up running into somebody just like themselves, only bigger, and then they get to see what it's like from the other side."

If only she knew how right she was. "I guess it could happen," I say. "But for me, I'd be happy if I never ran into them ever again."

"I don't blame you, Axel."

Now we're holding hands. I'm actually sitting on Flick's couch holding Chelsea's hand. I hope I don't sound like a robot, because my brain and my mouth are separate entities. I try not to stare at our hands. I try to focus.

Chelsea points to the TV and bursts out laughing. On the show now, two women brawl on stage. They pull hair, throw chairs, and scream at each other, though the sound is thankfully off.

"So Axel, I see you like the educational shows," Chelsea says, smirking. "Tell me the truth now. You didn't really miss school because of your eye, did you? You skipped out to watch ladies fight on TV, right?"

I like her sense of humour. "Okay, you caught me. You can't tell anyone, promise?" Chelsea is clearly amused, so I continue.

"Every day I sit and watch the clock at school, just aching to get home to watch those ladies have it out. Maybe I need help but ..."

Chelsea kisses me on the cheek. "That's for making me laugh," she says. And kisses me again. "And that's for all the nice things you've done for me."

Now my brain has left Earth. "Well, wow, I'm glad I can make you laugh. Doing what I did for you was easy, though."

"Thanks, Axel. Maybe easy for you 'cause that's the kind of guy you are."

I blush. "Speaking of nice, I can't believe you came all the way over here just to see how I was doing. That was a really nice thing to do."

"Well, you deserve it. I was just so sorry to hear about what happened Thursday. And I have to admit that I was a little nervous about coming over here. But now I'm glad I did."

"Me, too. This was actually a pretty crappy day until now," I add sincerely. Then I work up the courage. I kiss her this time. We kiss and hold each other while the world stops turning.

Chelsea glances at her watch. "Oh, wow!" She stands up. "I've got to go. I'm supposed to pick up my sister from her friend's place in fifteen minutes."

"Would you like me to walk there with you?"

"Oh, thanks, but you really don't have to."

"Well, then I'll put it another way. Can I please walk with you over there?"

She smiles warmly. "Sure, that'd be great."

I understand the expression now: 'walking on air.' Holding hands with Chelsea all the way to her sister's friend's place, I do just that.

As soon as I get back home, I dig out my allowance, what little I have, and run back to the thrift store to buy some better clothes. They have some decent blue jeans that fit me properly, and a few newer-looking t-shirts. They remember me from earlier in the day and give me a discount.

I'm broke again, but there will always be more allowances. If Chelsea and I are going to be an item, I need proper clothes.

My black cloud is suddenly grey.

CHAPTER 18
The Life of a Lie

At school Tuesday morning, I feel awkward with all the strange looks coming my way. My eye is healing well, but it's still bad enough to draw attention. I'm expecting the normal quips about 'the other guy' but that doesn't happen. Everyone knows the real story, thanks in large part to Donny, so they keep those comments to themselves.

Instead, I'm greeted with lots of "hey, looking good, buddy" or "you're the man" with high-fives and fist pumps. I search for Chelsea, but she's nowhere in sight.

"Good to see you, Axel," says Mrs. Watson as I enter the classroom. "Oh my," she adds, pointing to my eye. "Is it sore?"

"No, it just looks sore, but it's okay."

"Need any ice?"

"No, I'll be fine, thanks."

She smiles and shakes her head. I have the feeling she knows what happened and she's just being diplomatic. If she doesn't know, I'm not prepared to volunteer my story just yet.

"Oh, Axel, how did your almond sales go?" she asks as an afterthought. "We'd like to get everything in today."

I grimace. "Um, they went good, thanks."

"That's good to hear. I'll be talking to the class about collecting all the money and leftover almonds. Do you have that all ready to hand in?"

I am prepared for this. I had thought about it all morning and finally decided on a lame excuse, actually a lie, that might buy us some time. I thought about telling the truth as well, but in my mind it sounded even more lame than the lie: *well, you see, we were walking home and somewhere along the line I must have dropped the envelope with over six hundred dollars in it.*

I expect the reply to that would be something like *what bonehead loses an envelope with over six hundred dollars? You can't seriously tell me you're that stupid and irresponsible.*

Realistically, buying time will only be useful if there's a way to earn cash. That part still eludes me.

"Um, I don't actually have it with me right now," I reply.

"Really, Axel? I was hoping to get all the calculations done today. Could you bring it in tomorrow?"

"Um, well ... Mrs. Watson, could I please talk to you in the pod for a minute?"

She nods, puzzled. "Sure, Axel, in the pod."

I follow her in, close the door behind us and deliver my prepared lie.

"Okay, you see, my grandparents from Alberta came to Victoria for a quick visit on the weekend. And, well, they don't have much money and their car broke down. They were stuck, and I felt really bad for them so I went and loaned them all of the almond sales money so they could get it fixed. But they said they'll pay it all back as soon as they can."

I feel an awful guilt. I'm lying to one of the few people I trust, and the one person who trusts me enough to not to question me.

Mrs. Watson considers before she responds. "That was very generous of you, Axel," she says thoughtfully. "Yes, I must say, quite generous. Did they give you any idea as to when they could repay you?"

"Well, not exactly. Like I said, they just told me as soon as they could." I feel a knot in my gut. Will this ever end?

"Okay, Axel, I'm on the spot here. I assume you've told Eric about this as well."

"Um, not actually. Not quite yet. I was going to tell him today for sure."

"That'd be important, since he's your selling partner. And so is Frank, but I guess talking with him is out of the question right now."

She knows about Frank? I'm at a loss for words. "Um, yeah, uh," I stammer. "Frank doesn't know about this either. But I'll get in touch with him today for sure."

"Oh!" She looks startled. "So, Axel, you haven't been told?"

"Told what?" I reply anxiously.

"I assumed that being a friend you would have known."

My head feels light, empty.

"You see," she continues, speaking softly, "I got a phone call from Frank's mother just last night. She didn't say it was a carefully guarded secret or anything. But, Frank is in a coma in the hospital. He's in the ICU. She said he fell and hit his head. He could be there for a while. I asked her about visiting hours, but she said he was not allowed visitors at this time."

My heart nearly stops beating. I cycle through pity, sorrow, confusion. Then, rage. Had a bad fall? My ass he did! I try to imagine what I would've said if his mother had given me that line of crap. "No visitors?" I cry. "I can't even go see him?"

"Apparently not, Axel. Only his immediate family. But that could change as soon as he gains consciousness."

I bury my face in my hands. "That really sucks," I mumble.

"Yes, it does. I'm really sorry, Axel. I didn't know I would be the one breaking that news to you. Look, stay here until you feel you're ready to join us. And regarding the almond sales money, I guess somehow we'll just have to make it work, right?"

"Right." The less said from me on that topic, the better.

"I don't know what to say," Mrs. Watson continues. "This is a new one for me. Let me think about it, and I'll get back to you at the break. We'll work something out, Axel."

"Thanks a lot, Mrs. Watson."

The first fifteen minutes of class time is spent collecting money and leftover almonds, and sharing sales stories. I tune out completely.

Math is a blur. Percent, taxes, interest, and questions like how much interest would you earn on a thousand dollars if the bank paid four percent compounded over two years? Just calculations, meaningless calculations as far as I'm concerned. Give me that thousand dollars and then we're talking something meaningful.

Right now, a thousand dollars would be a life saver; it would take a million pounds off my shoulders; it would save all the kids in Africa that I hoped to save through the almond sales, plus more; it would almost solve everything.

But it wouldn't solve Frank's problems. I picture him on a bed in the ICU, a monitor beeping away. I see him hooked up to tubes and wires and hovered over by nurses, just like I've seen on TV. I know his father is to blame, but I'm responsible as well. Frank was not the intended target of the Cox brothers. If he hadn't been with me that night, none of this would have happened.

I manage to write down the assignment, but I get nothing done during class time. Whenever I look her way, Chelsea looks at me, smiling. I do my best to smile back. Thank God for her! She's my reminder to keep digging out of this quagmire.

The bell announcing the break rings and I instantly head for the door. Before I can make an exit, Mrs. Watson motions me into the pod. She closes the door and sighs.

"Axel, you're not doing so well, are you? You were half asleep for the whole math class. Are you okay?" She indicates my battered eye.

"Yeah, I'm fine, thanks. I didn't get a lot of sleep, though."

"I can see that. Well, you'll have to try and catch up on that tonight. So, Axel, I've come up with an idea. You say that your grandparents are going to pay you back whenever they can. Well, here's what I was thinking: we'll have enough money in our class funds to cover all your sales, enough for me to pay the supplier for all the product anyway. So, if you were to bring in money whenever you can, that would be fine with me. Whenever they send money to you, just bring it in and I'll keep track of it until it's all paid off. What do you think of that?"

"That would be great, thanks! But how long would I have to pay it off?"

"No panic. The field trip isn't for another six months or so, but I do have to make prepayments to the venues. So, four months at the outside? Of course, the earlier the better, but that should give your grandparents time to put it all together."

Strangely enough, I'm starting to believe my own story. I haven't even been in touch with my grandparents for several years. And here I am picturing them struggling to make ends meet in some rustic cabin in Alberta, trying to scrape money together to mail out to me.

My lie is becoming a reality. It just bought us some time, and lots of it. For that I'm thankful. I'm not proud of myself, but the temporary relief feels good. Four months might seem like a long time, but if I don't have the means to pay the money back it will feel like the snap of a finger.

"Yes, I think that should work really well for them," I reply. "Thanks a lot for helping us out. I'll bring it in as soon as I can."

"Good. Well, you still have a little break time, so you should take advantage of it."

"Okay, thanks."

I gulp water from the fountain, then find Eric.

"Where the hell did you go?" he asks. "I've been looking everywhere for you."

I tell him about my talk with Mrs. Watson and that we have four months at the most to pay back the money.

"Four months, eh? Any bright ideas?" asks Eric.

"You mean for making money?"

"Yeah, what do you think I mean?"

"Right, well, no great ideas yet. As far as I can see, all it does is give us more time to sweat before the shit hits the fan. You got any ideas?"

Eric smirks complacently and nods. "Yes, I do," he replies, all serious.

"You do? Well, let's hear it."

He looks around suspiciously, then whispers, "Later, okay? But hey, are we going to see Frank soon?"

"Oh, um, no."

"What do you mean, no?"

I look him in the eyes. "Look, Eric, I just got some bad news from Mrs. Watson."

"I'm listening."

"Get this. Frank's mother phoned Mrs. Watson last night to tell her that Frank is in a coma, and nobody can visit except family."

"What the f—!" Eric pounds a locker. Kids stop. Stare. He bites his knuckles to keep from screaming. The kids shrug and keep moving.

"I'm gonna kill his dad! That's what I'm gonna do! What the hell! I'm gonna ..."

I haul him outside.

"Take it easy, Eric. This isn't helping. We'll talk about Frank and deal with that later. We can't right now, though. So look, you said you have a money idea."

"Right," he replies, taking a deep breath. "Yeah, I have a way we can make money, and lots of it."

"Seriously?"

"Yes, seriously. You wanna hear it?"

"For God's sake, yes, I want to hear it!" I shriek.

"All right. Remember when I told you that my mom was getting real worried about the cops watching our place?"

"Yeah, I remember." Just then the bell goes. "Forget the bell. Finish what you're telling me."

"Okay, well, they've been watching our place like hawks, just circling around about twenty times a day, and always slowing down by our place like they're waiting for someone. So, you can guess what that's done to my mom's business, right? Like, she hasn't made any money in about two weeks now. Like, nobody will come to the door with the cops watching every move. So, buddy, that's where you and me come in."

"Come in? Come in where? Come in what?" I ask, confused.

"Me and my mom talked about it, and she said that the only way she could make a sale now is if I helped her. Like, it would mean that I would have to take the stuff in the packages and meet up with the buyers somewhere out of the neighbourhood. But she doesn't want me going alone."

"Of course not," I jump in. "Why get killed alone, right?"

"Oh, ha ha. She said it's not really that dangerous, but it would be at night when it's dark, and she doesn't like the idea of me being out on the streets alone at night. I told her about you and about the Cox beatings and the envelope. So she thought maybe you'd be interested." He raises his eyebrows theatrically and rubs his palms. "We'd make a lot of cash."

I'm at a loss for words. I clench my teeth.

"You okay, Axel?"

"I'm fine. Just have an upset stomach, that's all."

"So, what do you think of my idea for making money? Can you think of anything better?"

My adrenaline kicks in. "Better, you ask? Now that's an interesting way of putting it. Let's face it, anything legal would be better. Cleaning toilets would be better because you couldn't go to jail for it. Yes, I can think of better ideas, but I have to admit that none of them have much of a cash value."

"Exactly," says Eric with conviction. "That's my point. This is easy, fast cash."

"Just how much cash is it anyway?"

"One deal, twenty-five bucks. Two deals, fifty bucks. And we could easily do two or three deals in one night."

Dollar signs roll around in my eyes. "Fifty bucks in one night? Or maybe even seventy-five? Really? And how often do these deals happen?"

"Three or four times a week if we wanted, or maybe more. Mom always has buyers, so it would depend on when we could get together."

I scratch my head and groan. "God, Eric, how do I let you get me into these situations anyway? So we could actually make a few hundred bucks in a week between us, no problem?"

"No problem, buddy. Not much effort either. Just a little walking."

"Yeah, well, the last time we did a little walking together at night, it didn't end up so good."

"Don't even remind me."

"Sorry, I take that back, that was a low one." I'm not thinking straight. I feel sick at the mere thought of being Eric's accomplice again, delivering packages for Eric's mother.

"Not a problem, buddy. So whaddya think?" Eric persists.

"I'll think about it."

Eric shuffles, clenches his fists. "Make up your mind. This is a no brainer. It's like money in the bank. We'll pay for those bloody almonds faster than you can blink. Plus, we'll be able to pocket a bit, too."

"I hear ya. It sounds too good to be true. But, hey, I've gotta think about it a little more before I'm in a hundred percent."

Just then the front door of the school flies open and uppity Will, the do-nothing-wrong suck, appears. "You guys! Mrs. Watson sent me to find you. You're supposed to come to class."

"Well, Will, you found us," Eric replies with contempt, "so you can go back now. We'll be right behind you. Good job." He watches Will disappear into the school. "I hate that guy."

"Yeah, he's a suck."

"Okay," Eric continues, "call me tonight with your answer, but I'm only accepting the right one. And hey, before you go back in, I hate to bum from you again, but I left my damn lunch on the kitchen counter at home."

"I got peanut butter and jam. Half of it has your name on it. Plus, you get the banana and I get the granola bar. Deal?"

"Deal. Thanks, buddy."

CHAPTER 19
Two Blind Men

I'm losing sleep over Eric's offer. The obvious downside is that delivering Eric's mom's 'packages' is illegal. But there's a consequence only if I get caught.

The upside is I'd only need to participate for three weeks or less. If Eric wants to continue after that, that's his business.

Also, there's clearly more to this offer than just replacing lost almond money. Eric didn't forget his lunch at home again. There simply *is* no lunch at home. Getting those packages delivered would generate an income for his mother, Eric would have food once again, and I could have my whole lunch to myself.

Then there's the beating Eric took that weighs on my conscience. This is an opportunity for me to make up for that. And I haven't even considered Frank. I don't know what I owe him, but he sure deserves something positive in his life. He'll be out of the hospital one day, hopefully soon, and I'd like nothing more than to take care of his share of the lost sales money as soon as possible. After all, that money represents his first field trip.

Lots of upsides and one big downside. I believe I'm ready to give Eric my decision.

Late fall or early winter in Victoria is unlike the rest of Canada. We laugh about the snow storms and the ridiculous freezing temperatures like minus twenty and thirty degrees Celsius in other provinces. But they don't have to endure day after day of relentless rainfall, or wind storms that uproot trees, or dampness that chills to the bone.

I walk to school, shivering in my light jacket and no gloves. The temperature is slightly above freezing, rain pelts down, and gusts of wind push me sideways. I feel hypothermic by the time I make it through the doors. But there's Chelsea. My numbness disappears. She takes my hand, and we walk around the school making small talk.

I hear biting comments coming from the so-called popular girls as we walk by. I bet it drives them crazy that a good-looking, popular girl like Chelsea would go out with a loser like me. I really don't give a damn what they think, but obviously Chelsea does. She drops my hand and stares at a girl in a red bomber jacket.

"Shut up!" she yells. "What the hell is your problem anyway?"

The girl stammers, then walks off in a huff. A brawl with fuming, athletic Chelsea would probably be a bad idea. The girl's friends scatter.

I'm shocked, but I can't wipe the smile off my face. Chelsea grabs my hand and drags me in the opposite direction. She's on the verge of tears.

"Sorry," she says. "I hate that girl."

"I think I hate her, too. And I don't even know her."

Chelsea laughs and squeezes my hand. "Can we please pretend that that never happened?" she adds. "That wasn't exactly cool, was it?"

"I think it was great," I reply. "Sometimes people need to be told when to shut up."

"I guess, but I need to control my temper a little better."

"Not a big deal to me." Just then someone taps me on the shoulder. I whirl round—Mr. Davis.

"Axel!" he exclaims. "What in the world happened to your eye?"

Chelsea and I look at each other and smile. "It was her," I quip.

Chelsea jumps right in. "He deserved it. He was looking at me in class and I told him not to."

Mr. Davis laughs. "Okay, I get it. Axel clearly had it coming. How many times have I told you not to look at the girls in class, Axel?"

"Well, not enough, obviously."

"Okay, so I guess we need to have another meeting then, *right?*"

"Right," I return.

"Okay, what about right now?" he suggests. "I'll talk to Mrs. Watson about maybe being late for her class. How does that sound?"

"Sure."

"See you in my office in two minutes then." Mr. Davis hurries away.

"Sounds like you know Mr. Davis well," observes Chelsea. "You guys meet often?"

"Not that much. A few times, I guess. He's really a good guy to talk to."

"I suppose if he can help you, he can help anyone, right?" Before I can retort, she kisses me on the cheek. "You know I'm just kidding, don't you?"

"Yeah, sure. But you know what they say, that the truth hurts."

"You're so funny, Axel. I don't seriously think you need help, but whatever you guys talk about is none of my business. I'll see you later." She gives me quick hug.

We meet at his office door at the same time. Mr. Davis holds the door open and motions me inside. "Come on in, young man, and tell me a little more about that eye."

His office always looks the same, very neat and orderly. I hear the computer humming. We take our respective seats. Mr. Davis pushes something on the keyboard and the computer shuts off.

"Success," he says with a complacent grin. "So, Axel, this looks like a relatively new addition to your otherwise perfect face."

"Yeah, perfect face all right. Thanks for the compliment."

"Do you want to talk about it at all, or not really?" he asks, looking intently at my colourful eye.

"Sure. I don't mind telling you. Every kid in the school knows a bit about it, but only from gossip. You can probably guess who's behind it."

"You've got to be kidding! Donny? Did he actually come after you again?" He's trying to remain neutral, but anger infuses his voice.

"Actually, no. It wasn't Donny in person this time. He got his big brothers to do the job."

He rubs his forehead and stares at me. The only noise in the room now is the tapping of his feet. It feels like the calm before a storm, like something is about to explode. When he finally speaks, I almost jump.

"Seriously? His big brothers did that? How old are his brothers anyway?"

"Oh, I guess about grade ten or eleven. They're at the high school."

"That's unbelievable. I thought that kind of stuff was just all talk, like it was in my day. I mean, we always used the big brother threat to ward off bullies, but I really can't think of anyone who actually followed through with it. I can't believe what I'm hearing, Axel. This looks to me like a pretty serious assault. Have you talked to the police?"

"Well, no, I haven't."

"Any reason why not?"

"Not really. It was actually me and two buddies, and we all got beat up, but we didn't want to make it worse by talking to the cops. I don't know, maybe we should've, but I think it's a little late now."

"It's not too late, Axel. But it has to be your decision. Are you fearful of further retaliation?"

"That's part of it."

"If you want me to get involved, I'm willing to."

I almost jump out of my seat. "Um, please don't, Mr. Davis. I appreciate that, but, no."

He eyes me and nods. "Okay, I'll stay out of it unless I get the okay from you. But I might, just for my own sake, look into the history of those boys to see if this is a pattern. How did your buddies fare in this battle?"

"Not too good, I'm afraid, but they're with me about not wanting to get the police involved."

He looks off into space. "Axel," he continues, "my intention today was to touch base and have a friendly chat. But my goodness, I've really opened up a big can of worms. Those guys need to be stopped before they do some serious damage. And before they end up with criminal charges."

"They're scary guys, for sure. I don't know if I should say this, but I think they might get stopped."

"What do you mean?"

I've said too much. I look behind me, as if checking for eavesdroppers.

"This is just between you and me, right?"

"That's right, Axel. It stays in this room."

"Okay, so what happened was I told my foster brothers the whole story. And they guessed right away who I was talking about. That's the kind of reputation these assholes have. Sorry about the language."

"No problem. Please continue."

"Okay, well, I don't know if you know my foster brothers Ted and Ben Banting. But they were pretty pissed."

"Ted and Ben? I know them," Mr. Davis says animatedly. "They were both on my rugby team. I was the assistant coach. Between you and me, they couldn't seem to stay out of trouble. I always thought they were good boys, though. Just needed an outlet. Rugby was the perfect game. They were big, strong boys then, so I can imagine they're really big boys now."

"Yeah, and they said I'd never have to worry about those guys again."

Mr. Davis covers a smirk.

"Well, Axel," he says through his hands, "I just hope that this all gets resolved. You just don't need that kind of stuff in your life. Nobody does. Oh, and by the way, I hope I didn't interrupt anything between you and Chelsea. Nice girl. You choose good friends."

"Yeah, thanks. You didn't interrupt anything. We're kind of going out, but I guess I'll see how long she'll put up with me."

"At your age, Axel, enjoy the moment and have fun. Whatever happens, happens, right? Just keep your head high and be yourself."

On my way back to class I reflect on our talk. I think about the look on Mr. Davis' face when he realized that Ted and Ben were going to thump the Cox brothers. He's all for it, I'm certain. I guess revenge isn't always a bad thing.

I'm back in time for most of math class. It's pretty mindless percent work, which suits me just fine.

Mrs. Watson has us pack up our books early so she can get writer's workshop underway. Teachers are not very good at hiding their biases, and she's no exception. She has a short story that she's anxious to share with us to get our "creative juices flowing" before we continue on our personal projects.

"I'd like to read a story to you," Mrs. Watson says as she holds up an ancient-looking, hard-cover book. "It's a delightful little story, only three pages long, that has an important message, or I guess you could say a moral. But I'm going to let you decide what that message is. I'm very interested in your interpretations, so please listen carefully."

It takes a few minutes before everyone stops chatting and shuffling at their desks. When all is quiet, Mrs. Watson continues.

"Okay, the title of this story is "A Man Who Had No Eyes" by MacKinlay Kantor. The title causes a little chuckling, which dies off the moment she starts to read:

"A beggar was coming from the avenue just as Mr. Parsons emerged from his hotel …" The story is about two blind men. One of them, Markwardt, is a beggar, and the other man, Parsons, is a successful insurance salesman. It's ironic, and unbeknownst to the reader, that Markwardt has unwittingly accosted another blind man to use his rehearsed begging lines. Parsons realizes that he is approached by a blind man but doesn't let on at first. He patronizes the beggar by purchasing a useless item from him, which only leads to more begging.

We learn that both men were involved in the same disaster, the Westbury chemical explosion. They both made desperate attempts to escape, but the beggar was unable to avoid the explosion. And he lays the blame for his injuries entirely on the man who hauled him back and then leaped over his body to get clear.

At that point in the beggar's story, Parsons can no longer conceal his identity. He calls Markwardt by name, and challenges his version of the story, saying that it was the other way around, that it was actually Markwardt who had hauled him back and climbed over him.

Markwardt then realizes who he has approached, and is taken aback by the revelation that he is caught in his web of lies. Yet, he still feels that he deserves charity because he lost his eyesight. *Maybe (what you say is) so*, he cries. *But I'm blind! I'm blind ...*

Then the final blow: Parsons basically tells him to quit whining for he, too, is blind.

"What?" someone calls out. "He was blind, too? That's crazy!"

Mrs. Watson closes the book and smiles. "Yes, that's crazy, isn't it? That's irony, that's what it really is. And I'm sure most of you picked up on it, and also the message that the author so eloquently presents to the reader."

She writes on the whiteboard as she continues talking. "So, before you continue with your own projects, I would like every-one to put down the title and this subtitle: *What It Means To Me*. Just do a short write telling me what you feel the message is and perhaps how that message might have meaning in your own lives."

I have no idea whether or not the Westbury explosion was a real event, but I have a clear picture in my head of the two men and a mob of others fighting desperately to escape through the only available door before the building exploded. It would have been complete chaos. It would have been hell. It would have been ... just like Mr. Hunter.

I feel myself shaking as the pictures in my head shift to that unforgettable scene. All the pictures blend together with Parsons, Markwardt and Mr. Hunter all in the same smoke-filled inferno, all fighting to escape through an open garage door. Sweat drips down my forehead. Focus. Focus, I tell myself.

The message is clear to me. After a quick first draft, then some reworking and editing, I end up with this: *The two men had both ended up with the same fate: blindness. Yet, they chose completely opposite paths to go forward. Markwardt used his disability to get sympathy through begging. He could not accept his fate, and so he spent all of his energy blaming the world and insisting that everyone owed him something for what he sacrificed. Parsons accepted his fate and rather than dwell on his disability, he focused on his strengths and created a successful career selling insurance.*

For me, I think it means that we have to take whatever life throws at us, whatever cards we're dealt, and just make it work.

I'm reluctant to put more than that on paper in case it's read by someone other than Mrs. Watson. But on a personal level, the message has a lot of meaning. It makes me think about the way I've been approaching my own life.

I want to believe that I'm more of a Parsons, but I feel that Markwardt slips in there from time to time. When I ask myself if I accept whatever life throws at me, I have to say 'not always.' Overcoming all my challenges requires good decision-making. And as much I hate to admit it, I'm not always so good at that.

That reminds me. Eric is waiting anxiously for my decision about deliveries.

CHAPTER 20
Special Deliveries

Friday night, seven o'clock, I arrive at Eric's house as planned. His mother answers the door and welcomes me in. She's all smiles and a little giddy. I notice she's missing a few teeth.

"You must be Axel! Well, it's really good to meet you!" she exclaims as she offers her hand to shake.

"Thank you, uh ..."

"Call me Jeanie," she cuts in.

"Okay, thanks, Jeanie." I'm already getting cold feet. This just feels wrong, like I've just landed in a foreign country with a huge language barrier. But turning back now is not an option. I've made a commitment to Eric.

Her handshake is surprisingly firm. "Come with me," she says. I follow her through a dark living room area into the kitchen where she pulls out a chair from the table. "You just sit right there, and I'll go get that little rascal. I think he might be snoozing upstairs."

I sit and watch as she tears out of the room. Energy-wise, she and my foster mother Margaret are opposites. Jeanie, probably ninety pounds soaking wet, has a bounce in her step, but she looks much older than Margaret.

Jeanie's face is angular and leathery, her cheek beset with a nervous tick, her hair grey and scraggly.

Dirty dishes are scattered on the counter tops, table and stove. The plates on the table are caked with spaghetti sauce, possibly several days old. A pungent, musty odour fills the air.

Eric lives in a germ factory, yet he seems to stay reasonably healthy. I stay perfectly still for fear of touching anything.

Jeanie returns a few minutes later with Eric in tow.

Eric high-fives me. "Hey, Axel, right on time, buddy. You met my mom?"

"Well, yeah. I didn't come in on my own," I reply.

"That's my son," adds Jeanie as she gives Eric a loving pat on the head. "Always thinking."

"Okay, I get it. That was a stupid thing to say," replies Eric. "Anyway, you ready to go, Axel?"

"Yeah, sure."

"Okay, hold on a second, you guys," says Jeanie. She takes three small packages, actually just paper bags, out of the cupboard. They're bound with wads of scotch tape and numbered one, two, and three with a thick black marker. She pushes aside a few dirty plates and sets them on the table in front of me. Enunciating meticulously, she starts her prepared spiel.

"Now, listen carefully to my instructions. These are three separate deliveries and I wrote down the places to meet the clients on this." She hands a used, white envelope to Eric. Her hand has a slight tremor.

"You can see," she continues, "that each package has a number and there's an instruction on the paper for each one." She points to the number one on the envelope. "So, I wrote down exactly where to meet this guy for package one. It's at the Salvation Army at the bottom of Johnson. And I told him that he's number one, so all you have to do when you get there is look for a guy hanging around.

"He's supposed to be wearing a blue hoodie, but all you have to do is say out loud 'where is number one?' With two of you, you just make it sound like you're talking to each other. When this guy hears that, he'll come over to you and say that he's number one, and you just give him the package. Then he'll give you an envelope and it should be sealed. Tuck it in your jacket pocket and make damn sure it won't fall out."

Eric looks at me and rolls his eyes. I shake my head as if to say *don't even go there*.

"Are you guys listening?" she snaps.

"Yes," we both reply at the same time.

"Good, because we can't afford a screw up. It's basically the same thing for the other two clients, but in different locations. They're all close by, but I think it's better to keep them all separate so they don't meet each other. I think it's a safer way to go. The instructions are right there on the paper so just follow them exactly the way I wrote them down and it should all go just fine. Any questions, you guys?"

Eric looks at me and shrugs. I actually do have a burning question. "I don't mean to be critical or anything, but how can we be sure that these guys will just give us the envelope like you say without a problem? And how do we know that the full amount is there?"

"Oh, honey," she says, "that's the part you don't need to worry about. You see, these guys are regular customers of mine and they know that if they mess up the deal in any way, especially short-changing me, they'll never do business with me again. And believe me, they can't afford to lose me."

She sounds so convincing that I'm embarrassed for having brought it up. She gives me a long, glassy-eyed stare as if she's waiting for further questions. "You guys ready then?" she asks.

"Yeah, Mom, we're ready," replies Eric.

"Good then. I'm going to put these in here." Jeanie places all three bags in a plastic bread bag. "Now, one of you tuck this inside your jacket and zip it up tight."

"I'll take it, Mom," volunteers Eric. The bag fits so snuggly that, when his jacket is zippered up, there are no noticeable bulges.

Jeanie grins from ear to ear like a child at Christmas.

"Okay, you boys be careful out there," she says while patting our heads. "And come straight back home when you're done. You shouldn't be gone long."

"Okay, see you soon, Mom," says Eric as he leads the way out.

"Bye, honey. See you, Axel. Be careful."

"Bye, Jeanie."

It's like a final farewell before going off to war. My stomach churns, but jumping ship is not an option.

I'm oblivious to the light drizzle and steady breeze that accompanies us on our walk. Otherwise, my senses are much more acute than normal. Every person walking by and every car driving by is suspect. I feel like a flashing beacon. But my head is playing games with me. After all, it's dark, so nobody can see us clearly anyway. And two guys walking the streets at 7:30 don't exactly look suspicious.

We're walking down Ocean Boulevard Drive towards the bridge when a large sedan slows down beside us.

"What the hell," says Eric as he picks up the pace and looks straight ahead. "Is this guy really checking us out or what?"

"I don't know," I reply. "Let's just keep going."

The driver honks his horn. We both jump.

"Hello! Hey, sorry to bother you guys!" he yells out the passenger window. "I was just wondering if you could tell me how to get to the Oak Bay Beach Hotel."

We breathe a collective sigh of relief. Eric does the talking.

"Hello. The Oak Bay Beach Hotel? No, sorry, I can't tell you how to get there. But I know that if you stay right on this road, go over the bridge, and just keep going straight for about fifteen blocks or so, you'll eventually end up in Oak Bay. Or you'll be close to it. Anyway, you should ask somebody in that area and they'll probably be able to show you where it is."

"That's very helpful. Thank you very much. You boys have a nice night."

"Thank you. You as well," Eric finishes, using the politest tone I've ever heard. When the car is a safe distance down the road we have a good laugh about the whole thing. It helps to calm our nerves.

Close to the bridge is an expensive-looking hotel that I've never noticed before. It's right on the ocean. All the cars in the parking area look expensive as well. I can't imagine ever being able to afford luxury like that. Wealth is such a foreign concept to me. I wonder if people with that kind of money have any problems.

We both hold onto the blue metal railing as we cross the bridge. Looking off to our right is a nice view of the Inner Harbour, but we aren't exactly in the right frame of mind for sight-seeing.

There's a steady stream of cars crossing the bridge in both directions. I feel the soothing vibration of their tires on the metal waffle-iron-like surface. We pass the last girder and stand in awe of an ominous huge slab of concrete that is precariously attached to the bridge and about twenty feet in the air. Someone told me that it's a counterweight, necessary for a draw bridge of this type. But how it remains in place without crashing to the asphalt and ending up in China is beyond me.

"Crap. That's just not possible," says a wide-eyed Eric. "If that sucker came down, it would make pancakes out of the unlucky suckers driving underneath it. Remind me to never drive over this bridge again."

"Ah, don't worry about that kind of stuff," I reply. "The way I see it, it's like a lottery. Probably a few million cars have driven under that monster, and no one's been crushed yet. So they've all won the lottery. The odds are really good. But I guess if it ever does fall, some unlucky bugger loses the lottery."

"You got that right!"

Just a few minutes past the bridge is our first destination at the corner of Wharf and Johnson. The Salvation Army building looks a lot nicer than I expected. It is a sprawling, solid-looking brick structure about three stories high. The second floor extends out over the walkway, supported by a series of brick pillars and arches, creating an outside shelter. Two long-bearded men with dark hoodies stand at the entrance, one on each side. They pay no attention to us as we approach.

Eric stops and grabs my arm. "Hey," he whispers nervously, "do you think it's one of those guys?"

"Good chance," I whisper back. I take a few deep breaths to calm my nerves. "But holy shit, this is killing me. I feel like I'm gonna crap myself."

"You, too, eh?' replies Eric. "I can't believe we're here and we're really about to do this. But here goes nothing. Can't turn back now, right?"

"No, I guess not. We've come this far, so let's do it. I guess we just have to try out the line."

"Okay, right. So let's start talking right now and make it sound natural. Got an idea to get it going?" asks Eric.

"Well, not really, but I think I can do this. Follow my lead." With my back turned, making sure the two beards can hear, I start a contrived conversation. "So listen, I'm getting real tired of looking around. I mean, we found all the other ones." Then I increase the volume. "So where the heck is number one?"

Instantly, one of the men jumps to attention and jogs up behind us. "That's me," he says.

We start walking, the man following close behind, until we're clear of the building with nobody in ear-shot.

"Hey, I'm number one," says the man, sounding agitated.

We turn around. He's wearing a blue hoodie, which matches Jeanie's instructions. I nod at Eric.

"Okay, just wait here a second," says Eric. He walks up the block for privacy and to take advantage of a street light before digging out the bread bag. He returns with his jacket all zippered up and offers the number one bag to the client. "There you go," he says.

The man slips the bag inside his hoodie and hands Eric a sealed white envelope. "Thanks, guys," is all he says, and then strides away. We watch him until he reaches the end of the block and disappears around the corner.

"Done deal," quips Eric as he sighs in relief and smiles.

I give him a high-five. "On to number two. Let's go."

We cross the street and head back down Johnson. Just one block to the right, at the bottom of Pandora, is Swan's Pub where we're supposed to meet client number two. Again, it's an older building, nicely renovated with an abundance of hanging baskets lining the outside perimeter. It's too pleasant a place for a transaction of this nature.

A few people come and go through two separate entrances, but they appear to be pub clientele only. According to Jeanie's notes, we're looking for a tall, slender man with a shaved head and an anchor tattoo on his neck. Meeting time is between 8:15 and 8:25.

Nobody we can see fits that description, so we wait on the corner where we can monitor foot traffic on Pandora and Store Streets at the same time.

Just in case our client might be hiding somewhere in the shadows, we decide to try our line a few times:

"Where the heck is number two?" No response. We pause and keep trying, but after about ten minutes we're getting worried.

I shake my head in frustration and say, "I guess we missed him."

"Yeah, or maybe our dude is late," Eric replies impatiently. "It's 8:25 by my watch, so we're on schedule, but I can't imagine that these guys are big clock-watchers. We'll give this guy a few minutes. And if we have to, we'll leave this one for now and maybe come back after number three."

"I think we should give it a little more time," I reason. "I think your mom would be a little pissed if we miss him altogether."

"You got that right! So where the hell is number two?" he yells openly.

"I'm number two!" comes an anxious reply. Jaywalking across Pandora towards us is the man we're looking for. He fits Jeanie's description perfectly, but he's also one scary-looking dude. He's probably 250 pounds, has more scars on his face than I can count, and he's shaking uncontrollably. "That's me, I'm number two," he repeats.

Normally I'd give him a wide berth. To top it off, his black leather jacket flares open. Attached to his belt is a sheathed hunting knife with about a six-inch blade. I fixate on the knife and watch his hands as if I were his opponent in a gun fight. *If he goes for that knife,* I think to myself, *I go for the four-hundred-meter dash.*

Eric stays calm and simply follows the same procedure as before. "Hold on one sec," he says. He walks away and returns momentarily with the package. The exchange is made, the envelope is tucked away, and we start to walk away.

"Hey, you guys, hold on," the man calls before we get ten feet away. We freeze and turn around slowly. To our relief, he's smiling. "Good job, eh! But watch yourselves out here on the streets, eh. I'll see you boys again."

"Yeah, thanks," we reply in unison.

We start breathing again when we're a block away. "Whew!" I finally cry out. "This job is gonna take years off my frickin' life."

"You got that right, old man. Let's get number three done and get the hell back home."

According to the instructions, number three is just three blocks down Store Street in front of Value Village. Lighting is poor and most of the buildings are dilapidated in this dingy part of town. We pick up the pace and say nothing.

Just one block from our destination, we see the shadow of a man coming towards us pushing a cart. As he approaches, we see that it's actually a grocery buggy overflowing with his personal belongings. He stops right beside us, looks right past us and repeats the same phrase: "Odd job ... odd job ... odd job ..."

He looks ancient, but who knows. His grey hair is so long it almost touches the ground. He wears only a long-sleeved shirt, baggy pants and sandals with thick socks; he seems insensible to the cold. And he stinks.

"Odd job ... odd job ... odd job—"

"—Sorry, buddy," I say. "We don't have any jobs for you. We don't even work ourselves. We just—"

Before I can babble on any further, 'Odd Job' puts his head down and continues on his way.

Eric watches him for several seconds. "Remember what I said about living on the streets? I'd rather have a roof over my head. I don't give a damn what life is like underneath it."

"Yeah, I suppose so," I agree. It actually makes a lot more sense now. The street? Or Flick? I'm going with Flick, even if he can be an asshole. "It does make me wonder how it all happened, though. I mean, how does a person end up like that?"

Eric shrugs. "Bad luck, I guess. Maybe lost his job or something."

"Maybe. But a lot of people lose their jobs and still keep going. There must be some horror stories. And who knows, maybe they're happy where they are."

This gets a rise out of Eric. "Happy where they are? Are you kidding me?"

"Well, we can't get into their minds, can we? We'd have to ask them, wouldn't we?" I challenge.

"I'll leave that up to you, Mr. Charity. When you get a chance, you can come down here and get all their stories, all their horror stories that is, and then report back to me."

"I just might do that, Sergeant."

Before we can continue bantering, I see what appears to be our number three coming our way. We're looking for a short lady with long black hair and a shiny white ski jacket. It has to be her.

Wasting no time, Eric calls out, "Where is number three?"

"I'm number three," she replies in a soft voice. "So you're the guys doing this now. That's amazing."

I look at Eric and we both nod in agreement.

Without a word, Eric hands her the package and takes the envelope she's proffering.

"Thanks a lot," I say.

"Thanks, boys. And, hey, don't make a living doing this." It's more like a friendly piece of advice than a command.

"No, we won't. Have a nice night," I return cordially.

"Bye, boys."

She emphasizes *boys*. It makes us sound so young. Or maybe it makes her sound old. Either way, I like her advice. I won't be making a living doing this.

We put it in high gear all the way back to Eric's house. We're just two houses away when we see a police car coming up the road. It slows to a snail's pace as it nears Eric's house. We keep our heads turned away while making a beeline for the back door.

"You're back!" Jeanie cries the moment we enter. "Oh, you guys are just the greatest!" She gives Eric a big hug, and then pats me on the head. "Well, tell me, any problems out there?"

"No problems, Mom," Eric replies as he hands her the three envelopes.

"Oh, thanks, honey. That's fabulous! Wonderful! I'll be right back." Jeanie disappears to count the money and returns about five minutes later with one of the envelopes. It's open, and I can see several bills inside. A beaming Jeanie hands it to Eric.

"Here you go, you guys. This is for you, seventy-five dollars as promised. There's lots of small bills, so you can divide it up any way you like."

Eric is nearly salivating as he takes the envelope. "Thanks, Mom!"

"Yeah, thanks, Jeanie," I echo.

"Have fun, you guys. There's more of that to come." She gives a huge open-mouth grin, as if oblivious of all her missing teeth.

After she leaves, Eric removes a ten-dollar bill from the envelope. "Can I have this?" he asks. "I just want a little spending money to get me through?"

It's weird having Eric ask for my permission. I know how badly he needs the cash, so I'm not about to deny him.

"Yeah, sure, why not?" I reply, as I remove an additional five-dollar bill and hand it to him. "And take this as well just to be sure."

"Right on! Thanks, partner! So, what are you gonna do with the other sixty bucks?" he asks.

"Well, what do you think? We've got a debt to pay, right? So that's where it's going. I'm just gonna hide it at my place for now and wait until we do a few more deliveries before I start handing it in."

"Good plan. You're the banker. Put it under your mattress so you won't lose it." He laughs and pats me on the back. "Talk to you tomorrow, buddy."

"For sure, tomorrow."

I put the envelope in the inside pocket of my jacket. All the way home in the rain I keep my hands pressed against it. There's not a chance it can fall out.

CHAPTER 21
Down to Earth

Saturday is a day to sleep in. But it's only 9:00 o'clock and Ted and Ben are downstairs knocking on my bedroom door. This is the second time they've done this since my beating and I admit that I welcome their visits.

"Wake up, little bro," calls Ted as he opens the door.

I smile when I hear him say 'little bro.' Things are improving every day.

"Hey, you guys. What's going on?" I ask groggily. Both of them are in their pyjama bottoms, showing off their washboard stomachs and bulging biceps. The two of them look like tag-team wrestlers.

"News update," says Ted. "Ran into the Cox boys at school on Friday."

I jerk myself out of the covers and sit upright, my big ears all agog. "What happened?" I ask.

"Not enough," Ben jumps in. "Didn't exactly get a chance to finish the job, eh, Ted?"

"No, we didn't. We hunted down the little buggers and got them at their lockers. Ben and me each grabbed one and slammed them against the lockers, and we had 'em in a choke-hold when a teacher came by. He told us to cool it, and said if we kept it up he'd haul us down to the office. So that was about it."

"Yeah, but we left them with something to think about," adds Ben with a wild smirk. "We told them to make out their wills before we meet again." Ben and Ted laugh boisterously.

"And they seemed confused, like what the hell do we have against them?" Ben continues. "So we remind them about the night they beat up on you little grade eights, and then we said you were our foster brother. You should've seen the look on their chicken-shit faces. We thought they were gonna crap themselves, right, Ted?

They both laugh and slap each other on the back. "You got that right," Ted concurs. "And then they were squirming like little worms trying to apologize for the whole thing."

"So, what did you say to them?" I ask.

Ted responds, "I said, an apology won't exactly fix the damage you did to our foster brother and his buddies. I told him 'you do the crime, you do the time.' And the time is just a few minutes with us. Then those little whiners were almost crying, and trying to suck up more, and saying they'll make it up to you somehow."

"Make it up to me?" I say, confused. "Really? I can't imagine how that would work."

"No, me neither," says Ben. "We just laughed at 'em, and I told them to be sure and let us know how the hell they think they're gonna make up for the mess they made of three grade-eight faces. They cringed and that was about it. Their days are numbered, that's all I can say."

Ted shakes his head in disgust. "Yeah, it was a typical way for bullies to act. They can dish it out, but they sure as hell can't take it. So don't you worry about a thing. We'll finish the job sooner or later."

"Okay, well, thanks for letting me know, you guys," I say, unable to think straight any more. Ted and Ben getting revenge for me? Wow! "I'm glad you didn't get into trouble or anything. I really appreciate what you guys are doing for me, too."

"Not a problem, little bro," returns Ted. "And hey, it's after nine, time to get your ass moving."

"I'm getting up right now."

I put my head back down on the pillow feeling elated about 'my big bros.' Is this the same Ted and Ben that I was pulling pranks on not so long ago?

Somehow, I'll make it up to them later. But the more I think about the Coxes, the more uncertain I am that revenge is the best solution. It's clear that the Cox brothers are no longer a threat to me or Eric or Frank. I would really question their sanity if they're still willing to test my foster brothers after that encounter.

I'll be happy if the whole thing goes no further than this. Also, as much as I appreciate Ted and Ben's good intentions, having someone else do my dirty work doesn't sit all that well with me.

But right now, I don't have the power to call off the cavalry. The anticipation of their next meeting with my big bros must be nerve-racking.

Chelsea calls me just after lunch to ask if I'd like to go to see *Apollo 13* with her tonight. I really like this role reversal idea, the girl phoning the guy, especially since I'm still hopeless about initiating things.

"Yes, I'd love to go. What time is it showing?"

"Well, there's a 6:30 and a 9:30 at the Capitol 6, but I suppose the 9:30 might be a little late," she replies.

An alarm goes off in my head. This is a delivery night and Jeanie is counting on us. It's not something that can be postponed or even delayed. Jeanie made it clear that when she makes arrangements with her clients, she can't afford to mess it up. I do a quick calculation, and I figure if everything goes as planned, I can do the deliveries and still make it to the Capitol 6 by nine. But it would mean leaving Eric to walk home on his own. The walk between his house and downtown feels safe enough, so it shouldn't be a problem. It might not sit well with Jeanie, but what she doesn't know won't hurt her.

"Axel, are you still there?" Chelsea chimes in.

"Oh, sorry, Chelsea, I was just trying to decide which one was better. Actually, 9:30 would be perfect if it works for you."

"Okay, well, here's the thing." She giggles and clears her throat. "After the movie, I was hoping you could meet my mom. She can drive us home. It'd be close to midnight, though."

"Yeah, wow. That's pretty late for sure. Well, yeah, I guess if she doesn't mind giving me a ride that would be great."

"Not at all. She really wants to meet you. I told her how you rescued my sister's Hallowe'en candy and about Donny's brothers beating you up and stuff."

I'm cringing. "Maybe too much information," I say flatly. "But that's nice that your mom wants to meet me. Your dad, too?"

"Oh, my dad? Well, um, that's a different story. Me and him don't exactly get along well."

"Oh, sorry to hear that."

"Please don't be, Axel. He's just an asshole, that's all."

"I hope you guys can work that out, I guess."

"Oh, we won't. You can count on that," Chelsea states firmly. "Look, I'm sorry, Axel. I'll just say that my dad's done things that I'll never forget and never forgive. But, hey, let's stay positive here. My mom is great and she'll give us a ride."

"Okay, that's good then." I glance in the small mirror just above the phone table. "And hey," I add, "my eye is looking pretty normal now."

"You look just fine, believe me. It's all good, Axel. You're already in my mom's good books and she hasn't even met you. And believe me, that's not like her. Like, can you say overprotective? That's my mom. Pretty funny, eh?"

"Yeah, pretty funny, I guess." I would give anything to have an overprotective mother right now. That's how I remember my mother, overprotective but in a loving way. "Well, I'll see you there at 9:00. I've heard good things about the movie."

"Me, too. I'll see you then."

Jeanie is overly excited to see me again. After all, I now represent her meal ticket, possibly her whole subsistence. Today, with her tight ponytail and bright red lipstick, she looks slightly more girlish. But the deep wrinkles and dark bags under her eyes still tell the real story, and there's not enough makeup in the world to hide that.

Everything is packaged up and ready to go, and Eric has his jacket on. He's anxious to get going.

"Same three locations, same instructions," lectures Jeanie as she hands me the same sheet of paper we used for Friday's deliveries.

"Okay, Mom, we got it. Where is number one, and all that stuff," Eric says flippantly.

That gets a rise out of Jeanie. "Don't talk to me like a smartass! There's no room for mistakes here, you understand?" she yells.

Eric hangs his head like a whipped dog. "Yeah, sorry, Mom. Yes, I understand, and we won't screw it up."

"Good then." She hugs us both and holds open the front door. "Oh, and I'll need you guys for just two deliveries on Monday. Is that okay?"

Eric and I look at each other and shrug. "Not a problem with me," I say.

"I sure as hell won't have other plans, will I, Mom?"

"No, you won't, dear," she replies with a loving smile. "Now you guys be careful out there. And watch for cop cars, too."

"We will, Mom," Eric finishes as he pushes me out the door.

As if in answer, the moment we step outside we see a police car slowly cruising by. It slows almost to a complete stop when the driver spots us.

Eric grabs my arm. "Come on, follow me," he says in a panic. "Let's just go around to the back of the house. I get the feeling he's gonna ask us some questions or something."

We scurry to the backyard like a pair of wanted criminals. It's dark back here so we can peek around the corner without being seen. The police car is now stopped just slightly past Eric's house, and it appears that the officer is on his radio.

"I don't like the looks of this at all," I say to Eric.

"Ah, this is nothin' new," he replies with a wave of his hand. "They've been pulling off this crap for weeks now. Just give it a minute and he'll be gone, then we'll wait a few more minutes just to be sure."

"Whatever you say."

We wait in silence. I'm shaking the whole time. The only thing that calms me down is thinking about Chelsea.

"Hey," I whisper, "This would be as good a time as any to tell you that I have a date tonight."

"What the hell! You serious? With Chelsea? Tonight? Like when?"

"Well, like, that's what I need to talk to you about. So look, I'll do all the deliveries with you as we planned, but do think you could make it back home on your own just this one time?"

Eric grimaces and says nothing. The police car is gone, so we start walking. I finally get a response.

"Seriously? Why the hell would I have to travel alone?"

"Uh, well, I sort of, or Chelsea sort of set up a late movie. I mean, she actually phoned me so I just couldn't say no. It was either 6:30 or 9:30, so I figured I could do all the deliveries with you and still make it to the movie. But—look, I know I'm kind of putting you on the spot here. It would just mean ..."

"Relax, buddy," Eric cuts in. "I can handle it. I've done it a hundred times before. I'll just have to pretend I'm not carrying a bank vault full of cash, and I should be all right. I mean, why should it be any different, right?"

"Thanks, Eric. I really appreciate it."

"Not a problem, buddy. We really appreciate what you're doing, too. Mom's been in the best mood ever since we made those deliveries yesterday. She's like a different person when things are working out for her, and for me. Believe me, it's been hell living with her these past few weeks." He stops and looks at me intently. "I guess I shouldn't be telling you all this stuff, but you're the only guy I can trust to talk about it with."

"Well, thanks. I'll take that as a compliment, and you *can* trust me. Nothing we talk about ever gets out there, believe me."

He high-fives me. "I know that about you. You're a real friend."

I'm flattered and speechless. We walk in silence for a few minutes and I suddenly realize what a nice late fall evening it is. Cool, but no rain, no wind, and a clear, star-lit sky.

"Real hell," Eric says, continuing his spiel about Jeanie. "You seen her shaking?"

"What do you mean?" I ask.

"Her hands, her head. Did you notice the shaking?"

"Well, I guess I did notice it a little, but I didn't think too much about it. I thought maybe she was just over-tired or something."

"Over-tired all right. She's over-medicated, that's what she is. In fact, buddy," he states resignedly, "she's a junkie. That's my mom. I love her and I hate what she's become. She keeps saying that she's gonna stop and get clean, and I think she actually tries sometimes. But as soon as things go wrong, it's right back to the drugs."

I'm trying to think of something to say that might be consoling, but Eric is intent on getting a lot more off his chest.

"Today she was good," he continues. "That's because things are suddenly going good. But the slightest little thing goes wrong, and it's right back to square one with her. And then I have to look after her. I sometimes feel like I'm the babysitter. It's not fun, Axel. It's hell."

"Well, let's hope that things keep going well and maybe she'll actually stop everything," I say, optimistically.

"That would be something. I can only pray it works out that way."

"Never say never, right?" It feels good using that line now.

"Yeah, never say never. Never say never ... never say never ...," he keeps repeating like it's his new mantra.

The deliveries, thankfully, are going off without a hitch. It almost feels too easy, like we're already in a comfort zone. The buyers are there and on time, and they're always polite. We're starting to recognize some of the regular street faces as well. Odd Job does his thing with us once again, like a well-rehearsed routine.

I'm already getting a sense of the community that the street people have. They always greet each other with hugs, and they just seem to have a lot of respect for each other. There's a bonding that seems to keep them connected and grounded.

These downtown deliveries don't feel nearly as scary the second time around, which I suppose is a good thing. But I'm still constantly on my guard, still watching over my shoulders and closely checking every person who walks by.

It's a little past 8:30 when we complete the last delivery. "Well, Eric," I say, "I guess this is where I make my mad dash to the theatre. You're sure you're okay with everything?"

"Piece o' cake, buddy."

"I know your mom won't be pleased to know you were on your own coming home."

"No, but as far as she'll know, you were with me. You just went home instead of coming inside, right?"

"Right. Thanks for backing me up, buddy," I say with a firm handshake.

"Any time, partner."

I arrive at the theatre a little before 9:00. Chelsea is already waiting in line. "Axel, over here," she calls out. "I thought I'd get in line for tickets so we can get good seats."

I come up beside her in the line-up and she reaches for my hand. "Good idea," I say.

"Axel, you're breathing hard. Did you run here or something?"

"Well, yeah, part of the way," I reply, hoping the topic will change.

Chelsea looks at me confused. "Didn't you get a ride here?"

"Well, I had a few things to do downtown, so I just came from there."

"What, were you shopping or something?"

"Not exactly shopping, but I ... well ..."

"Hey, it's not my business," Chelsea cuts in. "You're here, so that's all that counts. My mom had things to do so she dropped me off about fifteen minutes ago. She'll pick us up at 11:45."

"That's really nice of her. I wouldn't even dream of asking my foster dad to pick me up from anywhere at any time, especially that late."

"Oh, really? That's too bad." Looking concerned, she adds, "You don't get along too well with your dad either?"

"Foster dad," I correct her. "Well, let's just say that we get along just fine when we don't interfere with each other's business. It's not really that bad. I'm used to it."

"It doesn't sound like much of a father-son relationship to me."

"You nailed it. It's more like I get a bed in his house, and Flick gets ministry money kind of relationship."

"Hmm, that's weird. Does he ever hit you?" she asks point blank.

"Actually, no. That's one thing he doesn't do. But he yells like hell. I'm used to it, though. And actually, I get a lot of freedom. Like going to a late movie with you was no problem. I think Flick probably does care a little, at least enough to check to make sure I get home and stuff. But he's not the easiest guy to warm up to. It's no big deal really."

Chelsea gazes at the sky.

"So, uh, you said you didn't get along with your dad, right?" I ask.

"Right. I said he's an asshole, because he is. He yells and puts me down and makes me feel like crap every day. I just don't like being around him."

Chelsea's face turns beet red, and she starts waving with her hands. "Like he's this big, good-looking jock, or at least he used to be. And he just thinks that the women in his life should jump whenever he snaps his fingers. He knows nothing about respect and I can't talk to him about it, because he won't listen to me. I hate jocks."

I'm stunned. I wait in silence.

"I'm finished," she says at last. "That's all I have to say about my dad."

"Yeah, well, that really sucks," I offer as I squeeze her hand. She squeezes back and smiles.

"But hey, aren't you a jock?" I tease.

"Me? Well, I guess I never think of myself as a jock, but I do like to play sports."

"That's good. Nothing wrong with that. Let's just say that you're the good kind of jock."

"Okay, I can accept that."

"And it's amazing that you'd hang out with me since I'm a star jock," I tease.

"You? A jock? I don't think so, Axel."

"Hey, you don't know. Have you ever seen me on the basketball court?"

"Are you serious, Axel? Do you really play basketball?"

"No, but I can spin the ball on my finger. I learned that when I sat on the bench all last year."

She laughs so hard that her gum flies out of her mouth. "You are too funny! I'm actually glad you're not a jock. But you're an awesome guy, and that's what I like about you."

She jumps up to kiss me on the cheek, and I turn every shade of red.

The movie is based on the true story of the Apollo 13 mission to the moon. The moon landing had to be abandoned because of an explosion which created a serious shortage of oxygen.

There they are, a hundred thousand miles up in space with a limited supply of oxygen and power, and they have to somehow complete the journey back home.

I'm transfixed by Jim Lovell (played by Tom Hanks) who is the commander of the crew. He has to somehow remain calm and collected while his crew is falling apart. The odds of making it back home are next to zero, and it appears that some of the crew are throwing in the towel, reluctantly embracing their fate. But there is a glimmer of hope, and Lovell insists they latch onto it as he refuses to give up.

I imagine myself being in that capsule, floating freely through space with an awe-inspiring planet Earth in view. In a sea of nothingness, all my Earthly problems disappear. Money has no meaning, so the lost envelope is meaningless, and there are no Cox brothers to worry about.

But Mr. Hunter is as real in space as he is on Earth. I have a commitment to him; he's in my conscience; he will stay with me no matter where I am. And Earth is where I need to be to do what's necessary to be forgiven.

Now I'm one hundred percent with the crew in the capsule dealing with one big problem: how to get back to Earth. The complicated issue of reaching Earth is now greater than any problem in the world. It's the only problem that exists.

My mind is toying with these thoughts when I feel Chelsea squeeze my hand.

"I have to close my eyes," she says. "If they're not going to make it, I don't want to watch."

The module is in the process of re-entering Earth's atmosphere. There's a long period of radio silence. Almost certainly, the module has burned up and disintegrated from all the friction. The tension is tangible.

"Oh, God, please make it!" Chelsea cries.

I actually know the ending, because I read about the real mission. I guess Chelsea hasn't, but I'm not about to spoil it for her. Plus, I like it when she cuddles up closely with me like she's doing.

Suddenly the vessel is spotted in the sky, contact is made with Houston, and it splash-lands safely in the Pacific Ocean.

"Yes! Yes! They made it! Yes!" Chelsea screams as she kisses me on the cheek. It makes me want to ask the projectionist to go back and play the ending again.

"It's unbelievable," I state as I wipe away a few tears of my own. "What a feeling that must've been landing back on Earth."

"Makes you kind of appreciate what we have here, doesn't it?" Chelsea adds with a wide smile.

"Yeah, you're right. It really does. Suddenly Earth feels like a great place to be. But holy crap, those guys went through hell, didn't they?"

"You won't catch me being an astronaut, that's for sure," she utters with conviction.

"No, me neither. I think I'd need a science degree for that anyway. Not much of a chance of that. But hey, thanks a lot for suggesting this movie. It was a good one."

"Thanks for taking me. And you really didn't have to pay for me either."

"I didn't?" I reply with a smirk. "Why didn't you tell me that earlier?"

"Oh, you're such a goofball!"

We walk out arm-in-arm, and her mother is waiting right outside the exit. Chelsea quickly lets go and becomes the daughter of an overprotective mom. We're on our best behaviour from that point on.

Her mother is a very nice, get-to-the-point lady, and I'm as polite as possible. If what Chelsea said about her liking me already is true, I'm not going to burst the bubble.

CHAPTER 22

The Grandparents Come Through

It feels like a normal Monday morning, but that feeling changes the moment I walk through the front doors of the school. Standing at the entrance with a goofy smirk and ready for a high five is Frank. I shake my head. Am I dreaming? Is he an apparition?

"Frank!" I scream "No way! You're back!" I mockingly run my hands over his head and shoulders. "Yup, it's really you, in person, in one piece!"

Frank gives me a friendly push. "Cut it out," he says. "Yes, I'm real. What did you expect, some kind of robot?"

"Well, you were in the hospital long enough for them to make a Frank clone, so you never know, right?"

"Oh, ha ha."

I hug Frank. Onlookers pause and smirk. Not manly? I don't care. Frank is surprised, even overwhelmed, but he smiles at the attention.

"So when did you get out?" I ask.

"Saturday."

"Why didn't you call? I would've come over. They wouldn't even let us see you in the hospital."

"Yeah, well, the doctor told me to just stick around the house and rest a lot. He said that a concussion like mine can take a long time before everything's back to normal."

"Well, you look pretty normal to me. About as good as it's gonna get anyway, right?" I laugh.

"Ha ha! So this is what I come back to, eh? One smart-ass line after another."

"Frank, it's great to see you back, buddy. We were worried sick about you, especially when they said you were in ICU and all that stuff."

"Yeah, it was weird up there. I don't even wanna talk about it. That's all done now, and here I am. So, what the hell have I missed?"

"There are a few things, but I can't say while there's people around. Stuff between just you, Eric, and me."

"Okay, I get it. And hey! I have something for you. You just might appreciate it, too. Come outside for a minute and I'll show you."

I follow Frank outside, coincidentally just as Eric is approaching the school. He looks as shocked as I was.

"Frank!" he screams. "Wow! It's you!"

Frank looks at me. "Here we go again." Then to Eric, "Hey, man, Axel already proved that I'm not a fake, like I'm here in person." They high five. "But no more questions. I just went through all the gears with Axel, so I'll fill you in about me later. You guys come over here."

Frank motions for us to follow him into the parking lot. He looks around carefully for other people before he takes off his backpack. "I think you might want this back," he says and pulls out a large envelope.

It's no ordinary envelope. It's *the* envelope. Eric and I stare at it in disbelief, our eyes bugging out, and our mouths hanging open.

Frank opens it up to show us the contents. "It's all here, you guys. Every last penny. Six hundred and forty-six buckeroos. I counted it."

This is two apparitions in a row. First Frank and now this. I'm certain I'm going to wake up any second now.

"You guys look like you've seen a ghost or something," Frank says as he waves the envelope in front of our faces. "You guys want it or not?"

"What the hell!" Eric and I scream in unison.

"Frank," I stammer, "we've looked high and low and across hell's half acre for this and ... and what the hell! There it is!"

"Yeah, here it is. I never expected you guys to be so glad to see it."

"Frank, where in hell was it? I mean, we walked you home that night and then just like that, it was gone. And holy crap, we traced every step over and over and over. I mean, Eric and I just about killed ourselves. Where did you find it?"

"My sister found it. That next morning, on Saturday, she found it just behind the shrub by the front door. It was right after I got sent to the hospital. She said she seen this envelope, soaked right through, and she was gonna grab it and throw it in the garbage. But damn good thing she looked inside first."

"That's crazy!" snaps Eric. "Can you imagine over six hundred bucks tossed in the garbage?"

"So, anyway, finish your story," I cut in. "Like why are we only getting this now?"

"Well, like I said, I was in the hospital, so there was nothin' I could do. Patty could still see your smudged writing on the envelope. I guess it said 'Almond Sales' or something. And she knew about me going out to sell almonds, so she said she knew it was ours. And when she saw how much cash there was inside, she said she didn't dare tell our parents. Believe me, if she did it would've disappeared for good. So instead she hid it in her closet until I got out of the hospital. So I guess you can thank Patty."

"Thank her!" I beam. "I would kiss her royal feet! She is now officially a goddess, the royal goddess of *saving the asses of idiots*. Frank, when we have a lot more time, we'll really fill you in, and then you'll know why we're insanely happy that this is actually in our hands."

Eric nods. He's still perplexed. "You have an amazing sister," he adds. "Can you imagine finding a soaking wet envelope with all that cash in it and then not taking a damn cent out of it? Like, holy crap, that sister is a keeper."

"Yeah, I guess," replies Frank. "She can get pretty annoying, though."

I take the envelope from Frank and kiss it. "I think I'm in love."

"I think I'm gonna puke," says Frank. "I can't wait to hear about everything now. Amazing how much can happen when you're away for a while."

"It is amazing," I agree. "But one thing's for sure, this envelope is not going to get lost again. It's going straight to Mrs. Watson, and the almonds are gonna be all paid up, and our field trips are gonna be all paid for, and Nutrition Solution is gonna save a bunch more kids, and life is gonna be just great!"

Eric chimes in. "Good sermon, Father Poomer." Eric and Frank both have a good laugh at my expense, but nothing can daunt my spirits. I'm holding in my hands the answer to a good number of problems in my life.

"I'm taking this to class right now before anything can go wrong," I state with authority.

"We're right behind you," replies Eric.

On the way there, I nudge Eric. "Hey," I whisper, "how did it go Saturday? Any problems getting home?"

"Like I said, piece o' cake, buddy. Mom was wondering why you didn't come in, and I just told her that you were in a hurry to get back home. No problem. Oh, hey, that reminds me. Here, take this." He pulls an envelope out of his jacket and hands it to me. "I don't know, maybe we don't even need this now that the envelope is back, but take it for now. Sixty-five bucks. I spotted myself ten again, if that's okay."

"You deserve it, buddy. Thanks for backing me up. The movie was great."

"Any time, man."

Mrs. Watson is busy writing notes on the whiteboard for the first class. The three of us step into the classroom. I hide the envelope behind my back. "You guys," I whisper, "let me do the talking, okay?"

They nod and stand behind me. Mrs. Watson turns around and almost throws the dry-erase brush at us.

"Oh, my goodness!" she yells. "You guys scared the wits out of me! How long have you been standing there?"

"We just got here now. Sorry to scare you like that," I respond meekly.

"Oh, it's fine, you guys. So what's up? Axel, you have something behind your back? Is it a surprise?"

"Yes, it is a surprise." I feel like a child as I place the envelope in her hands. "My grandparents came through and paid it all back in one payment."

Frank and Eric look at each other, puzzled. I try not to laugh at their confusion.

Mrs. Watson smiles as she looks inside the envelope. "Well, this is wonderful," she says. "It looks like we're all square. I'm so glad it all worked out so well."

"Oh," I add. "I think we might be two dollars short. I just remembered. But I'll bring it in first thing tomorrow."

"Oh, I think the bank can accept a two-dollar loan for another day, Axel. That's just fine. I'm very proud of the three of you for doing such an amazing job of selling. Not only did you cover your field trips, but you also made a significant contribution to our charity. Thank you so much all of you!"

We all mumble a "you're welcome" and made a quick exit.

"She sounded like you!" Eric exclaims. "Oh," he mocks in a feminine voice, "your field trips are paid for and you did so much for the charity."

I have to smile. "Okay, you made your point."

"And hey, how about those amazing grandparents of yours?" Frank cuts in. "Like what the hell was that all about?"

"Later, you guys. I know it all sounds ridiculous now, but you wouldn't believe the crap I went through to keep us alive. And yes, it was my imaginary grandparents who came to the rescue."

Eric grins and shakes his head. "We'll have to thank them when we meet them."

The bell sounds and we head right back to the classroom. Just before I get to the door, Chelsea pulls my arm from behind.

"Hey, don't be a stranger," she says with a bright smile. I wrap her in a bear-like hug. "Wow! Where did that come from?" she says, beaming. "You're sure in a good mood."

"Just feeling good, that's all. You know, Monday and all."

"But Mondays are usually a drag."

"Well, this is an unusual Monday. You're here, so that helps," I say with confidence.

"Wow! Nice compliments, too. And we're on Earth, so that helps, too," she quips.

"Great movie, wasn't it?"

"Yeah, and my mom really liked you."

"That's good to hear. I was on my best behaviour, you know."

I'm walking on air as I guide her through the door and to her desk.

"Try to stay awake today," Chelsea whispers.

"I'll do my best."

But as soon as I sit down and the routines start, sleep is the first thing on my mind. More to the point, school is the last thing. I still can't believe that Frank, or at least Frank's sister, had the envelope all the time. It's all like magic. Somebody snaps their fingers, and there's the envelope. Mrs. Watson is all paid up, there's no more debt, a lot of kids are going to be saved from starvation and, the most important thing of all, Mr. Hunter will be proud.

No more debt. The power of those words suddenly hit home. No more debt means no more deliveries for Jeanie. I no longer need the money. I feel like jumping right out my desk and screaming at the top of my lungs to celebrate. *I no longer need the money! No more deliveries! I'm free!*

Then, like someone hit me with a hammer, my excitement is quashed. I remember that I made a promise to do deliveries tonight. Damn! Now that I'm fully aware of the situation with Jeanie and Eric, I can't possibly back out of it either.

I don't know how it will go over, but this night's deliveries will be my last. Maybe I can assist Jeanie and Eric another way, but it will have to be a legal way, that much is certain. I'll have to think about how to broach the topic with Eric as soon as possible.

Now, what do I do with the drug money hidden in my room? Having that much cash on hand is nice, but it feels like dirty cash. Hard-earned, but still dirty. I'll consult Eric on that one as well. After all, it's his, too.

CHAPTER 23
The Finale

As usual, I'm at Eric's place at 7:30. Jeanie is in good form, full of positive energy and talking up a storm. With everything Eric has told me about her still fresh in my mind, I can't help but watch her more closely. The shaking really is an issue, but I also make another observation.

Jeanie never really engages us in a conversation when she speaks. It's always just her speaking, giving directions, nattering about something to Eric, or just babbling on about something irrelevant.

It's funny what you don't see or pay attention to when your nerves are on edge, which they always are when I'm picking up packages at Jeanie's. But tonight it becomes clear to me that poor Jeanie is a neurotic mess.

"Okay, you guys, just two deliveries tonight. Just the Sally Ann and Swan's and that's it," Jeanie directs us. "Just get them out and get home and everyone's happy, right?"

"Right, Mom," replies Eric flatly.

She gives him her glassy-eyed glare. "Do I detect another smart-ass comment coming from you?"

"No, Mom. No smart-ass anything. Just gonna do the deliveries like you planned."

"Good! Everything good with you, Axel?"

"Yeah, sure, I'm good to go," I reply with a feigned smile.

"Great to hear, Axel!" She hands the packages to Eric and the direction sheet to me, which seems redundant now that we know the routine by heart.

Then comes the part I'm expecting, but also hoping against hope won't materialize.

"Oh, so you guys," Jeanie adds as she rubs her hands together like an old miser, "I got nothing for tomorrow, but I got three deliveries for sure on Wednesday. Is that okay?"

This is really my cue, but I haven't had the chance to talk to Eric about my withdrawing from the Vic-East cartel. And this is clearly a bad time to suddenly spring my news on them. Shivers run through my body, and I nearly bolt. Eric consents. Jeanie's glassy stare is now on me.

I avoid their eyes when I commit to Wednesday's deliveries, knowing full well it's a lie.

"That's wonderful, you guys!" Again, she hugs us both and then holds open the door like she can't wait for us to get our asses moving.

It's another typical, cool Victoria autumn evening with a light drizzle and a soft southerly breeze. Eric is saying something, but I'm too preoccupied with my own thoughts to listen. I can't do this anymore. I have to broach the topic tonight.

"Hey, Earth to Axel!" Eric says loudly.

"Oh, sorry, I drifted away there. What did you say?"

"Nothin' important. But hey, did you see what I was talking about? You know, about my mom's shaking and stuff?"

"I did," I reply. "Was it a little worse tonight than usual?"

"No, it was about the same as always. Maybe even better than usual."

"You know, there's something I've been meaning to ask you, but you don't have to answer if you don't want to."

"Shoot."

"Okay, so we're doing this to help your mom because she's afraid of getting caught selling it herself. But where the hell does she get all the stuff in the first place? Like, how does the stuff get to your house without the cops noticing?"

"Special delivery, that's how. You know, like parcels carefully packaged up, stuffed up with paper and all kinds of filler crap to make them way bigger than any drug shipment would be. And they're sent special delivery so the postal guys actually deliver them right to the house. Pretty amazing, eh? Mom mails them cash for the shipments. So the banks don't see anything either. They're watching Mom every damn second of the day, and she doesn't even have to go anywhere to get what she needs. What they really watch for is guys coming to the house to buy the crap. And that was usually at night time, but they've really caught onto that.

"So," Eric continues, "Mr. Postee comes up to the house at about two o'clock in the afternoon with a big smile on his face, and he has no idea what the hell he's delivering. Mom signs the paper and she's all set. But that all stopped when no buyers could get to the front door with the cops watching us like hawks. If she doesn't sell it right away, she's out all that cash to the supplier. And Mom doesn't exactly know how to save, so just one screw-up in the whole operation, and she's hooped. And I'm hooped along with her, I guess."

"Wow!" I say, stunned. "So that's how it all works. It's like a real business, but maybe a little more stress than your average one."

"Like, a lot more stress."

"So, do the postal guys ever wonder why she gets so many deliveries?"

"Not really. My mom's good friends with all of them now, and I think she just tells them that they're all just supplies for her home business. And it's true," he adds, laughing.

"So that's where we come in," I say. "The missing link in the operation. The second special delivery guys."

"That's us," Eric concurs.

This discussion isn't making it any easier for me. The more Eric explains the whole thing to me, the more I realize that my pulling out of the operation will spell disaster for the two of them. I suppose Eric could possibly do deliveries on his own, but that wouldn't sit well with Jeanie, and it would actually weigh on my conscience as well. I need to leave it alone for now.

Before I know it we're in front of the Salvation Army and Eric is calling out for number one. It's a lady this time. She looks surprisingly unlike a street person, wearing a fashionable mid-length winter jacket and stylish high boots. She has short, dark hair and a youthful face. I'm guessing she's in her mid-thirties. She has a bright, cheerful smile and a friendly nature.

"Thank-you guys so much," she says in an upbeat voice after the transaction is made. "You guys are awesome. I'll see you guys again soon. You guys take good care of yourselves, okay?"

Eric looks at me, confused. "You're welcome," he mumbles.

The lady walks away briskly, like she's out for her evening exercise.

"I don't know," I say as we watch her disappear up Johnson Street. "It doesn't make sense, does it? I thought everyone who was buying this stuff was a frazzled mess. But then there's that lady. She looks like she could be from Oak Bay or something. It takes all kinds, I guess."

ISBN 142517718-2

9 781425 177188

"Yup," Eric agrees. "It takes all kinds. So let's get number two done, and our job is finished."

The rain has stopped, and the dark clouds are parting to reveal a bright full moon. Like a giant street light, its powerful beam erases much of the darkness and lights up the pathway to our next stop.

Again, it's a short walk to Swan's Pub. We stand on the corner and do a full 360-degree turn. I'm not sure if being able to see faces more clearly now is an advantage or a disadvantage. After all, it means that they can see us more clearly as well.

"Go ahead, Eric. You start the thing," I direct cautiously.

"Okay. Here goes nothing," he replies. Then loudly, "Okay, right, so where is number two?"

Instantly, a man with a short-cropped beard and a trench coat approaches us on our side of the street. He stares at us quizzically, like a disapproving parent. He doesn't match the description Jeanie gave us.

"Is it you?" I ask, thrown off.

"Yes!" he replies with a loud baritone voice of authority. "I am number two!"

Eric is shaking as he pulls the package out of his jacket and holds it out to the man. He grabs it and then—all hell breaks loose.

Lights from three vehicles start flashing. We're frozen on the spot and cops come at us from all angles like they're executing the takedown of the century.

All the oxygen is sucked from my brain. My legs feel like rubber. I'm about to faint, but before I collapse, two officers grab me and yank my hands behind my back. Then I'm handcuffed. I'm sure the same thing is happening to Eric, but everything is a blur.

"Yes, I'm number two," the trench coat officer repeats. "But I believe I'm your last customer."

CHAPTER 24
More Life With Flick

Eric and I ride in separate police cars. I feel like a caged animal with the woven metal protective barrier separating the front and back seats and no door handles. The two officers in the front are having a casual conversation about the bust, but the constant chatter on the two-way radio makes it impossible to hear what they're saying.

This is all too surreal. I'm trapped in a nightmare, suffocating in an inescapable black hole, in a time warp. Wasn't I walking downtown with Eric just a few minutes ago?

I hear the driver speaking to the dispatcher: *roger that, two suspects arrested for trafficking downtown.* That's us. Eric and I are now 'two suspects.'

Squeezing my eyes shut, I pray to be magically transported back in time. I should have quit the deliveries when I had the chance. I could have been in my room right now, or hanging out with Chelsea. Instead, I'm about to see first-hand the inside a jail cell.

My life flashes before my eyes, like they say happens just before you die. I see all my good intentions to make things right, to make the world a better place to be, to make Mr. Hunter proud, washed away by bad decision-making. I want to cry. I try to cry, but I can't.

We arrive at the police station. The door of the police car opens and I'm directed to step out. I hang my head low, fearful and ashamed, as an officer escorts me to a bland room with a table and chairs and nothing else. A large window in the wall facing me doesn't allow me to see out. I assume it has a one-way view from the other side, like the ones I've seen on police shows.

My brain is working overtime, replaying the events leading to my arrest, and thinking about my future. I know in my heart that I won't be capable of lying. I will tell them everything.

I'm asked to stand still while one of the officers removes my cuffs, then motions for me to take a seat. He sits beside me while the other officer sits across the table from us and starts the conversation.

"Axel. Axel Poomer, right?" he states.

"Yes, sir," I reply, unable to look up. My feet tap uncontrollably. My hands shake.

"I'm Constable McLeod and sitting beside you is Constable Purvis," he says. "Axel, you look a little anxious, and so you should be. But I'd appreciate it if you'd look at me when I'm talking to you."

I slowly lift my head.

"Thank you. That's better. Now, can I get you a glass of water?"

"Um, no, I'm good, thanks."

"Okay, Axel, let me know if you change your mind. Now listen, we're not here to grill you about went down tonight. We pretty well have all the information we need to go forward with this. We have the evidence, the package of, shall we say *goods*, that you and your friend Eric were selling; we know your source, and we know hers. We probably know more about you and your partner than you can imagine."

He pauses so I can respond, but I'm numb, unable to speak.

"Your friend," he continues, "is getting this same message in another room. And your friend's mother, I believe her name is Jeanie, is being arrested as well. So you see, there's nothing you could tell us that we don't already know except maybe for one thing: Why? Why did you ever get involved in this stuff?"

He says it in a way that reminds me of Mr. Davis. I sense he's on my side. The flood gates open up. Everything I've been holding inside gushes out in a torrent of tears. Constable Purvis pushes a box of Kleenex in front of me.

I blow my nose and sop up tears.

"I don't know what I was thinking," I finally manage to say. "I just ... I just had this debt and I ... I can't believe this is what I did."

"I hear you, Axel," Constable McLeod jumps in. "You had a debt, and I guess that debt led to all of this. I'm not going to lecture you here tonight about a million other better ways a young boy can pay off debts. Right now your foster father, Cliff Banting, is on his way here to pick you up. Charges of trafficking illicit drugs will be filed, you'll be released to the custody of your foster dad with certain conditions, including a curfew, and you'll be appointed a lawyer. That lawyer has experience with young offenders, and with you being in foster care, he will either work pro-bono, for free in other words, or the ministry will cover it.

"So, besides a fair bit of paper work to fill out," he continues, "we're finished here tonight. I'll be involved as the arresting officer, but the outcome is not in my hands. And Axel, I wish you all the best. You seem to be remorseful, and that's always a good start."

"Thank you," I say with a tinge of optimism. "So, I get to go home?"

"Yes, you get to go home. These are only charges, not convictions, so you'll have time to think about better decision-making before you appear before a judge."

I mumble another thank you. I'm not going to jail. That's a huge relief. However, Flick is on his way here, and the thought of having to deal with him makes jail a good option.

The officers lead me out of the dismal interrogation room into a proper office with a normal desk and chairs and windows that even allow me to see out. Flick arrives in record time, his face stern. Fortunately, anything he has to say to me will have to wait until after a lengthy conference in the office.

My conditions are made clear. I have to be home by 9:00 every night, be in attendance at school each day, and I'm not to be in the downtown area after 6:00 p.m. unless I have written permission or I'm accompanied by an approved adult. Lastly, I'm not to see Eric, except at school. I will be contacted by my lawyer in the next few days.

Listening to Flick flounder through the conference unsettles me. He shuffles and flicks his head like he's the one on the hot seat. Right now I have nothing but respect and sympathy for him. It's all because of me that he's been dragged down here and put into this humiliating situation. He avoids looking at me, likely because he'd rather break my neck.

I dread the ride home with him. But any abuse will be warranted. I'll suck it up the best I can.

We drive in silence for the first few minutes. The tension is so thick you can cut it with a knife. Flick's head keeps time with the song on the radio, the Eagle's "Lyin' Eyes." A volcanic pressure builds.

"Well, Axel," he finally starts, "what the hell do you have to say for yourself?" He's not yelling. He's eerily calm.

I ... I ... I," I stutter. "I don't have anything good to say for myself, Flick. I ... I'm really, really sorry that I did this and that you had to be involved. Really sorry."

"Oh, shit, don't apologize to me. What's done is done. That one officer mentioned something about a debt. What the hell was that all about?"

"Yeah, well, it was all about us selling almonds, and we sold a ton of them one night, the night I got beat up."

"I remember that," says Flick.

"We had a lot of money in an envelope, and I lost it that night."

Flick grimaces and tells me to go on.

I owe Flick the whole story. We're home before I finish, so Flick parks and waits until I'm done. It's the first time he's shown interest in something I have to say.

"Believe me," I add, "it was definitely going to be the last time I did those deliveries, but it all backfired."

Flick turns off the radio and looks straight ahead. His head is uncharacteristically still. "So that's what happened that night, eh? You got the shit beat out of you by those assholes, but they didn't steal the money. You said your buddy Frank had it all the time?"

"Yeah, well, he didn't know it because he was in the hospital, but his sister had it and kept it for him."

"And you really think that Frank's dad did that to him?"

"Sounds like it. Like, there was no way Frank had a concussion like that when we dropped him off," I confirm.

"Damn, maybe Frank's dad needs a little tuning up himself. Boy, you guys are really something. A bunch of bloody bozos, but bozos with good intentions, I guess, right?" He smirks.

"Yeah, I guess. But I can't believe I did those deliveries. Just stupid!"

Flick turns to look at me. "You know, I have a good mind to sic Ted and Ben on those bloody thugs. But I'd better not go there."

"No, I guess not." I want to tell him about Ted and Ben's involvement, but I think better of it.

"So how old are you? Thirteen?" Flick asks.

"Yes."

"Thirteen, eh? Isn't that something." Flick looks off into space. "Thirteen seems like the age when all the shit happens. Maybe our brains aren't developed enough to make good decisions. My god, I can tell you a story that happened when I was thirteen. You wanna talk about boneheads, well, I was the king. I was in shit all the time, and you think I'd get it and maybe stop gettin' into more trouble? No, not me. I'll tell you the one that made me king. You wanna hear it?"

"Yeah, sure," I reply. This is strangely therapeutic. At a time when I'm at my lowest, Flick is suddenly a real human being. My spirits lift.

"Okay, well, don't ever try to top this one, Axel. So there I was, me and two buddies that I won't name. My parents go out for the night to a friend's birthday party, and I know they won't be back till the next morning 'cause they're big drinkers and partiers, and they just left me and my sister on our own all the time anyway. She was a year younger than me.

"So," he continues, "we get into my dad's booze and it doesn't take long before the three of us are whacked out of our heads on whiskey. We're just havin' a hoot, eh! Dancin' and singin' and stumblin' and just being the biggest dimwits you could imagine. But it seemed like fun at the time. So what happens next? Well, my parents' friends drove them to the party, so guess what's still at home?" He laughs out loud, a goofy, childish laugh. I laugh with him.

He starts up again, "Right, so I get the keys to my dad's car, a big shiny new 1968 Buick Skylark. Baby blue. Oh, yeah, it was a beauty, too. I can hardly see over the steering wheel, and I don't know a damn thing about driving, but our brains are fried, so none of that matters. We get in. I back out of the driveway and hit a telephone pole. I get out and have a look. The bumper's dented, no big deal. We head down the street. I'm all over the bloody road, and I knock off a mirror on some parked car, then another mirror, and we're just pissin' ourselves laughing." He chuckles as he relives the events.

I know this story has a message, but I think Flick is losing sight of it. But he's enjoying this reminiscence, and so am I.

"You actually knocked off mirrors on other cars? That's crazy," I say encouragingly.

"Crazy as hell. But that was nothing. By that time—and if I'd had half a brain I would've guessed—somebody had called the cops. So, sure enough, about three blocks later, there's the cops."

"No way! Did they pull you over?"

"No, I pulled *them* over," he replies with raised eyebrows. "Bam! Head on into the cop car! My two buddies go flying into the windshield, no seatbelts, of course. They bang their heads, and they're bleeding like hell. The car is a frickin' mess, and I'm the only one not hurt. Of course, I'm crapping myself. Not because of the cops but because of my dad. He was a mean bugger and even being hammered, I knew this was gonna be painful, literally."

"So, did your dad give you hell?" I ask.

"You know what? He didn't. He surprised the hell outta me. He comes home that night because the cops called him, of course. He gets to the scene of the accident and he just stands there and stares at his car. I'm wondering how long it's gonna take before he beats the hell outta me.

"Finally, he walks around his car and pats it here and there like it was his little baby. I knew what he was thinking. His baby was hurt, and he felt the pain, but he wouldn't let on. He stopped to look at the damage, and then he walks over like nothin' happened and puts his arm around me. Didn't say a damn word up to that point. We just stood looking at that bloody car, me ready to put a rope around my neck. Finally, he speaks, and you know what he says?"

"I don't know, but I'm listening," I say anxiously.

"He says, 'Well, son, looks like I've gotta get my car repaired before I can get in the driver's seat again. And it looks like you've got some makin' up to do, right?' And he never raised his voice. That was like a thousand pounds off my shoulders."

"I can believe that," I remark.

"You got it, buddy. And to this day, I'm not sure what came over him, but I have the feeling that he'd done something bad in his day and maybe he got a break, too. He never said. But, I'm telling ya, I spent every waking hour for the next four months making it up to him. I'd shine his shoes, wash his car, cut the grass, clean the house, and do any damn chore with no complaining. And I spent about a week in Juvie, too. But that part was easy since everything was good at home." It was like the ending to a good movie.

"Wow!" I exclaim. "That's an amazing story. Is your dad still alive?"

"No. My dad had a heart attack just two years ago, God rest his soul."

"I'm sorry to hear that. I wish I could've met him."

"Yeah, well, he's still in here," Flick says with his hand over his heart. "But now here you are. You've got some thinkin' to do 'cause there's a damn good chance you'll be spending some time in Juvie yourself."

I'm aware of that, I feel faint just trying not to think about it. "Yeah, I know," I reply. "I guess I'll have to take what's coming to me. But I'm really sorry you had to get involved in this." "Look, I appreciate that, but it's not a problem for me. You're the one who's gotta get through this."

I'll accept any punishment. I'm more concerned about my dignity, what people will say behind my back. 'Axel the drug dealer' will ruin me. I might have to change schools, change cities, or maybe even change names. Unless people don't find out.

I know that young offenders get their names protected from the media. Only the police, Eric and Jeanie, and now Flick, know about this. I don't think I can hide the fact that I'm in trouble with the police, but the public won't know why. If I'm questioned about it, I'll need to have a good answer.

People get caught for vandalizing all the time, and nobody thinks much of it. Just rebellious youths who need to be taught a lesson. That could be me! A rebellious tagger who got caught spray painting downtown.

That's it! I'll get a hold of Eric as soon as I can and we'll get our story straight. But Flick would have to be in on it, too. I have nothing to lose, and Flick seems unusually approachable tonight.

"Flick, can I ask you a question?"

"Shoot."

"A favour, actually?"

"That depends. Don't push it now," he says, confused.

"Flick, can we keep this a secret, like between you and me and maybe Margaret? Like maybe just tell people that I got caught doing some vandalism downtown or something?"

Flick rubs his chin. "Hey, I'm all for that. Don't think people need to know anything about the drug stuff. None of their damn business anyway."

"So, you'd be okay with that?"

"Bloody right I would."

"Okay, so if anyone asks, I was just tagging downtown and that's why I'm dealing with the cops? Is that okay?"

"You got it. My foster kid's a tagger, and he got nailed. Doesn't sound so bad. And don't worry about Margaret. She's a hundred percent behind me."

"Thanks, Flick. That's going to be a big help."

"Okay. Let's get inside. I'm missing the Canucks right now."

I head straight down to my room. I put on Elton John's "Tiny Dancer" and rest my head on the pillow. So much happened today, but what stands out is Flick. He's a real human being. He actually talked to me like a father, an understanding father.

I get busted for pedalling drugs, get taken down by an army of cops, ride in the back of a cop car, and sweat my butt off at the police station. Yet it's Flick who wins the prize for throwing me off the most. For that I'm hugely grateful.

But Juvie is a good possibility. For that I'm hugely regretful.

CHAPTER 25
Apology

I wake up Tuesday morning with a new appreciation for the privilege of going to school. Nobody thinks of it as a privilege until the option is taken away. Funny what the threat of prison does to a person.

I have a lot on my mind. I tried calling Eric late last night, but nobody answered. My last call was just before midnight, so I worried about him all night. But when I arrive at school, Eric is there in the parking lot, waiting for me.

"You're alive!" I yell.

"Yeah, what did you expect? They didn't kill you, so why should they kill me?" He looks tired and he's not smiling.

"I called a hundred times. What the hell was I supposed to think?"

"I guess you'd think that I wasn't home."

"That's pretty deep thinking," I reply sarcastically. "A little beyond my abilities, buddy. So if you weren't home, then where the hell were you?"

"Well, let's just say that I was home, but it ain't the home I was hoping to be at. They put me in this bloody group home about two kilometers away."

"Really? Why?"

"Because Mom is being held at the cop shop until they get her charges straightened out and a lawyer and all that bullshit. I'm not *mature* enough to look after myself, even though I have been for the last two frickin' years."

"How long do they figure you'll be there?"

"They told me probably a couple of days. It's not all that bad. I get better food there than I got at home, plus they said I could buy a new pair of pants and stuff."

"They gave you money? I'm envious."

"Not cash. They don't trust me with that. I don't blame them. But they gave me a phone number and when I find something I want, up to fifty bucks, I get the store to phone them and get it approved. I guess I must look like a street guy." He laughs, poking his fingers through the holes in his jeans.

"Have you talked to anyone yet about last night?" I ask anxiously.

"Nobody. Not here and not at the home."

"Okay, so does anyone know why we're up the creek?"

"Not as far as I know. The cops dropped me off at the house, and I don't know what they told the workers there, but none of the other kids know a thing."

"That's good," I reply, relieved. "Listen, you and I don't want to be known as drug dealers, right?"

"Who, us? Too late for that. Can't change what's happened, right?"

"No, but if we can keep this all to ourselves then we won't have to deal with a 'druggie' label. You know what I mean?"

"Yeah, like our names are mud when they find out. I don't see how we can we keep this to ourselves. Like, what are you thinking?" asks Eric.

"Here's what." I lower my voice and Eric bends to hear me. "Okay, so we got in trouble with the cops, right? People will find that out somehow, for sure. But they won't know why because we're young offenders and they can't publish our names. So, here's what we do. We beat everyone to the draw by telling them today that we got caught for tagging downtown. That way nobody will gossip if they see us in a cop car or at the station, or if we have to make a court appearance. They might think we're idiots anyway, but big deal. Better than being a drug dealer, right?"

"Right!" Eric high-fives me hard. "It's perfect! I'm there all the way."

"Good. So, hey, you remember when you made me promise not to tell a soul about your mom?"

"Sure do."

"Well, that's just like this one. Promise not to tell anyone, including Frank."

"Why not Frank? He's one of us, right?"

"Yes, he is," I agree. "But Frank doesn't have anything to lose, so he might be careless. So, as much as we like Frank, we're taggers to him as well. Okay?"

"Okay. Done deal. We're taggers, end of story."

"Great. So, hey, did the cops tell you they're looking for a lawyer for us?"

"Yup. Should be any day now, they said."

"And paid for by the ministry," I add.

"Really? They didn't tell me that, but then I guess I'm not a foster kid," he jests, smiling.

"You are now."

"Shit, I never thought of that. Oh, well, if it means a free lawyer maybe it's worth it. So, anyway, I'm gonna take advantage of the free clothes while the offer's out there. Wanna come with me after school to check it out?"

"Sure, I'll tag along. Where to?"

"I'm just gonna check out Cedar Ridge first. Sometimes they've got some pretty good stuff in the thrift store. For fifty bucks I could probably get a helluva lot of stuff."

"Sounds good. I'll see you in class."

Class time is a blur. I can't focus. I keep thinking about the charges. I replay that last delivery over and over until my brain is about to explode. If I don't find a release valve soon, something is going to give.

Soon, this will be over. In the novel *A Wrinkle In Time* they used a tesseract to go instantaneously from point A to point B, from the present time to a point in the future, by wrinkling time. If I could do that, I could just move forward and never get into a predicament like this ever again.

I'm not exactly doing all the good I can do, Mr. Hunter, I say to myself. *Right now you can't possibly be proud of me, and thank God my mother is not around to have to deal with this garbage. But when I reach point B, everything will be different.*

Our plan works. Word about the 'tagging' spreads quickly, and we become the hot topic of the day. Whenever someone asks for more details, I just say it was a stupid prank, and that we were idiots for thinking we could get away with it. By the end of the day, the story pretty well dies out. I have a guilty conscience for not telling Chelsea the truth, though.

Eric and I meet up right after school and walk over to Cedar Ridge Mall.

"You know," I say, trudging along, "I really feel like crap. I just want this whole nightmare behind us. Like, get me a lawyer, and let's get this done."

"I'm with you on that. I wanna get back home, too. I want my mom to get back home."

"Yeah, poor Jeanie. She must be going through hell herself. Are you allowed to see her?" I ask.

"Not right now. I'll call again when I get back to the group home."

At the thrift shop, I wait outside while Eric does his shopping. After what seems like an eternity, he emerges with two huge bags full of clothing.

"I scored big time!" he says, beaming. "I've never had so many damn clothes! I got about five shirts, two pairs of pants, a couple of belts, a denim jacket, some other stuff and a scarf."

"A scarf?"

"Well, a bandana, I mean."

"Are you practicing to be a girl now or what?" I tease.

"Maybe. You wait, buddy. I'll wear this and next thing you know it'll be a trend."

"Oh, sure. We'll see how well that trend goes over. But hey, give it a shot, trend-setter."

"I will," Eric says with conviction. Suddenly his eyes bug out. "Oh, shit," he says, pointing over my head. "Look! Frickin' run!"

I turn to see what he's pointing at, and my heart stops. The Cox brothers are coming out of the second-hand store, no more than fifty feet away. Eric and I sprint to save our lives.

"Damn!" I yell. "This is just what we needed!" Eric is running as fast as he can, but the bags of clothing hinder him. I grab one. "Don't look back! Just go!" I scream.

We're not gaining on them. They're so close I can hear them breathing. Then one of them yells, "Stop, you guys!"

"Don't stop!" I order Eric.

"Please, stop, you guys. We just wanna talk to you! Please stop!" the Cox brother continues to scream.

"Did I hear him say 'please'?" asks Eric, puffing hard.

"Please stop!" he yells again.

"Yup, that was a please," I reply. "Weird, eh? They're polite assholes." My legs are giving out. I'm running short of breath.

Eric struggles as well. In between breaths, he utters, "They're gonna catch us anyway ... I can't stay ahead of 'em ... It's no use." He halts, bent over and gasping for air.

"Okay, I'm not leaving you here on your own, so here goes nothing." I stop beside Eric. The Cox brothers stand with us.

I'm shaking worse than Eric. "We haven't touched your brother since that night," I say defensively. "Just leave us alone."

Just like on the night of the beating, Daryl does the talking.

"Just relax, okay?" he says, holding up both hands. "We're not here to hurt you, believe me. In fact, look, we've been thinking about that night and Devon and me think that maybe we went a little too far, right Devon?"

"You got that right, Daryl. We went too far and we think we should apologize."

"Really?" replies Eric, shocked. "You guys think you should apologize to us?"

"Yeah, we do," insists Daryl.

My clogged-up brain jolts to life. It makes perfect sense. They want to apologize to save their hides from Ted and Ben. This is their feeble attempt to make it up to us.

Daryl is still talking, but I tune him out. Images and sounds of the almond sales night play in my head. It's all I can see and hear. Frank, Eric and me. Punches and kicks that never stop.

My heart beats. My blood boils.

After the talk with Ted and Ben, I wasn't sure I wanted them to finish the job. Now I'm certain.

"So, this is us apologizing, you guys. Okay?" says Daryl.

"Yeah, well, apology not accepted," I say firmly.

Eric looks at me like I've just blown a gasket. "It's not?"

I nudge him and whisper out the side of my mouth, "Trust me on this one. I'll do the talking."

Eric squints and shuts his mouth tight.

"Why not?" asks Daryl, stunned.

"Because we just frickin' don't want your apology, that's why," I reply, looking him straight in the eyes. "So keep it and have a good day." I nudge Eric and turn to walk away.

"Hey, wait, you guys!" Daryl calls. "Please don't go yet. Look, we're sorry for that night, and we really wanna make it up to you somehow."

"Look," I say, keeping my anger in check, "you beat the living snot out of the three of us and we just frickin' had to accept that, right? Like we didn't have a hope in hell against you guys. So here we are, and you could do it again if you wanted, but you want to apologize and your apology doesn't fix the crap we went through, does it?"

I'm on a roll. I can't stop myself. Eric tugs my arm and motions with his head to move on. Daryl and Devon say nothing in their defence, so I continue.

"Maybe one day you'll see what that beating was like. Then you'll understand why an apology doesn't fix a damn thing."

Devon turns white as a ghost. I think my last line hit home. I'm certain he's thinking about his next encounter with Ted and Ben.

"Look, you guys," he pleads. "Let's work this out right now. So, okay, we get it. We need to do more than apologize. So how about something like ... like." He can't think on his feet, so Daryl takes over.

"Like maybe you guys get to punch us to pay us back," he jumps in.

Punch them? So tempting.

"Yeah, you guys could punch us," Devon reiterates, following his brother's lead like a puppy dog.

"So how would that work?" I ask. "We punch you and then you have a good reason to kick the crap out of us again?"

"No," replies Daryl. "It means you guys get to punch us, and we do nothing. It'll all be even, and then maybe we all just, uh, just sort of leave each other alone from now on."

"Leave each other alone? Are you afraid of us?" I challenge. "Hell, you're twice our size."

Daryl and Devon shrug, defeated. But they don't give up yet.

"Look," says Daryl, "here's how it could work. You guys punch us, we're all even, and then you tell your foster brothers that we settled everything, and then they leave us alone, too."

"Oh, you mean Ted and Ben? Have they been bothering you?" I ask, straight-faced, but smiling inside.

"Well, yeah, I guess. You guys wanna pay us back or not?" asks a frustrated Daryl.

Eric whispers, "Your call, buddy. You're doin' the talkin'."

"Yes," is my reply to the Coxes. "We'd like that. So how many punches do we get?"

"Devon, what do think, maybe one or two punches each?"

"Yeah, sure," agrees Devon. "One or two each and we're even."

"Where can we punch you?" I ask.

Daryl raises his hands to offer his whole body. "You pick your spot," he replies. "But, hey, let's do this behind the mall. Come on."

We all follow Daryl to the back of the mall where the deliveries are made. It's all quiet and nobody is in sight. The butterflies in my stomach are making me nauseous. The anticipation is killing me.

For me, this is not about the beatings alone. It's also everything directly and indirectly related to the beatings: Frank ending up in the hospital, the envelope getting lost, Eric and I risking our lives in the drug world, and, sadly, getting busted. And it's possible that the worst is still to come. A few punches will feel great, but the Cox brothers, in my opinion, will still come out the winners.

"Two punches each, right?" I clarify.

"Right," replies Daryl.

"That means you each get four punches, two from each of us."

"Fine. Go for it."

Eric and I turn away to have a private discussion. Squeezing my fists to calm my nerves, I whisper my strategy.

"Okay, listen, let's just forget the two each crap. You just do your four on Devon, and I'll do my four on dickhead with the big mouth. And remember, they think they're getting off easy 'cause it's just little punks giving them punches. Wind up just like Daryl did with Frank and let's make these assholes regret they ever made a boneheaded deal like this with us. Got it?"

Eric's not convinced. "Yeah, I got it, but this feels really weird," he says, shakily. "I sure as hell hope they don't change their minds and do another number on us."

"Trust me, they won't. If they did, they would be living in fear for the rest of their days. Look at 'em. Ted and Ben have them absolutely crapping their pants. They won't touch us, believe me."

Eric smiles. "I'm looking forward to this."

"Let's do it."

I stare at Daryl. "Okay, so it's basically four punches each, so we're gonna just make it simple. Eric will do his punches on Devon, and I'll do mine on you."

"Fine with us," he agrees. "Fire away."

"You go first," I say to Eric.

I see red in Eric's eyes. He has that goofy look that everyone misreads, but he's ready and he's angry. Devon doesn't have time to brace himself before Eric winds up and punches his nose.

Devon stumbles backwards and holds his hand to his face. He freaks out when he sees the blood running through his fingers.

He's about to say something when Eric lets loose with his left hand. He scores a hit to Devon's right eye.

"Wait!" he screams. "Just a sec!"

"No time outs," says Eric as he plants another right and left.

Devon falls to his knees and cries. This is the guy who punched us relentlessly and kicked us when we were down. Now, four punches and he's reduced to a pathetic, snivelling weasel.

Daryl looks at his brother, dumbstruck. At a loss for words for the first time. He stands his ground as I step forward. He's visibly shaking, which, strangely enough, makes me even more anxious to strike him.

My first blow is, like Eric's, smack in the middle of the nose. And it's equally effective. Blood spurts out, but he just lets it bleed. He stares me down and shrugs.

But then he does something that flicks a switch in my brain. He smirks and does the 'bring it on' motion.

In a rage, I swing hard with my left, then my right, then my left again, then my right again, and I just keep on punching. Daryl is determined to stay on his feet while I, Ali, the crazed prize fighter, pummel him into oblivion. I can't stop myself. With all the pressure built up inside me, this is the release valve I've been looking for.

Daryl is trying to say something, probably that I've had my four punches, and I wonder why he doesn't fall down to avoid more hits. When I do finally stop, I realize why. Daryl is basically knocked out. Still standing, but technically knocked out.

His eyes are rolled back; all I can see are the whites. He staggers for a second before finally collapsing, first to his knees, then flat on his back groaning in pain.

I turn to Eric who, shell-shocked, silently mouths a "what the hell just happened?"

"I don't really know," I reply. "But it's all over, buddy." My fists are red and sore, but I ignore the pain. What I do feel is relief. A huge weight has just been lifted from my shoulders.

Devon is barely back on his feet and Daryl struggles just to sit up. It's done. The score is now settled, and there is nothing more to be said, except one thing.

"Apology accepted. I'll tell the bros," I finish. Then I turn to Eric. "Let's get the hell outta here."

CHAPTER 26
RJ

After supper the same day, I invite Ted and Ben to my room and tell them the whole story. They go insane. They almost piss themselves laughing, high-fiving me and patting me on the back.

"You really took care of things, didn't you, little bro?" Ben yells. "I can't frickin' believe what I'm hearing. You and your little friend beat the ever-living shit outta those guys? And they just let you do it? That's just beautiful! 'Apology accepted.' You actually said that? That just kills me!"

They continue for some time, and I'm right in there with them, revelling in the so-called victory. Oddly enough, it's a victory for the Cox brothers as well. They are now free to walk the halls or to roam the city. But I suspect they'll go into hiding for a few days while they lick their wounds.

"But what's this crap I'm hearing about you tagging downtown?" asks Ted. "And you got caught by the cops?"

"Uh, yeah. I'm in a bit of a bind, I guess. Just stupidity. I don't know what's gonna happen exactly."

Ben looks at me quizzically. "Dad said you're gettin' a lawyer. Is that right? Do you really need a lawyer just for tagging?"

"Well, yeah, I guess. But I don't think it will be a big deal, and the cops said it probably won't cost anything."

"Well, you better bloody well learn something from that," Ben adds, suddenly turning serious.

"Yeah, and Ben speaks from experience," Ted chimes in jokingly. "You learned a lot in middle school, didn't you?"

"Right, smart-ass. And you were my teacher," Ben responds with a poke to Ted's chest.

"Hey, you guys, it won't happen again, believe me," I cut in.

The conversation ends when Flick barges in. "Axel, you've got a meeting at the cop shop tomorrow after school," he announces. "They've got a lawyer all set up, so don't miss it. Four o' clock." He sounds a little more like the old Flick, but he isn't yelling.

"I won't miss it. Promise," I reply.

"Good."

Everyone leaves my room and within minutes, exhausted and still in my clothes, I fall asleep. I don't wake up until my alarm goes off the next morning.

The meeting is in the interrogation room, the one with the one-way window. Constable McLeod leads me inside. I'm surprised to see Eric and a man in a suit already seated and ready for business.

I stand on one side of Eric and ask, "Hey, where were you? I looked everywhere."

"Left school early," he replies. "Had something to do."

Constable McLeod clears his throat and starts the meeting. "Axel, this is your lawyer, Mr. Roy Chambers. "Mr. Chambers, I'd like you to meet your other client, Axel Poomer."

Mr. Chambers politely shakes my hand. "Nice to meet you, Axel. And please feel free to call me Roy. You as well, Eric."

I was told this was going to be a casual meeting. Roy looks pretty formal in his pin-striped, three-piece suit and shiny pointed black shoes. He also looks younger than I expected with a full head of dark brown hair, not one of them out of place, and a smooth round face.

"Please take a seat, Axel," he directs, pointing to a chair beside Eric. Eric manages a nervous smile and gives me a subtle high-five as I sit down. Constable McLeod sits at the head of the table. He defers to Roy to lead the discussion.

"Well, boys," Roy starts, "this could possibly be the shortest meeting of your lives, depending on what you two decide. And let me explain what your choices are." He pulls a document out of a binder and puts on some reading glasses.

"So, what I see here," he continues, "is that you two are charged with possession and trafficking of illicit drugs." He takes off his glasses and rubs his eyes. He shakes his head. "These are very serious charges, and you are very young boys. These are not the kind of convictions you'd like to have on your record. Would you agree?"

"Yes," Eric and I reply simultaneously.

"Now, of course it's my job to do what I can to either reduce or negate these charges altogether. But I have to admit, given all the facts and evidence that I've seen, this is by no means going to be an easy task. In other words, I cannot guarantee that you will walk away free of these charges. Convictions carry a range of penalties up to and including time spent in the Youth Detention Centre."

He pauses, still staring at us. I shift uneasily in my chair, and I look over to see Eric with his head buried in his hands. Roy coughs lightly and continues.

"I can't say more about that because ultimately it's up to the presiding judge. Neither of you have previous convictions. First-time offenders could get a lighter penalty. Again, that's up to the judge. Even as first-time offenders, the judge might decide to make scapegoats out of you guys and lay down maximum penalties, as a deterrent for future offenders."

He wipes beads of sweat from his forehead with a Kleenex, the room being hot and stuffy. Roy looks from me to Eric and nods.

"Do you have any questions or comments?" he asks.

We both shake our heads. "No, sir," I reply.

"How about you, Officer McLeod? Would you like to add anything?"

"No, you're covering everything just fine. Please continue," he replies.

"Okay, good. I just described one scenario. Here's another. A better one." He clears his throat. "Restorative justice. Have you ever heard of that?"

We look at each other and shrug. "No," I reply.

Constable McLeod says, "You two are fortunate. Restorative justice, or RJ, isn't for everyone. The police first make this recommendation, and then the Crown has to agree. The Crown, or shall we say, the prosecutor, has to agree to allow your case to go to RJ, which means it could bypass the criminal justice system. That could be significant for both of you. You see, if you go through the whole RJ process and everyone reaches terms of agreement, and you fulfill your part of the agreement, nothing will ever show on your record. Is that correct, Officer McLeod?"

"That is correct," he concurs. "I, and a few other officers, spoke to the Crown. As you have no previous convictions and have shown genuine remorse, we thought RJ would be a good way to go. Your case would be dealt with outside of the criminal justice system. So no lawyers or judges, and you would likely come out with a clean record.

"But," he adds sternly, "if something goes wrong and the RJ process is sabotaged for whatever reason, your case gets referred back to the Crown, and you're dealing once again with criminal charges."

"Thank you for that clarification, Constable McLeod," Roy says. You boys have any questions?"

Like I'm sitting in school, I put up my hand.

"Axel, go ahead. And no need to use your hand."

"Um, I appreciate everything you're saying. But with RJ, how do we reach an agreement?"

"Good question, Axel. Constable McLeod?"

Taking his cue, he shoves his chair back and stands. "With restorative justice, you will first be assigned a mentor. That mentor will be your guide, your advisor, your advocate, your go-to guy or gal. He or she won't necessarily be your friend, but will prepare you for the eventual RJ dialogue or facilitation.

"That means," he adds, methodically, "you'll need a clear understanding about the nature of your offence, and how it affects not just you, but everyone around you. The whole community. At the facilitation meeting you acknowledge what you've done, and agree as to how to make it up to society. Everything is summed up and finalized in that one big meeting. Does that all make sense?"

"Does to me," replies Eric.

"Me, too," I agree. "But just one thing. How long before that final meeting?"

Roy jumps in. "That depends entirely on you guys. If or when it looks like you're ready to move into facilitation, the parties involved come up with a date that works for everyone. It's not something they rush through. They want the process to be effective, and the Crown needs a measure of justice served in lieu of the criminal system." He raises his eyebrows. The room is quiet.

"Um, thank you," I say.

"So, boys," Roy continues, his hands clasped like he's praying, "criminal justice system or restorative justice? If you two want a few minutes to talk about it privately, go to the far side of the room. We'll wait here."

I whisper to Eric, "RJ for me. What about you?"

"RJ for sure."

"Okay, we have our decision," I say aloud.

"Which is it?" asks Roy.

"We'd both like to do RJ."

"You've made the right decision," Roy says with a big smile. He shakes our hands first, then Constable McLeod's. "So, you guys just put me out of a job," he jests. "My work is done here, but I wish you guys all the best for a successful RJ facilitation and for a very bright future."

Eric and I both thank him, several times each. Constable McLeod offers us a ride home.

It's a kind offer, but I don't want to be seen in a police car. "Oh, we're okay, but thanks," I respond. "We need the walk."

"Fine, boys. Be good out there. I'll be talking to you soon. I'll contact the Restorative Justice Society. They'll set you up with a mentor as soon as possible."

"Okay, thanks a lot," I finish.

Once away from the police station, we take a few deep breaths and then laugh so hard we almost go into convulsions.

"I haven't felt this good in a hell of a long time," Eric says, wiping away tears.

Ambling down the street, my arm around Eric's neck, I reply, "Me neither. RJ, eh? Maybe we're not criminals after all."

CHAPTER 27
Three Stories

The week drags on. Eric and I wait on pins and needles for our mentor to call. We're anxious to get on with the whole RJ experience and, ultimately, with our lives.

It's Friday. We're outside on our lunch break at school, just the three of us, when Frank shocks us.

"My dad is being charged with assault," he states, then bites into his sandwich.

Eric and I stop eating.

"And I'm the reason he's being charged," he adds.

"Really? Did you rat out your dad to the cops?" asks Eric.

"In a way, maybe. Whatever, right? He had it coming, that's for damn sure," Frank proclaims. "It was all the ministry. I mean, I wasn't even conscious, for god's sake. I guess someone from the hospital got suspicious and reported everything to the ministry, and they did all kinds of investigations and stuff."

"So, what the hell really happened anyway?" Eric prods.

"You mean besides the Coxes kicking my brains in?"

"Yeah?" Eric's eyes bug out of his head.

"Well, you guys probably guessed it, eh? Like, my dad kicked the crap out of me after you left. Nothin' new there. I'm used to that routine. But this time he really went whacko on me. And I was mouthing him off, like I always do. And then ..." He stops. His face is beet red.

"You okay, Frank?" I ask.

"I'm fine."

"You don't have to tell us any more if you don't want to," I add.

A tear runs down Frank's cheek. He dries it with his sleeve. "I'll tell you guys, but just keep it to yourselves, right?"

We assure Frank we will.

"Okay, so then the bastard chases me up the stairs with a frickin' baseball bat. I mean, you know what I was like? I could hardly frickin' walk. So I'm scrambling up the damn stairs, and then I feel this whack on the back of my head, and that was it. Don't remember nothin' after that. I seen stars, then black. I wake up in the hospital three days later."

Eric scowls. If his thoughts are similar to mine, Frank's story is filling him with a combination of guilt and anger and 'if only.' If only we had taken Frank to one of our homes instead; if only Frank hadn't done sales with us that night; if only we hadn't run into the Cox brothers, everything would be different.

"So how did they find out the truth?" I ask.

"Well, like I said. They investigated even while I was unconscious. I guess they were suspicious about the dent in the back of my head. When I woke up, two men were there, asking me all kinds of questions. And at first, I made up a bunch of crap to get rid of 'em, but they knew I was lying, and they weren't leaving till they got the truth."

Frank clears his throat and continues. "I asked myself why the hell I was protecting my old man. It was stupid. My dad's just a mean, frickin' alcoholic. Like I have stories that would blow your minds. And I never know what the hell to expect when I go home. I usually just sneak in and hide in my room and hope he doesn't know I'm home. And how do I get food, right? Well, I set my alarm and wake up at three in the morning 'cause he's always passed out by then. I make myself a sandwich or something, and go back to bed and set my alarm again for six-thirty, so I can get the hell outta the house before he wakes up. That's the life of Frank."

He takes a long drink from his water bottle. Eric and I are dumbfounded. We wait in silence. Frank takes a deep breath and starts again.

"They gave up at first, but they came to the house after I got out of the hospital. I could tell they knew I was lying. Like they asked me at least twenty times who caused the damage to my head and with what. I finally told 'em the truth. Said it was my dad with a baseball bat. And they say 'oh.' That's their reply: 'oh.' Then they thank me and go and arrest my dad."

He rubs his eyes with his sleeve again. Eric and I are speechless.

"You're frickin' amazing, Frank," I finally say. And I mean it. I wouldn't trade my life for Frank's for the world.

"I don't think so," replies Frank.

"Yeah, you are," Eric jumps in. "You don't see it the way we do. From our side, you're frickin' amazing."

"Okay, whatever you guys say. Thanks, I guess."

Eric adds, "Well, since we're telling stories, I've got one, too."

I nudge Eric playfully. "You're not gonna top Frank, are you?"

"Not a chance. This is a good story. My mom came home last night. So I get to go home in the next few days."

"Really? That's great!" I exclaim. "Is she free and clear?"

"Well, not really. But she probably won't have to go back to jail. Believe it or not, she gets to do the same thing we're doing with RJ."

"What's RJ?" asks Frank.

"Short for restorative justice," replies Eric. "It's where you make up for your crime instead of going to court and maybe even prison."

"Is that what you guys get to do for the tagging?"

"Yup. It's RJ for me and Axel. But Mom might have to do a little more than us since she's an adult. But she won't mind a bit. You know, it's weird. They found her a job at the bottle depot, and she'll be working like forty hours a week. Like, how does that work, right? You bust your ass trying to make ends meet, but you can't so you do what my mom was doin'. And then after you get busted and go through all that legal crap, they find you a job that you could never find yourself. Unreal. I mean, they're still watching her closely and everything, but she's happier than hell right now."

Frank chuckles. "What's really weird," he says, "is that your mom gets busted for drugs at the same time you guys get busted for tagging. You're all a bunch of crooks."

"Yeah, I guess," I join in. "So, look, since everyone is telling good stories and I don't have any of my own, I think now would be a good time to tell Frank about the Coxes."

"What? You haven't heard about that?" Eric asks, surprised.

Frank's eyes light up. "Okay, you got me. What about the Coxes?"

"You tell 'im," says Eric.

I get my thoughts together. "Okay Frank, tell me. How much would you like to just punch those Cox brothers' faces in?"

Frank punches the air like a shadow boxer. "I'd like to tee off on those bastards so bad and so hard that they don't wake up till the middle of next week," he says, continuing to punch the air. "I'd love to see their faces smashed in. I'd like to—"

" Okay, we got the picture," I jump in. "And I think you're gonna like this story. On Tuesday Eric and I punched their faces in." I wait to see Frank's reaction.

"What? No way. You didn't beat up those guys," says Frank. He smirks like he's waiting for a punch line.

"Yes way," I say with a straight face. "We did."

"You guys are full of shit, right?"

"Wrong," corrects Eric. "God, you shoulda been there."

Frank beams. "I can't wait to hear this."

I tell Frank the whole story. I add as much drama as I can, and I don't leave out a single detail. "... and I keep punching and punching until he just drops, like a sack of cement. And before we leave these guys, and they're still just crawling around and right out of it, I say that their apology is accepted."

"He really said that!" Eric chimes in, bent over laughing.

The retelling of the story is so satisfying, like being avenged once again.

But Frank's face is what really makes it worth telling. No more pathetic lost soul look, now he's the Cheshire cat, grin and all.

"You guys," he remarks, "that's the best frickin' story I've ever heard!"

CHAPTER 28
Who To Tell

The phone rings and I jump out of the kitchen chair to answer it, but Ben beats me to it. It's Sunday, and I've been staying close to home all weekend in case the mentor calls.

"It's for you, lover boy," Bens says. He throws me a kiss as he hands over the phone.

Holding the phone against my chest, I ask Ben politely to give me some privacy.

"Oh, not a problem, lover boy. Anything for the lovely couple." Then with exaggerated movements, he picks up his sandwich and takes baby steps into the living room.

I hear Chelsea's voice. "Are you there, Axel."

"Hi Chelsea. Sorry for the delay, but how's it going?"

"Well, not so great. Just hold on a sec." I hear nose blowing in the background. "Okay, I'm back now," she says, sniffling.

"You don't sound so good."

"Yeah, I've been better. Hey, Axel, can we talk? I really need to vent right now. Either that or just move the hell away from my dad."

"Yeah, for sure. I can meet you right now."

"Good. How about the back of the school in half an hour?"

"I'll be there."

I find Chelsea behind the school, sitting on her jacket, her back resting against a tree. We share a long hug. Her eyes are glazed red. "Thanks for coming on such short notice."

"It's not a problem. Not like I was doing anything important. But I'd come even if I was."

"I believe that," she replies softly.

"What's happening? Why are you so upset?"

"Oh, Axel, I'm sorry. You're the only one I feel I can talk to. Normally I could talk to my mom, but not about this."

Confused and curious, I reply, "Tell me anything you want."

"It's my dad. I told you before that he's just an asshole. But he's really worse than that. He's a frickin' monster. A fooling-around monster."

"Fooling around?" I echo.

"Yeah, it's true. My friends saw him kissing someone. I just didn't want to believe them. I refused to believe them. But then yesterday, I saw my dad's car parked right across the street from our house. With a woman inside. My friends weren't lying. Can you believe it? They didn't see me, though. I wanted to go over and scratch her eyes out."

"Wow! I don't blame you. What an asshole," I say, reaching for her hand.

"Yeah, well, I made the mistake of asking him about it today. And I told him what I saw. I should've expected it. He let loose on me. Called me every name in the book–slut was his favourite one–and just went insane, and he almost hit me. At the end, he says I'd better not tell mom because I'd be responsible for ruining our lives."

"You'd be responsible? Your dad is whacko!" I exclaim, my blood vessels about to explode.

"He is, you're right. Hey, let's walk," Chelsea suggests, leading the way. "Thanks for listening."

"Listening is easy," I say. "Dealing with your dad isn't."

"No, well, let's change the topic. So, what about you? What's happening with all that tagging stuff anyway?"

"Um, not much, I guess. Eric and I, well, we have some meetings coming up."

"You're not going to jail, are you?" Chelsea asks, smiling.

"No, I don't think so."

"It's just tagging, for god's sake. They need to get over it, right?"

"Yeah, I guess," I reply, weighed down with guilt. After Chelsea laid out her life to me like an open book, I can't continue this lie. "Hey, Chelsea, we weren't actually tagging."

"You weren't? So why are you in trouble then?"

"We were doing deliveries for Eric's mom."

"Axel, you're confusing me. Since when do deliveries get you in trouble with the police?"

"Since the deliveries had drugs in them. Illegal drugs."

She drops my hand. "You're kidding, right?"

"I wish. Please don't think I'm a drug dealer or anything."

"I'm still listening," she says calmly, looking me in the eyes.

"Okay, thanks. So, remember the beating we took?"

"How could I forget?"

"So that night we lost all our almond sales money, and we had to find a way to make it up."

"That's not a good reason, Axel."

"I know. Don't think for a second I'm not kicking myself about this. But the other reason, the main one for me, was that Eric was actually starving. Like, they had no food in the house. His mother was a dealer, and the cops were watching her, so she couldn't make any money. And it just got more complicated, you know. She's an addict and Eric was a real mess. So those deliveries were going to save them, too."

Chelsea touches the tear running down my face. I didn't even know I was crying.

"So, there it is," she says, now upbeat. "Once again, it's Axel to the rescue. I can't believe it. In my mind, anyone who pushes drugs deserves to go to jail. But you just changed my way of thinking. And, like I said before, that's what I really like about you."

"Yeah, well, I think you're amazing, too."

"Me? I don't think so."

"I do. Look at you. I just told you that I'm busted for pushing drugs, and you didn't even run away."

"I'm not going anywhere. Maybe it wasn't the best decision, but it was for a good reason. It doesn't change a thing for me."

"It might change things for your mom."

"Yeah, well, I did tell her about the tagging, and she's fine with that. You're still in her good books. But I won't tell her about the drugs." She kisses me on the cheek. "What does happen now? This is a more serious charge than tagging."

"Yeah, for sure."

I explain to Chelsea about RJ and how it works. When I finish, she says, "It makes perfect sense, doesn't it?"

"I guess. I like it, for sure. Why do you think so?"

"It's your first offence. If they send you to Juvie or something, like what good does that do? It makes more sense for you to make it up or pay back something. Does jail make you a better person? I don't think so. What do you learn, right? Like nothing."

"I guess. So that was the option, and we took it."

"That was smart, Axel. I guess a smart thing and a dumb thing makes it all neutral." She squeezes my hand.

"Well, you wouldn't hang out with a dumb guy. You're too smart for that."

"Touché!"

Feeling confident, I kiss her on the cheek.

I toss and turn the whole night through, my mind racing out of control. One minute it's restorative justice, then it's Chelsea and her dad, then it's Chelsea and me and my fear of that bubble bursting.

I'm in and out of dreams that blend with reality: *my mother and Mr. Hunter are calling out to me and I try to run to them, but they keep getting farther and farther away. I keep running, only to hit a wall of fire and smoke. Choking and screaming ...* I wake up soaked in sweat, then try to go back to sleep, and the cycle continues.

Monday morning. When my alarm goes, I'm exhausted, but I force myself to get moving. I need to talk to Mr. Davis.

I knock on his office door, and he's there in an instant. "Axel!" he exclaims. "What a nice surprise!" He opens the door wide. "Please have a seat."

Do I get special treatment from Mr. Davis? Maybe not, but I do feel special, and I'm glad I came.

"What a nice way to start my Monday morning. How have things been going for you, Axel?" Mr. Davis starts, now seated on his side of the desk.

"Okay, I guess, thanks."

"Good to hear, Axel," he replies, stroking his goatee. "So, what's on your mind?"

"Nothing serious. I just thought I'd come by."

"I'm glad you did. When we last talked, as I recall, you were doing pretty well even though I tore you away from Chelsea."

"You didn't tear me away. It was all good. Still is, in fact."

"So I didn't ruin everything? You're still good friends?" he says light-heartedly.

"We're still going out, if that's what you mean. Not sure why she stays with me, though, but I'm not complaining."

"Still enjoying the moment, eh? Good to hear. Well, you're a good person, so that doesn't surprise me."

"Yeah, I guess. Thanks."

There's a long pause. Mr. Davis rests his chin on his clasped hands, wearing a half smile. Finally, he breaks the silence. "Axel, it seems you think you're not Chelsea's equal. Well, I believe you're anybody's equal unless you convince yourself otherwise."

"I suppose you're right," I agree. "But she's good-looking and popular, and, well, I'm kind of the opposite."

"Have you heard the old saying that opposites attract?"

"No."

"Well, it's true. We often like people who are different. People who might have different opinions, or they're involved in things that make them more interesting. But the truth is, we're attracted most to people we have something in common with. You think Chelsea is attractive, and she probably thinks the same about you."

"I can't imagine that," I say, chortling.

"You say she's popular, and you think you're not. She might find that an appealing quality; someone who's humble but has lots of character, like you."

I look up, beaming. "You really think so?"

"I really do, Axel. You have a lot of things going for you, but you just don't realize it yet. Like I said before, enjoy the moment and if that moment lasts a lot longer than you expect, all the better."

I smile wide. I'm speechless.

Mr. Davis continues. "Now, I need to ask you about something. I ignore the grapevine news for the most part. But, not this news."

"The tagging thing?"

"That's the one. Everything okay there?" he asks matter-of-factly.

"Um, yeah, it's all, uh, well ..." I catch myself before going any further. I realize I can't lie to Mr. Davis. "It's all a bunch of crap." Mr. Davis sits up straight. "Seriously? The whole thing is just a rumour?"

"Yes."

"Well, there you go. Now you know why I ignore most of what I hear unless it comes straight from the horse's mouth."

"No, it's only crap because I made it up. Me and a friend of mine, that is. We didn't want anyone to know what really happened."

"Why'd you and your friend create that story? Is that something you'd like to talk about?"

"Actually, yes, it is." I rub my eyes. "You said you'd keep everything confidential."

"I did."

"Okay, I've been lying to everyone, except Chelsea, and the lie just keeps going and going. It's driving me crazy. But I know I can trust you."

"Thank you, Axel. You can trust me. So now, you've sure got my curiosity up."

"Me and my friend got busted for trafficking drugs." I can barely look at him.

Mr. Davis squints and says, "Okay, that's very surprising to hear. How long were you involved with drugs?"

"Look, I don't do drugs and I don't really traffic them either. I was doing it for reasons that nobody would believe, so why bother explaining, right?"

"What were your reasons?"

"I was helping out my friend's mother. She and my friend were really struggling to make ends meet, so she needed our help to make these deliveries. It was because the police were watching her. But I also needed the money to pay back a debt, and this was the quickest way to pay it back."

Mr. Davis stands and paces. "So, Axel. This was the quickest way to pay it back, but there were obviously other means available to pay it back. You also wanted to help your friend's mother, which is commendable, but it does surprise me that you made that choice. Is it really as simple as that? You had good intentions, but you just made a poor choice?"

"Nothing is simple in my life, Mr. Davis. But yes, I definitely made a poor choice. I was feeling a lot of pressure, but it was really pressure I put on myself, I guess." I pause to get the sequence of events straight in my head. I can't decide where to start. Every event has another event that precedes it. And it all leads back to the original event: the fire.

"Can I get you some water, Axel?" Mr. Davis asks.

"I'm good, thanks."

"You said you were putting pressure on yourself?"

"Um, yeah, that's for sure," I reply. "It's always pressure and it goes way back to when I was small."

"Now, you told me that when you were small you did something bad and that you felt responsible for a lot of things that followed, right?"

"You have a good memory," I say, smiling. I'm reassured that Mr. Davis is indeed a good listener.

"I think it goes with the territory."

"Mr. Davis, do you have a little more time?"

"I have as much time as we need. You're missing class time, but I'll take the blame when I talk to Mrs. Watson."

"Thanks," I reply. "Okay, this is going to shock you, believe me."

Mr. Davis closes his eyes as though he were meditating. "Shoot," he says.

"Okay. So, do you remember my story starter? The one where I said that I'd murdered my best friend when I was four?"

"Almost five?" he adds.

"Yes, that's the one. Well, I lied to you that day."

"About what?"

"I really did murder my best friend when I was four, almost five. I didn't make that up."

Mr. Davis starts pacing again. "I'm waiting for a punch line, Axel."

"There's no punch line, Mr. Davis. That's where everything bad in my life started."

He sips from a glass of water and looks down. "I'm sorry, Axel," he finally says. "This is really absurd."

I leap out of my chair. "Okay, look, you don't believe me and why the hell would you anyway, right?" I hear myself yelling, but I can't control it. "It sounds like a bunch of crap, and I'm just wasting my time! I thought you were the one person I could tell, but I was wrong!"

I turn to walk out, but Mr. Davis grabs my shirt sleeve. "My goodness, you *are* telling the truth, aren't you? I'm so sorry, but please try to see it from my perspective. You tell me that you lied during that first visit, and then you tell me this. What am I supposed to think?"

His hurt look almost brings me to tears. "I'm really sorry for giving you mixed messages. I really am telling you the truth now. I just couldn't unload it during that first visit. I didn't know you, and I really wasn't ready to tell anyone anyway."

"Let's both take a seat and three deep breaths," suggests Mr. Davis, sounding more like his old self. "Well, Axel, you have my undivided attention. But do I need to brace myself for the next part?"

"I don't think so," I say, able to smile again. "But I can't leave you hanging now, right?"

"No. Please continue."

"Okay. Well, all I ever wanted to do was to help my friend. I was small and happy and my favourite thing in the world was visiting my friend Mr. Hunter."

"Your friend was an adult?" he asks.

"Yes. I don't really know how old he was, but I didn't really have any other friends, so Mr. Hunter had to be my favourite. He was a handyman, always in his garage building things or fixing cars. I would ride my bike over to his place whenever I could, and he always took the time to talk with me and show me things, or give me advice. And there was one piece of advice that sticks in my mind, and it keeps me going every day. He told me that I should always do something good for other people because good things would come back to me in return."

Mr. Davis nods his approval.

I continue. "So, one day we had a conversation. I know it might sound weird that I would remember a conversation from when I was just about five, but I remember it like it was yesterday. He said there was never really enough time in a day to get everything done.

"Well, that's what got me thinking I could do something for Mr. Hunter to help him get everything done. He was always doing me favours, so this was my one chance to pay him back." I hear the bell, marking the end of first block. "Is it okay to continue?" I ask.

"Please don't stop there, Axel. I'm on the edge of my seat, literally."

"Okay, well, I came up with a plan to help him. It had to do with getting rid of a big junk pile at the back of his garage. He said that it was another thing on his list of things to do, so that was the one I decided to help him with." I stop there, face buried in my hands.

Mr. Davis pauses, then comments, "I'm picturing this little boy trying to help his neighbour. Very touching, actually."

"Mr. Davis, the rest is going to be hard for me. So if I stumble, please don't be surprised."

"Can I get you some water, Axel?"

"Yes, please." I wait anxiously while Mr. Davis walks to the staffroom to get a coffee mug of water. By the time he returns, I've gone over the next sequence of events in my head, and I'm already in tears.

Mr. Davis puts a hand gently on my shoulder. "Axel, is this too much to talk about right now?"

"I want to do this. I want you to know why I am where I am."

He hands me a Kleenex box and I go through a few tissues before continuing. Stumbling, stuttering and pausing frequently, it takes several more tissues to get through my story. When I get to the part about Mr. Hunter in the burning garage, Mr. Davis is fighting back tears of his own.

I push on, barely pausing to breathe. "And he died in that fire. And that's what caused my parents to break up, and why I ended up in foster care, and why I'm such a screw-up. And that's why I sold all the almonds. It was so I could make enough money to save kids in Africa from starvation. Everything in my life goes back to that fire, and all I want to do is to keep doing things for other people to please Mr. Hunter." I stop there.

"A screw-up?" says Mr. Davis. "Axel, that is exactly what you're not. Look at you? You're one of the most thoughtful boys I know. And a murderer? That's just ridiculous. You're making yourself out to be some kind of evil criminal. That couldn't be further from the truth. Now just give me a minute here. I'm still shaking for goodness sake."

I'm shocked at how strongly my story affects Mr. Davis.

"It's also why I got into this trafficking thing," I add. "All our almond money went missing and I wanted pay it back so more kids could be saved, but, man, did I screw that one up."

"Hmmm. I suppose it's fair to say that things got very complicated," Mr. Davis says, serene. "But your intentions were so honourable that I can't think that what you were doing was even illegal. Axel, when I wade through all this, what I see is a very good human being who had a terrible misfortune. But I also see a very bright future for you."

I wipe away the last tear. "I hope you're right. Right now I just need to get past this drug thing."

"Right!" he exclaims, upbeat and smiling. "What exactly is happening with that?"

"Well, turns out that my friend and I are doing restorative justice."

"Restorative justice? That's great. I know that the police are pretty selective about cases they send to RJ. When is that happening?"

"We're waiting for a mentor to call us and then I guess we'll get things started."

"Good. Use me as a reference if you like. You'll get a glowing one."

"I appreciate that. So, uh, I guess I should get back to class."

"I suppose so, Axel. But, one last thing: Donny Cox's brothers. Did that all get resolved?"

"Yes, it did," I reply with a wide grin.

"Good. You look particularly pleased. How did it go?"

"We beat the crap out of 'em," I reply triumphantly.

He laughs. "Who's we?"

"Just me and my friend Eric. We beat the crap out of the Cox brothers."

"What? I thought these were big high school guys."

"A heck of a lot bigger than us. I'll tell you the whole story another time, but it's all over, and everyone's agreed to leave it alone forever. But we honestly did beat the crap out of 'em."

Mr. Davis shakes his head and pats me on the back. "Well, I don't quite know what to say about that, Axel," he says. "But I do look forward to hearing the rest of that story. Boy, and this is only Monday morning. I hope everything goes smoothly with RJ. Please come and tell me all about it."

"Thanks, Mr. Davis, I will. You have a great day, too."

CHAPTER 29
The Mentor

I usually look forward to the holiday season. But this year I'm having a hard time embracing it all. Christmas is about four weeks away, and I'd like nothing more than to put my biggest problems behind me before the big day. That doesn't seem possible.

Tuesday, just one day after my meeting with Mr. Davis, I receive a call from our mentor. Her name is Willow Robertson. Friendly and soft-spoken, she puts me instantly at ease. She tells me a bit about her role, but doesn't wish to get into details on the phone. Her schedule is flexible, and I tell her I can meet after school any day, the sooner the better.

She suggests tomorrow evening at 7:00 at our local Tim Horton's. After getting Eric's approval, she gets back to me, and it's all settled.

Willow is already waiting when Eric and I arrive together. It isn't busy, so she picks us out right away and meets us at the entrance.

"Axel and Eric?" she says.

"Yeah, that's us," I reply. "I'm Axel, that's Eric. Hi Willow."

"Nice to meet you both." She shakes our hands and smiles.

I think she's somewhere between forty and fifty. She has greying hair parted neatly in the middle and wears a denim jacket over a loose-fitting blouse, faded blue jeans, and open-toed sandals. I'll bet she was a hippie once.

When she smiles, her whole face lights up.

"I'd like to buy you guys a beverage," she says. "You name it."

We both choose hot chocolate.

She directs us to the far corner of the coffee shop.

In no time, we're all sitting together with drinks. Willow says: "So, you guys, I've only had one other case before this one, so I'm not exactly a veteran, but I will do my best. Do you both understand my role?"

"You're a counsellor?" I suggest.

"I'm not actually a qualified counsellor, but I will be guiding you through the RJ process so you'll know exactly what to expect during the facilitation. I'm a neutral person. I don't have anything to do with the final decisions, but I'll be there to support you guys. Does that make sense?" she asks.

We both nod.

"Good. First, how are you coping?"

I respond first. "Stressed out, but okay."

"And you, Eric?"

"Same. Just wanna get this done."

"I can imagine, but we can't rush things." She sips her tea. "Tell me about yourselves? Anything. I want to know you better."

I point to Eric. "Okay, I'll start," he says. "I'm thirteen years old, in grade eight at Pacific Shores Middle School. I live with my mom and I don't have any brothers or sisters."

"Does your mom work?"

"She just got a job at the Bottle Depot."

"That's great. And you guys get along?"

"Yeah, we get along great," Eric replies curtly.

"That's fabulous! We don't always hear that with teens and their moms. How about you, Axel?"

"Same as Eric. I'm thirteen and in grade eight at Pacific Shores. But I live in a foster home with a foster mom and dad and two foster brothers."

"How long have you been in foster care, Axel?"

"For about eight years now."

"Oh, so quite a long time. And how is it working out for you?"

"It has its ups and downs, but I'm pretty happy with things right now."

"Great to hear that, Axel. I appreciate you guys sharing that info with me. As for me, I'm a single mother of two daughters aged eighteen and twenty-two. They still live at home with me. They see their father regularly, so that's all good. It hasn't been all roses bringing up my daughters. They've caused me a few extra wrinkles." She smiles, showing her laugh lines. Eric and I smile back.

"But I love them dearly," she continues. "I work as a receptionist in a dental office, and now that my daughters are a little more independent, I decided to also volunteer with the RJ Society. I did my mentor training just six months ago."

She takes another sip of tea and gives her contagious smile. "I'm thrilled to be your mentor. I read all about your case. I know about the trafficking charges, but I'll need to know more. Tell me how you feel about your actions and the charges. Eric?"

"Me? I feel awful about everything. The charges are what we deserve, and we need to make it up."

"Okay, thanks, Eric. Axel?"

"I agree with Eric a hundred percent. What we did was so wrong, and we deserve to be punished. I don't know what we can do to make it up, but I'm willing to do almost anything."

"That's good to know. Thanks, Axel. It's uncommon for mentors to work with two responsible parties—that's you two—but they thought this might work well for this particular case. You both accept responsibility for your actions, so that's a good start. Now, I have a question. Who would you say is affected by a crime of this nature? In your case, we don't have a specific victim, but there are indirect victims. Who would they be?"

Eric and I reflect before responding. I picture the two of us out on the streets making deliveries. The clients and all the street people are still clear in my head. I also recall my comments to Eric about the possible reasons people end up living on the streets.

I reply first. "I think people who live on the streets are some of the victims. What we were doing could make it worse for them, because maybe drugs force people on the streets."

"Insightful. Thanks for that, Axel. Would you like to add to that, Eric?"

Eric looks contemplatively out the window. This topic really hits home for him. "Um, I agree with Axel. I think we just made it easier for people to get hooked on drugs. If drugs weren't easy to get, a lot of those people wouldn't become junkies and spend all their money on getting fixes."

Looking pleased, Willow writes on a notepad. "I don't want to forget anything important that should be shared with the facilitators. Any notes will be shredded as soon as we have the facilitation. I only share them with people in the RJ Society. Besides them, everything we talk about is strictly confidential."

She writes slowly and meticulously, pausing often to get her thoughts together. She finally looks up and says, "Good progress here. Now, I'm going to pry a little deeper. You both seem to have a solid grasp of the problems associated with trafficking, so what was your motivation for getting involved in that business? What was your mindset?"

"It was all about money," I respond without hesitation. "That's all it was. Eric and I and another guy sold a bunch of almonds for a school fundraiser, and we lost the envelope with all the money. So, basically, we panicked because it was a lot of money and there was just no way we could pay it back. And when we found out that we could make a lot of money making these deliveries, we thought we could just do it for a few weeks and that would be it." I look at Eric. He's looking down, shaking his head. "But it didn't work out that way, and now we realize that the whole idea was just stupid."

"Wow. I see. So tell me," Willow says, "how in the world did you ever get this connection for drug trafficking?"

"Oh, well, we sort of, uh ..." I've cornered myself. I look around helplessly.

Eric jumps in to rescue me. "It was my mom. She got us to deliver it. She got busted, too, and she's doing her own RJ for it."

"I see," says Willow, shifting uncomfortably. "We won't talk at all about your mother's case. I'll leave that entirely up to her. But at least this is all making sense. Not good decision-making sense, but it does explain your motivation. Just out of curiosity, did you make enough money to pay it back?"

"No, we didn't," I answer. "We made a little before we got caught, but then we found the stupid envelope. So we did pay it all back."

"So you made some extra money?"

"I guess we did," says Eric.

"You might want to think about what you should do with any profit you made. And that leads me to the other part of our meeting. This is going to be the most important part of the facilitation. They're going to ask you for suggestions for an agreement. I can help you with this, but we need to come up with ideas for ways you can make it up to *whomever* for your crime. *Whomever* could be the street people you talked about, or it could be society in general. It's whomever or whatever is affected by drug trafficking. Think about it for a few minutes and then we'll do a little brainstorming."

Willow continues to take notes while Eric and I put our heads together. We agree on volunteering: cleaning up the downtown, picking up garbage, or scrubbing graffiti off walls.

"That," Eric whispers, "would make sense to people, since we said we were tagging."

I agree. "And if we're cleaning up the mess from vandals or whatever, we're sort of paying back society even for trafficking, right?"

Willow looks up from her notes and smiles. "I heard that. I like it, too. I'll write that down. Any other ideas?"

"We're thinking that our volunteer hours should help the street people since they're the ones affected," I reply.

"Uh huh. What about places like the Salvation Army or the food bank? They're always happy to have extra hands. Possibilities anyway. Don't forget, you guys have to be under supervision since you're only thirteen. Also, they'd need to keep track of your hours so they can report back to RJ."

"Sounds good to me," I reply.

Willow continues to document our suggestions. "It's all a part of making a positive contribution to the whole community of people in need. Another possibility is the Soup Kitchen. Many there have been affected by drug or alcohol addictions. But it would depend on whether RJ thinks a place like that would be appropriate for younger guys like yourselves. I've never heard of any issues there. People are usually respectful to all the volunteers. Shall I write that one down?" she asks.

"Yes," we both reply.

"Now, what about the profit? What to do with that?" asks Willow.

Eric looks at me.

I shrug, then say, "We could donate it somewhere, like one of the places we just talked about, like the Salvation Army or the food bank maybe."

"Good choices. How much money are we talking about?" she asks.

I do a quick calculation. We completed two nights of deliveries, making seventy-five dollars each night. But Eric took fifteen dollars the first night and then ten dollars from the envelope he brought home on his own. "One hundred and twenty-five dollars," I confirm.

"Hmm. That's a lot of money. You could split it up any way you like, or give it all to one charity. We'll bring this up at the facilitation to show you are good guys at heart. Anything else?"

"Nope," I reply.

"Great. More suggestions might come up during the facilitation, but your willingness to accept responsibility for your crime and to put in the hours of restitution will make for a successful dialogue."

She closes her notepad. "I don't think I'll need this anymore," she says, smiling again. "You guys are making my job easy, and I really appreciate that."

"Thanks, Willow," I say. "We're really happy that you're our mentor."

"Yeah, thanks a lot, Willow," Eric echoes.

"My pleasure, guys. Now, you need to meet the facilitators. They might ask you a few questions, too, but nothing formal. It's a get-to-know you kind of a meeting."

"When?" I ask, anxious to move the process along.

"Well, I'll do my best to get a date set up tonight. One last thing. You can bring in a support person to the facilitation. He or she wouldn't contribute to the conversation. They can just be moral support. You can tell me later what you decide. Now, can I offer you guys a ride home?"

"Oh, no, thanks, Willow," Eric says. "We'll just walk."

I shake my head at Eric. He brushes me off with a flick of his wrist.

The wait is short. Eric and I get the call Thursday morning. Willow arranged the first meeting for Friday. "We just might have an agreement before the Christmas shut-down," she says.

Willow picks us up Friday evening. She drives us to the RJ office located in a converted character home near Fort St. and Stanley Avenue. Our facilitators, Daniel and Andrew, greet us. Daniel is in his late twenties to maybe early thirties. Andrew is probably a good ten years older.

The meeting room, formerly a living room, is cozy with a small wood fireplace and French doors. We sit in comfortable padded chairs arranged in a circle. Eric and I face each other. Daniel and Andrew also face each other a few chairs away.

They're both friendly, but business-like. Eric and I follow directions and answer questions. They sound pretty much like the ones Willow asked us at our meeting, exploring our mindset, our motivation, and our willingness to make up for our crime.

Then Andrew explains their reasons for the seating arrangement. "We want you guys to be completely independent with your responses. You will be asked questions separately even though many of them will be similar.

"The other chairs," he continues, "are for the other participants: Willow, Constable McLeod, support people if you choose, and one or two community members who will offer their input regarding the nature of your crime and how it affects the community in general."

Then we have an open-ended conversation to lighten the mood.

Near the end, Andrew states, "The facilitation will be Monday if that works for everyone. Okay?"

We both nod excitedly, and Willow gives her assent.

"Great," Andrew finishes. "So, everyone enjoy your weekend, and we'll see you at 7:00 Monday evening."

Willow smiles. She calls us over to the door. "That's amazing," she says. "This is even speedier than I expected. No weeks of anticipation for you two. Come on, and let's get you home."

CHAPTER 30
RJ In Action

The RJ facilitation goes smoothly. Surprisingly, Flick is there as my support person. Eric doesn't have one; Jeanie is having a hard enough time keeping it together for her own RJ case.

Constable McLeod speaks in our favour. He believes wholeheartedly that we deserve the opportunity to show how remorseful we are by volunteering our time. He also goes on at length about the faith he has in youths today, citing several examples of groups he's worked with and acts of kindness he's witnessed.

There is only one community member, a middle-aged, well-to-do-looking lady. The last person on the list of speakers, it's over two hours into the facilitation before she gets the floor. Ignoring the fidgeting, she gives us a lengthy lecture on all the "consequences and ramifications" of being involved in the world of drugs. I'm fighting to keep my eyes open when Daniel jumps in to save the day. He thanks her politely for her input and then quickly moves us on to the terms of agreement.

In the end, Eric and I agree to one hundred hours each of community service. The Soup Kitchen, the food bank and general downtown cleaning are the three options we choose. The drug money that is still in my room will be split between the food bank and the Salvation Army.

We both thank and hug Willow. We're to report to her about our progress until we've completed our hours. A lot of hand-shaking, more thank yous, a little paper work, and restitution is on its way.

Monday morning, my alarm goes off and I wake up feeling like a new person. The facilitation is actually over, and I can't wait to start my community service.

I run all the way to school, anxious to see Chelsea. But the first person I run into is Eric. He's wearing his bandana, red with white polka dots. Tied in a knot at the back of his head, it covers most of his forehead.

"Hey, Cheech!" I howl. "I can't believe you wore that!"

"Never mind, I'm getting good reviews," Eric returns, laughing and waving his arms. "Everyone wants to know where I got it. I'm telling you, it's gonna be the trend, buddy."

"You know, it suits you. It's the new you. Keep it on."

"I will. So hey, when do you think you'll start the service stuff?"

"I'd start tonight if I could," I reply. "If Willow doesn't call by supper time, I think I'll give her a call."

"Yeah, if you do call, tell her I'm ready to get started, too."

"For sure, I will."

Someone taps me on the shoulder. It's Mr. Davis. "Axel, good morning. How's life?" he asks.

"Pretty good, thanks. Please come over here for a sec," I add, leading the way to a spot near the canteen where we have a little more privacy. "So, I had my RJ facilitation last night," I tell him, glowing.

"That's great! And ... what?"

"Well, me and my friend have to do a hundred hours of community service each."

"Sounds fair. Are you okay with it?"

"I sure am. I can't wait to get started and to get it all over with."

"Where at?"

"The Soup Kitchen first."

"I'm sure you'll come out of this whole thing a better person. You might even learn a lot out there while you're at it."

"I hope so. But thanks for all your help, too. Your talks really helped."

"That's great to hear. Thanks, Axel. You just made my day. And don't stop coming in to visit, okay?"

"I won't, for sure."

I turn to see Eric now surrounded by a throng of students pointing and laughing at his bandana. Eric stands his ground, a big smile on his face. "You guys are just all jealous!" he yells, waving his hands wildly.

I watch him, amused and amazed.

Frank approaches. "Hey, what's with Eric anyway? Like what the hell is that all about, the headband and everything?"

"It's all about Eric starting a new life," I reply.

"What the hell? What do you mean starting a new life?"

"I can't really explain it, Frank. It's just a hunch I have. But he's doing okay over there. How about you?"

"I'm good."

"Anything more happening with your dad?"

"Nah. They're slow with the charges. But you know what? He's been good lately. It's like he's on his best behaviour now that the cops are on his case. So as far as I'm concerned, they should take their bloody time. My life is good right now."

"Really? Glad to hear it. That's weird, though. Maybe it is good that they're taking their time."

I keep a constant eye out, but Chelsea is nowhere in sight. The bell goes and there's chaos in the halls as everyone heads to class. Mrs. Watson stops me before I get two steps in the classroom.

"Axel! Good morning!"

"Good morning," I reply sheepishly. I know what's coming next.

"Come here for just a second," she requests, stepping outside the door.

Reluctantly, I join her in the hall.

"How in the world are you anyway?" she asks, concerned.

"I'm okay, thanks. In fact, I'm really good."

"Really good, eh? Well, I'm really glad to hear that. Axel, I heard about the trouble you got yourself into. I was worried."

I'm sure she's referring to the tagging charge. I can't imagine Mr. Davis breaking his promise. "Um, yeah. I, uh, did a stupid thing and now I'm dealing with that."

"Does that mean it's all getting resolved?"

"Yeah, I guess you could say that. I'm paying the price." Is she angry? No. She's calm and relaxed. "It's being dealt with," I add, "but I think I disappointed people by being such an idiot."

"We all live and learn, right?" she states in a motherly tone.

"Yeah, I guess so. I wanna believe that."

"Axel, if you're concerned about disappointing certain people, that's a good thing. But it's you that counts the most. If you feel you've disappointed yourself, then you need to do what's necessary to get your head up high again. I was concerned when I heard about that incident with the police. But I wanted to believe you would rise above it all. Did you?"

"Yeah, I think so. I'm starting some community service soon to make it all up, and when that's done I don't ever want to be in this situation again."

"Good. And just for the record, I never thought less of you because of that. You can always count on me for having your back, even if you happen to mess up again. Not that that's possible, right?" she says sarcastically.

I crack a half smile. "Thanks for not writing me off, Mrs. Watson."

"Oh, and by the way," she adds, "I just got around to reading the responses to that story I read aloud, "A Man Who Had No Eyes." Part of yours really stuck out in my mind: *Take whatever life throws at you and just make it work.* It's like the old adage *if life gives you lemons, make lemonade.* Your insightfulness and your personal drive always amaze me, Axel. I know that life has thrown a lot of curve balls at you, but you seem to be able figure them out and knock most of them out of the park. I'm proud of you for that," she finishes.

"Thanks." Red-faced and beaming, I head to my desk. Still no sign of Chelsea.

Concerned, I phone Chelsea that night after supper. I don't recognize the voice that answers.

"Um, is, uh, Chelsea there?" I ask hesitantly.

"Axel, you goofball, it's me," Chelsea replies, her voice an octave lower than usual.

"Oh, sorry, but you don't sound like yourself. I was just wondering if you were sick or something. Didn't see you at school today."

Sighing heavily, she replies, "Oh, Axel. I'm really not well. Not really sick, but not well."

"I don't get it."

"Well, let me just say I'll be getting better and better as the days go on."

"Now I'm really confused. Like, are you sick in bed?"

"No, it's nothing like that. What it is, Axel, is the shit hit the fan yesterday. My mom found out about my dad, and my dad is gone. I actually feel great that he got the hell out of here. It's my mom that I worry about. But she's strong, and she leans on me, and we're going to be all right. Thanks for calling to check on me, Axel."

"If I can help, I'd sure like to."

"You just did help. Thanks. You take care, and I'll see you at school tomorrow."

"Yeah, you, too."

Willow calls Tuesday evening. She has arranged for my first shift at the Soup Kitchen on Wednesday at five o'clock. Eric's first few shifts are garbage duty downtown. Nervous and excited, I have another restless sleep.

Flick drives me to St. Andrew's Cathedral down on View Street. I walk around back as instructed and find the Soup Kitchen sign on the first door I see. I take the stairs down to the basement. It's really a cafeteria with several tables that are already filled with hungry people wolfing down the offerings.

My supervisor drops what he's doing to greet me.

"I assume this is Axel," he says in a high-pitched voice. We shake hands. "Am I right?"

"Yes, sir," I reply. I'm surprised to see that I tower over him.

"I'm Anthony Baldwin. Your friend Willow told me you were coming. Nice lady, that Willow," he adds, smiling warmly. A short, stout man with a thick black and grey beard, and a shiny bald head, Anthony reminds me of a leprechaun.

"Yeah, she is nice," I agree.

"Nice to have you here, Axel. I know you have your reasons, but you don't need to explain. In the soup kitchen, we're all equals. Everyone of us has a past, but nobody needs to know about that, so we never pry. Come, follow me."

Anthony leads me to the food counter where two ladies are serving food. "That's Becky and Emma," Anthony says, loud enough for them to hear. They smile and wink.

Two more staff clear away dirty dishes, and three cooks are in the kitchen. Anthony says there will be time to meet them all later.

"So Axel, you can start by bussing, just like Ellen and Hannah out there." He hands me a bin. "Collect the dirty dishes, put the compostable scraps in a designated bin, the other scraps in the garbage, and leave the bin on the counter for the dish washers to collect."

"Okay, should I just go out there now?" I ask, starting to sweat.

"Yup. But just a few rules: don't ask too many questions, and think carefully before you volunteer any personal information. Do that, and you won't have any trouble down here. You're a good-looking young man, so don't be surprised if you get some attention. Just use your common sense."

"Okay, thanks for the advice, Anthony." I'm not quite sure what he means by 'attention.'

I see a few familiar faces, but I doubt any of them recognize me. Most say very little as I clear away their dishes. Periodically I hear a 'good lad' or a 'thank you.'

I'm sure I stand out like a sore thumb, but I don't feel unsafe.

This is a three-hour shift, and time flies by. Some of the guests are here the whole time, which I'm told is discouraged. The majority have their meals and move on to make room for the steady turnover of the needy.

At the end of my shift, I'm just about to leave when an elderly man with a long grey beard approaches me. "You're a good lad," he says. "My name is Simon."

"I'm Axel," I return.

"Axel. That's a fine name. My girlfriend and I want to thank you for your time," he says, pointing over to where a grey-haired lady sits, her head hanging over the table. "It's very nice to see a fine young lad lending a hand. I'm here most every night, so if you come back I'll see you again."

"I'll be back, for sure," I reply. "I hope to be doing a lot of shifts here."

"That's wonderful. Have a beautiful evening, Axel."

"Thanks, Simon. You have a nice one yourself."

CHAPTER 31
An Offer

According to Willow, my next shift won't be until Saturday, same place, same time. I look forward to it.

With the nine o'clock curfew, Friday night is a quiet one. I'm in my room reading and listening to music when Margaret barges in with a message.

"Axel, your father phoned when you were at school. He's coming to Victoria tomorrow with two of his children. He said he's coming over just to see you. He sounded so anxious to see you. I believe you told me you were going to the Soup Kitchen at five, so I said it would have to be before then. Is that okay?"

I look up from my novel, my heart palpitating. Margaret, standing in the shadow of the hallway light, her hair in curlers, is a vision of my mother. For a split second, I'm in a time warp. Four-year-old Axel is waiting for his mother to come and say good-night. I must look like I've just seen a ghost.

"Why are you looking at me so strangely?" she asks, sounding put off.

I squint hard. "Oh, sorry, I was just, uh ... Wow. My dad's actually coming here tomorrow? With two kids you said?"

"That's what he said."

"I guess he didn't say which ones, did he?"

"No, he didn't. What the heck difference would that make anyway? Are you close to them at all?"

"Um, no. I've never met them. I was just wondering if he was bringing the kids that are actually his, or the ones that she already had before they got together."

"Oh, it's one of those relationships, eh? Too complicated for me. I have no idea who he's travelling with. I guess you'll find out tomorrow, right?"

"Yeah, thanks a lot, Margaret."

"You're welcome."

Suddenly my Friday night is full. My father is actually coming over here to see me. To see me! I spend the rest of the night wondering about everything: what he might look like, what his kids might look like, what he might say to me, what I might say to him.

I play reels of my life over and over in my mind's eye, starting with my father's days as a travelling salesman and me riding Maynard in and out of driveways that represent his destinations.

Reels with multiple frames of an absentee father, a missing mother and an angry boy. So many fragments and cracks. The projectionist needs to stop periodically to put things in perspective. The reel eventually makes it all the way to the restorative justice meeting. And now I wonder what will be playing on the next reel.

I watch from the living room window as a red Mercury Villager minivan pulls up to the curb in front of Flick's house. Everyone in the van stays put for several minutes. It has tinted windows, so I can't make out the faces inside. If my father is as nervous as I am, the delay makes perfect sense.

Finally, the doors open and two boys emerge, followed by their father, my father, I pay no attention to the boys. I'm totally fixated on the man who has become a distant memory. He stands on the sidewalk holding the boys' hands, staring at the house.

My window and about thirty feet are all that separate me from embracing him. Standing there in living colour, like an image on a TV screen, I can't help but smile as a childhood memory surfaces. I recall wondering why people on the other side of the screen couldn't see me. I would scream at them to get their attention and never get a response. My mother would just laugh herself silly. I don't believe she would find humour in this.

The boys spot me and point me out. My father waves wildly and makes his way to the front door. He has a full head of dark brown hair with hardly any grey. It's close-cropped and neatly combed and parted. He's wearing an expensive-looking brown leather bomber jacket and fashionable hiking boots.

In my mind, the picture of my father has always been that of an old man. From a four-year-old's perspective I guess all adults look old. But when I do the math, I know he was in his early thirties when he left us, so he must be about forty now. He's tall and slightly overweight, and he has my ears. Or I have his ears. It gives him that Alfred E. Newman look from *Mad Magazine*. I like it.

Margaret has been standing behind me the whole time. She runs to the door to open it before my father has a chance to knock. I hear all the introductions, then Margaret yells, "Axel, come here and see your father!"

As I approach the door, the boys come running at me like I'm a candy tree. Margaret takes her cue and disappears.

"Axel!" they both scream. "It's Axel! Axel, Axel, Axel!" Then the smaller one jumps up and I catch him in my arms. He wraps his arms around my neck and squeezes tight. The older brother hugs me from the ground, his head buried in my side.

"Okay, boys, take it easy on poor Axel," my father says with a huge smile. "They're not usually like this, believe me. That's Stephen you're holding, he's eight, and that's Jerry his older brother, and he's nine," he states. My eyes meet my father's over Stephen's head.

We stay locked on each other while the boys argue about whose turn it is for me to hold.

I finally break the ice. "Are these my real step-brothers?" I ask.

"I guess all my kids are your step-siblings," my dad replies. "But yes, these two I had with Theresa. So they're more closely related to you than their sisters, I suppose."

I smile when I look at them. Almost twins, they have identical flat-topped hair styles and matching winter coats. If not for the difference in height, they would be hard to tell apart. My own flesh and blood, my brothers. I do my best to fight off tears.

"Okay, Stephen, come on down now and give Axel a break," my father says firmly.

Stephen does as he's instructed, and both boys stand quietly beside me, each one holding an arm.

"Axel, can I give you a hug?" my father asks.

Slowly, I wrap my arms around his waist. He presses the back of my head into his chest and holds it there. We stay like that for a full minute, my tears now flowing freely. When he finally loosens his grip and I stand back, I notice that his leather jacket is stained with my tears. His eyes are red and watery as well.

"Why don't you put on a jacket and come on outside," he suggests. "I think the fresh air might be good for us."

I grab my coat and shoes, and we all step outside. It's a cool December day, overcast with a light breeze, and no rain. He tells the boys to play by the van while we finish our talk.

"How have you been keeping, Axel?" my father asks, one hand on my shoulder

"Oh, good, I guess."

"You look good. How are things at school? Getting decent grades and everything?"

"Pretty decent, I suppose. About a B average, I guess."

"Nothing wrong with Bs. I would've given my left arm to have Bs in eighth grade. I was more of a C student. Not very focused in those days. So, I'll bet you have lots of friends, too."

"I have a few," I reply. "I know lots of guys, but I only hang out with a few of them."

"A few good friends are all we usually end up with. That's good to hear, Axel. So, you're keeping your nose clean, I suspect."

"You mean staying out of trouble?" I ask, my hands shaking.

"Yeah, you know, within reason. Nobody's perfect, right?"

"Right. Well, I'm not perfect, that's for sure." Do I want to open up to my father so soon? I side-step it for now. "But I'm pretty much staying out of trouble," I add.

"That's good to hear, Axel. I just know that you're a good boy and, Axel, there's something I want to ask you." His attention is drawn to the boys who are screaming and throwing pebbles at each other. He yells at them to settle down, and all is quiet again. "Sorry about that. Now, where was I?"

"You just said that you wanted to ask me something," I reply.

"Yes, I do. It's something I really want you to consider seriously." He pauses. "Axel, me and the boys, Theresa and the girls, Shelley and Simone, want you come and live with us in Vancouver. We're all settled in there now, my job and everything, and we'd love to have you join us. There's still stuff I'd have to work out with social services, but I think I could clear those obstacles fairly soon."

In shock, I'm unable to respond.

"I know you'd get on well with Theresa," he continues excitedly. "She's chomping at the bit to meet you. And the boys? Well, look at the boys. They do have two big sisters from Theresa's first marriage, so having older siblings is nothing new to them. But having a brand new big brother would be very exciting."

"Um ... I ... uh ... well," I stammer.

Stephen and Jerry are standing beside me again. "Yeah, Axel, please come and live with us!" they plead. "We need a big brother. Our sisters are evil, but maybe you can fix them!"

I laugh openly. Amusing and flattering, the boys are making it difficult for me to say no. I really like the idea of two little brothers looking up to me. But it's not that simple.

I have a life here in Victoria. I have friends, a girlfriend, and I have a lot of community service time to do. I can't leave everything and start all over in Vancouver.

"Well, look, Axel," my father cuts in, "I don't expect you to make a decision right now. Give it a little time to sink in. I could arrange to have you come over to visit us a few times so you can see what it's like, too. Theresa is a great mom, a natural with kids. Does that sound fair? Just think about it for now? I sound like a broken record, don't I? What do you think, Axel?"

My mind goes blank. I need time for all of this to sink in. But there is one lingering question that's been haunting me.

"I do have one question, Dad," I finally say. "I, uh, just never could figure it out. Like, why did you never come back to help look for Mom?"

The colour drains from his face. Looking down, wringing his hands and shuffling back and forth, it takes a full minute before he's able to respond.

"That was a long time ago, son. I made some bad mistakes, some seriously poor decisions, and I know that some of them can't be fixed. Your mother and I were going through a tough time and I know that a lot of it was my fault. I wasn't a model husband, that's for damn sure. We weren't going to make it as a couple, Axel. I knew that, and I needed to just be away. But then there was you. I'm still banging my head against the wall for deserting you. You were always on my mind, but I just didn't have it together."

Another long pause and lots of hand wringing. I wait patiently in silence.

"I told you about my AA meetings," he continues, "and they've helped me to see what alcohol did to me and to everyone around me. It hasn't been all roses with my family in Toronto either. And, well, I don't think I can ever forgive myself for leaving you like that, or for not coming back to look for your mom. But I'm going to try to make up for things the best I can."

Then, sounding a little more upbeat, he says, "One thing I'd like to do, Axel, is to set up a fund so I can pay for all of your post-secondary education. It's just one small thing, but I think it's a start."

I'm not sure how to respond to that. It sounds like a generous offer, but it's so far in the future that it doesn't have a lot of meaning for me right now. I look up and say, "Thanks, Dad. That's nice of you. I guess we'll see if I ever make it to college."

"Oh, you will. I'm sure of that. But Axel, I don't know what else to say about what I've done. I could make up a whole lot of other feeble excuses, but you're looking for some real answers. I'm afraid I don't have them."

"That's okay, Dad," I say, now anxious to give him an out. "I was just wondering. But I'll definitely think about what you said."

"I hope you will. Well, I guess it's time to go." Then to Stephen and Jerry, "Come on boys, let's jump in the van."

"No, you come with us, Axel!" Jerry yells. The two of them hold onto my legs and I drag them all the way to the van.

I have a knot in my stomach as the van pulls away. This feels like some hit-and-run incident. He comes. He makes an earth-shattering offer. And he leaves, all in about twenty minutes.

How ironic. A conversation with my father that doesn't end with a hollow promise. I'm truly excited about being a part of a real family again, but I know I'm not ready for it.

I also know that Margaret will be picking my brain as soon as I go back in. But if I tell her the gist of our conversation, it will likely stir things up around here. I might even be asked to leave. I'm not ready for that either. For now, the offer to move to Vancouver will stay strictly between me and my dad.

CHAPTER 32
Something About Simon

The forty-minute walk to the Soup Kitchen helps clear my head. But I regret wearing only a light jacket. I'm shivering cold by the time I get to the bridge. I'm pretty sure, though, that part of my shivering is just nerves. The bridge brings back vivid memories of the bust, and my dad's visit is still fresh in my mind.

It's almost dark by the time I arrive. Standing out in front of the Cathedral, I notice how impressive it is. This gothic-style structure of old brick and towering spires stands out as a Victoria landmark. It strikes me as an unlikely location for the Soup Kitchen. But it is a church after all, so it makes sense that the needy would be cared for within its walls.

Anthony greets me once again. "Hello, Axel! You know the routine," he says genially, handing me a tray. "Relax and enjoy yourself tonight. When you see fit, get some supper for yourself. Then sit at one of the tables and try to blend in a bit. I learn something new from these people each and every day. Just remember those rules, right?"

"Right, I remember. Don't ask personal questions, right?"

"Yes, good! And don't volunteer too much personal stuff about yourself."

"Okay, got it. Thanks."

Dozens of guests are lined up holding trays. They move along slowly while the serving staff fills their plates and bowls with generous portions of vegetables, potatoes and soup. More and more faces are becoming familiar to me. Odd Job is sitting at a far table hunched over his plate with four other men, all of them jabbering away loudly and animatedly.

Few people actually take notice of me while I'm bussing. I try to make eye contact so I can at least say hello. But I soon discover that many of them are not capable of a conversation. Oblivious to me, and everyone else for that matter, they talk to themselves or to invisible people.

There are also many who appear to be perfectly normal, happy-go-lucky individuals. When the time comes for me to sit down and eat, I'll make sure some of them are at my table.

After about an hour of bussing, I get my own plate of food and take a seat at my pre-selected table. At first, it's like I'm invisible. Nobody seems to acknowledge that a newcomer has joined them. So I just sit quietly and eat my food until, finally, someone speaks to me.

"A gift from God, isn't it?" says the clean-cut gentleman with a short grey beard, and sporting a tattered brown blazer. I had singled him out earlier as one of the normal ones.

I look up to see that he is indeed speaking to me. "Uh, yes, it is," I reply, confused.

"All the rest is an illusion," he continues. "Like government and capitalism. Nothing is what it seems to be. We are all but servants in this great illusion and God is our provider. We ..."

He continues on in that vein but I soon lose interest. It's clear that he doesn't need an attentive audience anyway. He doesn't even appear to notice when I pick up my plate and change tables.

The people at the next table, three men and one woman, welcome me with open arms. I notice a flask being passed around under the table. I take a seat, and there's no mistaking the reek of alcohol. I find it hard to breathe, but I don't want to be rude by leaving too soon. This is friendly group. Loud, jovial and inquisitive, they take turns peppering me with questions:

"What do your parents do for a living?"

"How many siblings do you have?"

"How did you ever end up working here at the Soup Kitchen?"

And so on. Keeping in mind Anthony's rules, I try to be selective with my responses.

"My father is a salesman, and I'm an only child." Regarding the reason for my being here: "I did something illegal, but I'm not allowed to talk about it. But I'm actually glad that I get to work here."

"You're a nice boy!" one of men yells joyfully, followed by a round of cheering from the group. The alcohol continues to flow and stories start to flow freely. Everyone speaks at once; nobody listens. I hear bits and pieces of different stories about an abusive relationship, alcoholic parents, a drug addicted partner, or runaway kids.

The more I hear, the more nervous I get. Anthony's rules were clear. I'm being careful not to give away too much about myself, but these guys are spilling their guts to me. I just keep turning my head from one story teller to the next until everyone finally runs out of steam. Everyone except Vivian, the sole woman at the table.

The group quiets as she continues her tale. "... and I was just a rebellious youth who took to the streets, got addicted to meth, and was never able to leave. And I had perfect parents who did everything by the book. I lived in a really nice neighbourhood, and I was spoilt rotten. But I despised everything my parents represented, so I rebelled."

No response from the group. The flask is still being passed around.

"Do you ever talk to your parents?" I ask.

"I haven't heard from them in over fifteen years," she replies, looking off into space. "I guess I got what I asked for, but it's not what I would ask for today."

"I'm really sorry to hear that," I add.

"Oh, don't be sorry for me. Just don't ever do what I did." She gives me a Jeanie-like glassy-eyed stare.

"Yes, I suppose that's good advice," I say, hoping there's nothing more to be said.

"You're damn right, it's good advice," Vivian concludes.

I thank them all for letting me join them at their table, then pick up my tray and get back to work.

A short time later, I feel a tap on my shoulder. It's Simon, the old man I met just as I was leaving my last shift. He has a complacent grin on his face.

"Axel, join me for a friendly chat," he requests, pointing to his table in the far corner.

"I don't see your girlfriend there."

"You remember that I have a girlfriend!" he returns. "That's marvellous, Axel! You do pay attention, don't you? Well, you're right, she's not here tonight. Laloo wasn't feeling up to it tonight, so she just stayed in her suite. I'll get her out tomorrow, I'm sure. So you'll come and join me then?"

"Yes, I will. Thank you. I'll try to come over there in a few minutes." Simon is so polite and positive. And he seems perfectly normal so far. I look forward to getting to know him better.

I continue on until my bus bin is full, then drop it off for the dish washers before taking Simon up on his offer.

Welcoming me graciously, he pulls out a chair. "For you, my friend."

His long hair blends with his long beard to make a solid mass of grey hair. Tall and slender, he walks like he's floating. Once seated again, he looks me up and down.

"I've been watching you a little, and I don't want you to take that the wrong way, but I'm impressed with you."

"Well, thanks, Simon. I'm not doing anything special, though."

"You're doing something very special," he responds warmly. "You're helping people like us, and you add a breath of fresh air to this place."

Not quite sure how to take that compliment, I thank him again anyway.

"If you don't mind me asking, how old are you, Axel?"

"Thirteen," I answer, forgetting about Anthony's rules.

"Oh, my. Your life is just beginning, my friend. Thirteen," Simon repeats. "Up to this point, you should think of life as an apprenticeship. Learning the trade of life," he adds. He seems to be looking right through me. "So, what are your interests, Axel?"

"Well, uh, I read a bit and I have a girlfriend." I feel a pang of guilt for breaking the rules once again. But Anthony did say to use my common sense, and I don't feel that Simon is a threat.

"Good for you! Young people these days don't read enough. Maybe girls get in the way." He chuckles. "Do thirteen-year-olds actually have serious girlfriends these days?"

"Well, I don't know. We just hang out together and maybe go to a movie and stuff."

"A woman in your life just makes every waking day that much brighter. But this is coming from an old fart. I never had a girlfriend when I was your age. You see, my mother, God rest her soul, wouldn't allow me to even think about girls until I was in high school. She was terrified I'd get someone pregnant and end up in the same predicament she got herself into at age fourteen."

"Your mom was pregnant at fourteen?" I ask, surprised.

"Yes, with me," he says, laughing. "And I wasn't an easy child, believe me. But I suppose your mother is a more liberal thinker than mine was."

"Um, well, I don't really have a mom," I reply. "Just a foster mom right now."

"I'm so sorry to hear that, Axel."

"Yeah, it's not easy to talk about, but it's been quite a few years now."

"Your mother. Is she no longer with us, Axel?" he asks sympathetically.

"I pray that she still is, but I just don't know." I pause to reflect. "You see, well, it's a long story. And I don't think you wanna hear all this stuff."

"I'm trustworthy, my friend, and I'm all ears," he replies affectionately.

Feeling completely at ease now, I open up even more to Simon. "Okay, well, I'll tell you a little more. What happened was, when I was just a kid I did something that really messed things up and my parents split up, and I ended up in a bunch of foster homes."

Still continuing to look through me, Simon responds, "Life is an unpredictable journey, my friend. But true strength is acquired by embracing all those unpredictable things that are thrown at us and forcing ourselves to move forward. I believe that's you, Axel."

"I guess. I try to move forward, but sometimes I step backwards."

"That's because you're human. We don't really learn unless we make mistakes."

"Yeah, well, I've sure made lots of those."

"So, no father either?" Simon asks.

"I have talked to my dad, but he has a new family and lives out of town. And my mom? She had a breakdown and was in a hospital for a while. Then she just disappeared. I always think about her, but I'm not even sure if she's alive."

Simon takes a sip of coffee. "Hmm, let's leave that one alone for now."

"Do you mind if I ask you a question?" I say, curious to know how an intelligent man like Simon ended up here.

"Not at all. Anything you like."

"Do you have any kids?"

He almost drops his coffee mug. He takes a few moments to compose himself. "That's a fair question, Axel. Yes, I have two boys. I've not been in contact with my boys for ... for far too long. They're all grown up now, but I don't even know if I have any grandchildren." He strokes his beard.

"I'm sorry I brought that up, Simon."

"Not at all, my friend!" he exclaims, springing back to life. "If we can't deal with the past, we can't move forward! Are you a good listener?"

"I think so." I should walk away now, as Anthony suggested, but I'm glued to my seat.

"Good, because good stories require good listeners. Mine is not a happy story, but I'll tell you more so you and I can be on open terms. Tell me, what do you think I did for a living?" Simon starts.

"I have no idea. A lawyer maybe?" I reply.

"No, not a nasty lawyer. I was a philosopher. I was the head of the philosophy department right here at the University of Victoria. And I believe I was a very good philosopher. I especially loved teaching. I loved stretching the parameters of young minds. Yes, it was a wonderful profession. It was the only profession as far as I was concerned."

"How long did you do that?" I ask.

"As long as my mind was intact. You see, when life takes a sudden detour through the gates of hell, your mind goes with it."

"I don't understand. Your mind seems really good to me," I comment.

"Thank you, Axel. I've worked hard to get my mind back. As I said, I was good at what I did. I studied my discipline and I read voraciously. You see, there is no end to learning, yet I was determined to find an end. Well, that was a preoccupation that occupied every waking minute. There was no time for anything else. Just learn and learn and read and read, and there was simply nothing else that mattered. What folly, right?" he asks, looking at me intently.

"I guess. It sounds like a bit much to me."

"And to my wife!" he exclaims with conviction. "I had such tunnel vision, I lost sight of what was really important in my life–my family. My wife became so fed up with a husband who had no interest in the daily domestic duties of a marriage such as showing affection or being a father, that she did what any wife would do." He pauses for a few sips of coffee while I wait anxiously for the next line.

"She left me, of course. And she absconded with my boys. They started a new life. She received almost full custody plus a lot of money from me. Damn, nasty lawyers sided with her, said I was too neglectful.

"So, well, here I am, right? My life just spiralled and spiralled downhill from that point on. I took a leave," he continues with regular pauses. "But that eventually ran out and then the money ran out as well. I had nothing. I was nothing and I had nothing." Pause. "My wife tainted the boys, you see. To the point where they didn't want to see me." Pause. "But, Axel, I am rebuilding. I am here. I have friends in this street community. I have a lady friend. And I now believe I have a new friend sitting here with me. Am I correct in that assumption?"

"Yes, you are, I answer without hesitation. "I'm your friend, Simon."

"Then life just got a little brighter. So, friend, take this glass of water." He hands me a half-full glass. "And let's have a toast to our new friendship."

I clink my glass against his coffee mug and drink down the water. Simon holds his drink out to the whole Soup Kitchen. "I toast everyone here," he announces in a low tone, intended for my ears only.

Watching my mysterious philosopher friend with admiration, I feel a tingling sensation. His story hit a nerve. I try to imagine what he went through losing his kids. It makes me wonder what my mother might have gone through.

It dawns on me that Simon, just minutes ago a virtual stranger, has shared the intimate details of his life. I'm privileged.

"I'm happy to be your friend, Simon," I proclaim.

Beaming, he replies, "That means a lot to me, Axel. Thank you."

Aware of the time, I glance around. Several tables need to be cleared.

"You're falling behind in your duties," Simon jests.

"Yeah. But it's been great talking to you, Simon."

"Indeed, it has, my friend. I trust there will be many more opportunities for us to converse in the future. I'll see you next time, with Laloo, I hope."

"I look forward to meeting her," I say, smiling.

"Good. And Axel, why not bring your girlfriend along as well."

"Oh, uh ... well, I could check." No way Chelsea wants to hang around the Soup Kitchen. But it can't hurt to ask.

"And when might you be gracing us with your presence here next?"

"Monday for sure."

"Until then, my friend."

CHAPTER 33

Introductions

First thing Sunday morning, I make four phone calls. The first is to Eric to find out how his community service is going.

"Like shit," he says. "My hands are blistered from scrubbing walls and my back is killing me. I'm gonna try and get some shifts at the Salvation Army."

"That's a drag," I reply. "How's your mom?"

"Oh, she hasn't had her RJ meeting, but she's keeping her nose clean, and I mean that both ways," he adds, laughing. "And she still has her job."

"Good to hear, buddy. I'll give you a call later."

"Later, Axel."

The next call is to Willow. I tell her I want to do all my community service at the Soup Kitchen, and that I want to bring a friend along. It's all good to her. She gives me Anthony's phone number so I can call him personally.

The third call is to Anthony. He tells me how proud he is of me, and that Chelsea's welcome, as long as she follows the rules as well.

"I would like to have a chat with her first," he says. "A young girl can be a potential target. But it would be wonderful having her there."

I thank him, even though I'm not even sure she'll agree to come.

My fourth call is to Chelsea. "Axel! What are you up to?" she asks.

"Not much. Just doing my time at the Soup Kitchen."

"Right! What's that like?"

"Different, that's for sure. But really interesting people," I reply.

"Like what do you mean, different?"

"Like, it's a whole different world. But it's a really cool feeling when they accept you. There's an understanding, you know, like I don't judge them, and they don't judge me."

"That sounds pretty cool," Chelsea agrees. "So, you're actually meeting those street people. The ones we never pay any attention to."

"Exactly!" I exclaim. "And you should see Simon! He looks like an ancient Greek philosopher, and he actually is a philosopher and he's the smartest guy I've ever met!"

"You're really excited about that place, aren't you?"

"Well, yeah, I am," I reply, calming down. "Sorry if I just took your ear off."

"I like it, Axel. It's great you're having such a good time. It sounds a lot better than my boring life. So, when do you go back there?"

"Okay, hold on, Chelsea. I wanted to ask, would you like to come with me tomorrow to the Soup Kitchen?"

Silence. "Seriously? Oh, I don't know, Axel."

"Why not? It's perfectly safe. Anthony the manager has complete control of the place, and everyone there is just happy to be getting a good meal, so it's all peaceful. You don't have to worry about a thing."

Dead silence on the other end.

"Chelsea? Are you still there?"

"Just hold on. I'm not hanging up."

I wait for several minutes. I'm just about to hang up when I hear muffled talking in the background, followed by a loud cheer. "I can go, Axel!" Chelsea yells into the mouthpiece. "Mom says that it's okay as long as she can drive us there and back. I'm excited about this! What time do we go?"

"Five, and we're done by eight for sure, or earlier if we want."

"Great! My mom will be by to pick you up at a quarter to five."

"Okay, great. See you tomorrow at school." I hang up, elated. Suddenly, I see the humour in this: Simon and me bringing our girlfriends to meet each other. The two of them are probably fifty years and several worlds apart.

Chelsea's mother is punctual. Chelsea and I are at the Soup Kitchen by five. Anthony gives Chelsea his orientation spiel. I grab a bus bin and go to work.

More people are acknowledging me tonight. I want to blend in as much as possible, but I'm fully aware that they are living in a world to which I don't belong. Being accepted here is good, though.

A short time later, I feel the familiar tap on my shoulder.

"Axel! You're a man of your word!" exclaims Simon. "Right on time as usual."

"Hello, Simon." I set my bin down and turn around. "It's good to see you."

"You as well, my friend. And did I see you arrive with a lovely young lady?"

"You did. I didn't see you when we came in."

"Oh, we're tucked away over in the corner. Out of the spotlight as usual. So, are you going to introduce me to your girlfriend?"

"You bet," I reply. "I'll see if Anthony's finished talking to her." He has. Chelsea is already busy carrying bus bins into the kitchen.

Simon follows me over to her. "Simon, this is Chelsea. Chelsea, this is Simon, the philosopher I told you about."

Chelsea looks shocked.

They shake hands and Simon gives her a penetrating gaze that glues her to the spot. "Chelsea. What a lovely name," he says calmly. "So, I have the privilege of meeting a friend of my new young friend Axel. How wonderful that you would join him here on the other side of life."

"Oh, thanks. And nice to meet you, Simon," Chelsea replies, grinning nervously. "So, you're a philosopher?"

"That I am. But philosopher is merely a title, and an insignificant title at that. I am a friend. That is the title that's important. And I'm delighted to see that my friend has been successful in talking you into this. I'd love for you to meet my lady friend Laloo." He points to his table in the far corner where, again, I see the grey-haired lady with her head bent over the table.

"And, Axel. I want very much for you to meet Laloo as well," Simon adds.

"Sure. I could meet her right now. Or would it be better to wait?"

Simon's eyes light up. "Why wait? But before we go over there," Simon instructs, holding an arm out in front of us, "Laloo is a woman of few words. So don't be alarmed if she doesn't speak to you. Just know that she is absolutely delighted to meet you. She told me so."

Simon leads us over to his table, then rests one hand on Laloo's head. "My dear," he says softly, "our friends Axel and Chelsea are here to meet you."

As Laloo slowly lifts her hand, Simon continues. "My dear Laloo understands everything very well, but she says little. In fact, I dare say that she understands all the nuances, all the peculiarities, all the complexities of life far better than I."

Simon is still talking when Laloo reaches up for my hand. She clasps it firmly with both hands and won't let go. Simon doesn't notice. Her eyes are inquisitive, and her mouth hangs open, as though she is about to say something to me. Instead, she continues to stare. I'm glued to her dark, glowing eyes. Though child-like, they're surrounded by deep wrinkles that must have a story in every fold. Dimples show when she smiles. I notice two large, yellow, butterfly barrettes holding her thick, greying hair in place.

"It's very nice meeting you, Laloo," I say, not expecting a reply. Her grip tightens, making me more and more uncomfortable. I try to pull away gently, to no avail. Finally, with a little force I manage to break free. I motion for Chelsea to follow me over to the serving area.

"Why did you do that?" she asks, angrily. "I didn't even get a chance to shake her hand."

"Did you see the way she was looking at me? And she wouldn't let go of my hand. She was squeezing the life out of it. It was too weird."

"I didn't notice that." Returning to her calm self, she asks, "Any idea what she meant by that?"

"I have no idea. Maybe nothing. Sorry."

"It's fine, Axel. You don't need to apologize. I hope Simon doesn't take it the wrong way, that's all."

"Don't worry about Simon," I reply, hit with another pang of guilt. "Let's get back to work then."

We grab our bussing trays and go our separate ways. A short time later, Simon approaches me, looking horrified.

"Axel," he says, trembling, "come."

I follow him to the washroom entrance. He seizes me by the shoulders. "What did you say to Laloo? She is absolutely beside herself."

"Nothing," I reply defensively. "She grabbed my hand like she wasn't going to let go. I pulled away and then left. I'm sorry."

"No, Axel, that's not it at all. She's in tears for god's sake, and she's gone completely mute." He chuckles. "Now, I admit you make good first impressions, but this is beyond reason. I've never seen Laloo act like this before."

I take a minute to put everything in perspective. None of this is making sense. Simon waits patiently. I finally break the silence.

"Laloo," I say reflectively. "Where does that come from?"

"Oh, it's just a pet name that I bestowed upon her. You see, she has this delightful ritual. At the end of every evening, just before we part company, she sings me a lullaby with that name. It begins like this ..."

Tears well up in my eyes the moment Simon starts to sing. I feel like someone just hit me on the head with a hammer.

Simon stops and looks at me quizzically. "Axel, my goodness, you're crying."

I wipe my eyes. "I am, Simon, but please sing it anyway."

Simon continues to sing the very lullaby that lulled me to sleep each day and night when I was a little boy. When he gets to the second verse, the melody still as clear in my mind as the day it was last sung to me, I do my best to join in:

Laloo laloo laloo laloo laloo la
Underneath the silv'ry shining moon.
Hushaby, rockabye, mama's little darling,
Mama's little lullaby a coo.

Chelsea is soon beside us, hands clasped and smiling. When we finish, she yells, "Bravo! Bravo! That was a wonderful duet!"

I smile through my tears. "Thanks, Chelsea. You make a good audience."

"Axel, you're crying. Are you okay?" she asks, all sympathy.

At this point I don't know whether to laugh or cry, but the tears keep coming. "Believe it or not, Chelsea," I say haltingly, "I'm perfectly fine."

"Okay, I get it. I'll leave you guys alone for a bit." She kisses me on the cheek and goes back to her duties.

"All right, Axel," says Simon with his penetrating gaze, "tell me about those tears, and about that lullaby. It's not a common lullaby. I'd never heard if before Laloo sang it to me. And yet you know it well. Why, my friend?"

I shake my head in disbelief, almost too stunned to speak. I place one hand on each of Simon's shoulders and look him in the eyes. "There's one hell of a good reason why," I reply, laughing and crying at the same time.

"You're confusing me to the nth degree, Axel. Please enlighten me."

I hug him gently. "Simon, Laloo is my mother."

CHAPTER 34
A Hug For a Four-Year-Old Boy

"This is impossible, is it not?" says a stunned Simon. He glances at Laloo sitting upright now, looking distraught. "How can you be sure?"

"It all makes sense now, Simon. That's why she was squeezing my hand and looking at me so intensely. She recognized me! And the lullaby. That's my mom's lullaby. Laloo is my mother. I'm sure of it!"

Simon looks from me to Laloo and back again. Then shaking his head in disbelief declares: "This is truly a miracle."

"Yes, it is, Simon," I agree. "And I can't stop shaking." Never really believing this day would come, I'm unprepared for the flood of emotions.

I dab at my eyes again. "Simon, I feel like I'm just dreaming. Did I really just shake hands with my mother? And that look in her eyes. She just knows, doesn't she?"

Simon grins from ear to ear. Tears sparkle in his grey beard. Shakily, he replies, "A mother knows her son, Axel."

"Well, this is just stupid now, isn't it?" I say, snapping to life.

"Why would you say that?" asks Simon.

"Because here we are talking about this miracle, and there's my mother sitting by herself. I don't even know what I'll say. But I guess it doesn't matter, does it?"

"No, it doesn't. A long-lost son need say nothing. Come, my friend," he says, leading me by the hand. "Let's go see your mother."

It feels as though I'm having an out-of-body experience, like I'm watching myself from above as I approach her.

My mother stands with open arms and an angelic smile. Her eyes are closed. It's a surreal moment when she locks me in a tight embrace. And we stay like that for what seems like an eternity.

"Axel ... my son. Axel ... my son," she whispers over and over.

Chelsea, curiosity aroused, makes her way over. Simon accosts her and explains the miracle unfolding before her eyes.

Arm-in-arm, Simon and Chelsea take in the extraordinary reunion. Anthony and others catch on that they are witnessing a magic moment. It becomes a tear-fest. Tears of happiness rain everywhere.

Closing my eyes tight, I drift back in time. I am a four-year-old boy being coddled by my mother once again. I am snuggling up for my nap, lying in the dark with my back resting against my mother's tummy. I can feel her rhythmic breathing as she gives in to a peaceful slumber. And now I can hear her singing the lullaby: "*Laloo laloo laloo laloo laloo la* ..." It's not my imagination. My mother really is singing it in my ear.

I whisper in her ear to sing it again. Softly, for my ears only, she continues to sing. I glance up to see Chelsea with her head resting on Simon's shoulder, Simon mouthing the lullaby.

"Keep singing," I say to my mother, fearful this will end too soon. "Please keep singing."

I lose count of how many verses my mother sings to me. She is equally determined to preserve the moment. Then, her voice begins to fade away and she's slowly collapsing in my arms. Simon notices and rushes over to help her to her chair.

"You must rest," Simon says, assisting her as she slowly lays her head on the table. Then to me, "I must get her home for her medication. She should be taking it right about now. Just let her rest here for a few minutes. It's only a few short blocks from here."

"Is she going to be all right?" I ask, panic-stricken.

"Oh, yes, she'll be fine," Simon reassures me. "It's anxiety. This was too much for her. She'll take her medication, and everything will be just fine."

"Okay, good," I say with a sigh of relief. "So Simon, how can I contact my mom? That would be okay, right?"

"Absolutely, my friend. But she has no phone, so I'll give you my number and you can relay any message you like through me. How would that be?"

"That would be great," I reply. "And I'll give you my number as well."

Anthony overhears our conversation and hands us a notepad and a pen. We exchange phone numbers and I walk my mother and Anthony to the exit door.

"Can I help you get her home?" I ask anxiously.

"It's best that Laloo calms down. More excitement might trigger a reaction."

"Okay, I understand." I hug my mother, then Simon.

As the door closes, Simon says to me, "This has been a night to remember."

I nod and step outside to watch them disappear around the corner of the cathedral.

When I arrive home that night, Flick and Margaret are watching TV and drinking eggnog. For the first time since I've been living with them, I sit down and join them. Confused, Flick reaches for the remote to push the mute button.

"So, what's up?" Flick starts.

"I have some news," I say, straight-faced.

"Well then, we're all ears, aren't we, Margaret?" Flick responds, putting down his drink.

"Yes, we are," Margaret agrees. "What is it, Axel?"

My news is simple. Four words will do. "I found my mother," I say, fighting back tears.

They jump off their chairs. Flick yells, "You what?"

"It's true," I confirm, still holding it together. "I found her and I hugged her." Then I race to the bathroom to blow my nose. When I return, they're both sitting again, quietly sipping on their drinks.

Beaming, Margaret says, "Axel, this is amazing news! Where did you find her? When did this happen? Where is she now?"

I'm overwhelmed. They believe me, and they want to hear the whole story. I tell them about Simon and how he befriended me, and how he came to introduce me to his girlfriend Laloo.

"That's an odd name," interrupts Margaret.

"Yes, it is," I agree. "That's how I made the connection because Laloo was the lullaby my mom used to sing to me every day. And it was a nickname Simon gave her."

At the end of my narrative, Margaret is sobbing.

Flick runs to the kitchen and returns with a small glass of eggnog. "Well, this calls for a celebration," he announces excitedly. He hands me the glass. "Cheers!"

We all clink glasses in a toast. My eggnog contains alcohol. I drink it anyway, no complaints.

"So, are we going to meet her?" Margaret asks.

"Well um, I hope so," I reply. "I can't see why not."

"I have an idea!" Flick jumps in. "Why don't we invite her over for Christmas dinner?"

Margaret scowls. "Flick, that's when all my relatives come over, and you know what they're like?"

"I sure do. I wouldn't wish that on anyone," he replies. He tries to laugh but starts choking and coughing instead.

"Why not have an early supper for your mother and her friend," Margaret suggests. "Nothing wrong with having two Christmas dinners."

"I'm for that," Flick throws in.

I look at them and smile. "Really? Thank you. Thank you," I repeat. "I'll phone Simon tomorrow. Should I set it up for Wednesday?"

"Wednesday will be fine, Axel," Margaret confirms. "We can get the fixings and a small turkey tomorrow."

"Thank you!" I repeat, wanting to hug them both, but staying put. This is a different side of Flick and Margaret, a compassionate side that I never knew existed.

I call Simon right after school the next day. He is delighted to be invited to a Christmas dinner, but he adds that if we want to surprise Laloo, we should order Chinese food.

"She's been dreaming about that," he says. "She absolutely loves Chinese food, but neither one of us can afford that kind of luxury."

"Okay, I'll check that out and get back to you, Simon," I finish.

When I tell Margaret about the Chinese food request, she looks relieved.

"That's a whole hell of a lot easier than cooking up a Christmas dinner," she declares. "What could be easier than Chinese food? One phone call and it comes to your door."

"So that will work then?"

"Works for me, that's for darn sure. Flick will eat chicken fried rice till the cows come home, and the boys love the whole nine yards."

"That's great! Thanks! So, just one last thing. Can I invite my girlfriend as well?"

"You mean I'd actually get to meet the mystery lady?" Margaret says, mockingly. "You bet. We'd love to have her join us."

"I really appreciate this, Margaret!" I step forward with the intention of giving her a hug. Awkwardly, she turns sideways.

"Not a problem, Axel," she replies. "We're happy for you."

I make my second call to Simon to confirm the Chinese food dinner date and time. He's overjoyed. "That's marvellous! We shall be there promptly at five o'clock!"

"Great! And Simon," I add, "I'm not working at the Soup Kitchen tonight, but could I stop by to see my mother anyway?"

"Unfortunately, Axel, poor Laloo hasn't recovered from all the excitement last night. However, I'll be going over to her suite soon and I'll pass on the news of the invitation and I know she will be very pleased. She already has a glowing smile that I haven't seen for some time, my friend.

"And," he chuckles, "I asked her how she recognized you so readily. Well, she had a good laugh over that one. She said one clue was your name, Axel, which is not a common one. And then she pulled on her ears and said that those were really what gave you away."

"Hah, I always knew that God gave me these flappers for a reason," I state. "What better reason could there be than that one, right?"

Simon laughs. "You're a good-natured lad, Axel. Until tomorrow."

CHAPTER 35
Forgive Me, Mr. Hunter

Chelsea and the Chinese food arrive at about the same time, just after five. The dining room table is set for eight with a large poinsettia in the centre to help put everyone in the holiday spirit. Everyone is cheerful, the conversation is upbeat. Mouths are salivating as Margaret empties the delivery bags, placing container after container on the counter, enough food to feed an army.

We have double containers of chicken-fried rice, chicken chow mein, steamed rice, and sweet and sour chicken balls. Plus, single containers of Szechuan beef, chicken chop suey, chicken and broccoli, and honey garlic pork. On top of that are the standard egg rolls and a ton of Wonton soup.

The dress is pretty casual, no suits or ties or dresses. Chelsea looks great in her black slacks and white blouse. I don't make any comments about that for fear of giving Ted and Ben ammunition for later on.

Fifteen minutes pass. Simon and my mother still haven't arrived. By five-thirty I'm concerned.

"Maybe you should call your mom," suggests Ted, staring hungrily at the food.

"Okay, I'll give it a try." I dial Simon's number and let it ring at least twenty times. "No answer. Maybe they got lost or something," I say defensively. "Just give it a few more minutes."

"In a few more minutes, I'll be eating the food and the containers whole," Ted grumbles. "This is gettin' ridiculous."

Flick pours us soft drinks while he and Margaret sip on white wine. We do our best to make small talk. I check my watch again. Five-fifty. I'm just about to suggest that we start without them when the phone rings. Everyone jumps. I'm nearest to the phone, so I answer it.

"Hello."

"Axel, it's Simon." He sounds agitated.

"Hello, Simon!" I yell. Everyone watches me eagerly. "Are you and Mom on your way?"

"Axel, we're not on our way at all. I'm afraid that the idea of having dinner at a stranger's house is causing Laloo too much anxiety. She wants nothing more than to see you, but this is entirely out of her control, even with medication."

Feeling faint, I hold the receiver away and see all the anxious faces waiting for me to say something.

"Where are they?" Flick whispers.

"Just a sec," I reply. Back to the phone. "Simon, where are you right now?"

"We're at the entrance to Chinatown. We went for a walk to calm her down. I'm at a phone booth and Laloo is resting on a bench right here beside me."

"Okay, just a second, please, Simon." Then to Flick, "They're down at the entrance to Chinatown. My mom is having an anxiety attack about eating at a stranger's house."

Flick and Margaret shake their heads in frustration.

"So, they're not coming?" Flick says.

"Flick," I reply, frustrated, "she wants to come badly, but she just can't do it. I don't know what to say."

Margaret pipes up. "They're down by Chinatown, you said? Down by the gate?"

"Are you down by the gate at Chinatown?" I ask Simon.

"Exactly. It's but twenty feet away," he replies.

"Yes," I return to Margaret.

"Okay. Your mom isn't able to eat at a stranger's place, so we'll bring the food from the stranger's place to her!" she yells excitedly. "Ted, Ben, pack up those containers and put it all back in the bags. Flick, reach up in that cupboard and get those paper plates left over from last year. I'll pack up some utensils and cups. Axel, you gather up the drinks, be sure the lids are on tight, and put them in plastic bags. And let's get our coats on and head to Chinatown to have a Chinese food feast!"

"Simon, are you there?" I yell into the mouthpiece.

"I'm here, my friend."

"Did you hear any of that?"

"I could hear a lot of commotion, but I'm not sure what was said."

"Simon, please go and sit on the bench with Mom and just keep her there. We're on our way. We'll meet you there in ten minutes!"

"Axel, are you sure?"

"I'm sure. Please don't go anywhere."

"This is an extraordinary thing you people are doing. I will keep Laloo here. I will promise you that."

"Good! Thanks, Simon!"

We load all the food and supplies into the trunk and back seat of Flick's car. We can't all fit in one vehicle, so we use Ben's ancient Honda Civic as well. Ben has his 'N' which means he's not supposed to have more than one underage passenger. He brushes aside the rules for this occasion.

"Get in," he says to Chelsea and me. "And make room for this." He hands me a ghetto blaster. "If we're gonna be dining out, we might as well have music, right?" he says, chortling.

Chelsea and I laugh along with him. I feel like applauding as well. This is all for my mother, and I'm humbled by all the kindness.

Ted takes the front passenger's seat while Chelsea and I jump in the back, and we follow Flick and Margaret down to Chinatown.

Simon and my mother are huddled together on a bench staring at *The Gate of Harmonious Interest* located in the middle of Fisgard Street at the entrance to Chinatown.

Margaret gives orders for unloading the cars. I run to my mother and sit beside her with my arm around her shoulder. She looks at me with a tender smile and whispers, "Axel, my son. I'm so happy. I'm so happy."

"Me, too, Mom. Me, too," I return.

Chelsea sits beside me. I hold her hand. "I'm sorry, Chelsea. This must be kind of weird for you. Are you okay?"

"I'm loving every minute of this. It's so refreshing to see a family actually being reunited. This is your night, Axel. Yours and your mother's. That's all that matters right now, okay?"

"Thanks, Chelsea." We hug for a long time, and then I introduce everyone to Simon and my mother.

As expected, Simon is very warm and gracious. My mother, on the other hand, nods gently at each person as they shake her hand, but barely utters a word.

The food containers with serving spoons are spread on the ground in front of our bench. Paper plates and forks are handed out and, within minutes, people are sitting with heaps of Chinese food.

Next, Margaret passes around coffee mugs and fills them with wine and soft drinks. Then, standing with her own mug held high, she calls for everyone's attention. "I would like to propose a toast to two very important people. Simon and Laloo, here's to you."

Everyone stands but my mother. Then we all clink glasses and drink up. Ben turns on the ghetto blaster to an AC/DC tune.

"Oh, for god's sake, turn that garbage down, or off!" orders Flick.

Ben turns *Problem Child* down to a background level. He smirks and I start laughing. AC/DC at a Christmas gathering does lighten the mood.

My mother squeezes my hand. I squeeze back and she whispers in my ear once again. When she repeats herself, I just smile. *This is my mother talking to me,* I say to myself. *If she wants to repeat herself a thousand times, I will listen to every word a thousand times.* Just as I'm embracing that thought, she stops.

Then, like a switch has just been flipped, my mother is suddenly lucid. "Axel, my son, I'm so happy. I'm so very happy. It wasn't your fault. It was never your fault. You were just a little boy. I was a neglectful mom and I thought I'd lost you forever."

She squeezes her eyes tightly shut, and adds, "I'm so happy, and so should you be."

"I am happy, Mom. We'll never lose each other again," I reassure her.

While everyone continues to eat, drink and be merry, I amble over to stand in the middle of the Gate to Chinatown. I'm actually standing right in the middle of the road. Looking around at all the Christmas lights adorning the lamp posts and store windows on Government Street, I feel warm all over.

This is an early Christmas dinner, but for me it's Christmas day. *What gift could be better than this?* I ask myself. Life is good. I do wonder what lies in the future, but right now life, yes, is good. And I can think of no reason why it shouldn't stay this way.

I look at Chelsea still sitting on the bench near my mother. She is a big reason why my life is good. I still have to pinch myself. I know Mr. Davis said to live for the moment, but I really hope that the moment never ends.

My father's offer suddenly comes to mind. I've decided that I will visit him in Vancouver as planned, but whether or not I ever move in with him is an unknown. Living with my foster family is not a bad option for now. In fact, life is just fine with Flick, Margaret, Ted and Ben. I'm proud of all of them, especially Margaret. The way she came through for me to make this all possible—that was really something.

Whatever is going on in my life in Victoria, I will visit my mother every day, even if I don't see her at the Soup Kitchen. And I hope Simon stays with her forever.

And I'm now certain that doing community service will always be a part of my life. It will be my way of doing something good for others. I may have saved a good number of kids in Africa through my donations to Nutrition Solution, but I can see now that people right here in Victoria need help as well.

Looking up to the stars where I know Mr. Hunter is watching me, I have a private chat with him:

I believe I have made you proud. I have followed your advice and I think I am a better person for it. Doing good for others has brought more good into my life than I ever could have imagined. But the most important thing of all is that I believe you have forgiven me. I can now move forward and one day we will meet again. Merry Christmas.

Printed in Canada